Spring Into SciFi
2023 Edition

A Cloaked Press Anthology

Published by:
Cloaked Press, LLC
P. O. Box 341
Suring, WI 54174
https://www.cloakedpress.com

Cover Design by:
Fantasy & Coffee Design
https://www.fantasyandcoffee.com/SPDesign

Cloaked Press is Proud to Present:

Karl El-Koura

Alex Minns

James Wymore

Barend Nieuwstraten III

Rebecca M. Douglass

A. J. Lewis

Cheryl Zaidan

Damian Karras

Elizabeth Estabrooks

Maraki Piedras

Jason E. Maddux

Ray Daley

Greg Eccleston

G. A. Babouche

Sharon McDonell

Rob Younger

Table of Contents

The Mind-Meld

by Karl El-Koura

All of his life people had underestimated Lou Gare. From age one to age one hundred and twenty-three, no one expected more from him than he'd already proved. His biological parents had signed him over to the responsibility of the state when he was two, but he'd learned from that experience, resetting his cycle so he wasn't cranky during the day and energetic at night. He found grade school boring, but after his first bad report card and the threat of being held back, he taught himself to sit still and listen and behave enough of the time to get passing grades. Then much better grades in high school, when he realized just getting good grades meant a free ride at any college he chose. On and on … no one expected him to graduate top of his class from MIT. His graduate thesis, demonstrating that emotions experienced by one highly trained person could be detected with reasonable accuracy by another highly trained person, was *interesting*, according to his advisor. Certainly no one on the committee who granted him his doctorate expected him to turn his interesting but impractical idea into a business, or for him to transform that business into a multinational corporation that generates billions of dollars each year.

And now—was he going to start underestimating *himself*? The computer models proved he'd succeeded; the animal trials

1

confirmed it. Was he going to balk now because it was time to finally find a willing human participant?

The Mime Corporation's Board of Directors wanted him gone and forgotten, had already pushed him out as CEO of his own company. And he'd let them, so he could devote all of his time to the problem that had obsessed him since Marissa had … well, since she'd slammed her racecar into a concrete wall on the three-hundred-and-thirty-ninth lap of the Daytona One Thousand and burned to death in a fiery ball of expensive metals, the majority of her thirteen million followers experiencing her agony with her.

Marissa had died … five years ago now … but he had found a way to bring her back. Now he just needed to take that final step.

"I'm sorry," Lou said. "What was the question?"

The young journalist with his full-toothed smile nodded knowingly.

Senile. That's how the journalist was categorizing him. Rather than *focused* or even *absent-minded*, as he might have been described ten or twenty years earlier.

Sam Something or Other from the Hourly Someshow said, "I was asking about Marissa Adrostky. Some people say you haven't been the same since her death."

They sat in Lou's private box above the Daytona International Speedway. When they'd walked in, Lou had waved off the young woman who approached them from behind the bar at the left side of the large suite, but Sam Something had said he'd love a cold one.

The bartender ducked back behind the bar and poured the drink into a tall glass, then handed it to Sam with a very pretty smile. She seemed familiar, so Lou said to her, "It's nice to see you again." The surprised look she gave made him second-guess himself, and probably planted the seed in Sam's mind that his subject was as senile as some people claimed. But his slip-up wasn't a sign of old age; Lou had never been good with faces. It was his body getting old and tired; his mind was as sharp as ever.

Still, it could be used to his advantage. "Do you know why I called it a mime?" he said, instead of talking about Marissa to this stranger.

The journalist blinked at the abrupt shift in topic. He tried to hide his confusion by taking a sip from the gently bubbling amber liquid, then licked off the bit of foam that stuck to his upper lip and said, "Short for mimicry, right?"

In the curved window that filled the front wall and looked out over the ant-like army of workers below, busily getting ready for the big race, Lou could see his own dim reflection. An old man's face with its two days' growth of patchy white stubble, the hair struggling to grow on his cheeks like grass on arid land; wrinkled skin and cracked lips; tired eyes.

He turned to the journalist, and the contrast between the half-resolved reflection and the fully-resolved, fresh-faced, clean-shaven young man threw him for a second.

"It's not mimicry," Lou said flatly.

"It makes sense, though," Sam continued undaunted. He tapped the silver crown—the mime—running around his head. "We see what they see, hear what they hear, feel what they feel. Mimicry."

"It's not mimicry," Lou repeated, turning to face the glass and his aged reflection again. "It's based on an old TV show—you know what TV was?"

"Sure I do," Sam said enthusiastically. "Like holos, but two dimensional, right?"

For whatever reason—his youth? his sharp, good looks, dark hair perfectly pressed back? Lou waking up on the wrong side of the bed that morning?—the reporter had gotten on his nerves. He didn't like watching races alone, not since Marissa's death; usually he enjoyed the company, and was especially tickled that that this younger generation was still interested in this old man's thoughts.

Sam Something was staring at Lou, with a friendly but curious look. "So … where's your mime?"

"There was a TV show way before your time," Lou said. "Before mine, even. *Star Trek*. And in it, they did this thing called a mind-meld. That's where I—you *do* know that I'm the inventor of the mime?"

"Of course!"

"Well, that's where I got it. Mind-meld; mime. Get it?"

"Yes!" Sam said, but Lou wasn't sure. Sam took another sip of beer and said, "So where's yours?"

"I like to watch the whole thing," Lou said grumpily. Then he tried to shake off the feeling of malaise as the alarm bell sounded to indicate the race was about to begin.

The bartender walked over to turn the window into a holoscreen. She was tall and shapely, and Sam regarded her appreciatively when she reached for the button on top of the window, her shirt riding up to flash her lower back. There was a day when Lou would've been watching her, instead of watching Sam watching her.

Sam lowered his mime around his neck, as if to show solidarity with Lou's regressive ways.

The bartender approached and asked Lou, in her sweet voice, if he'd changed his mind about that drink. He felt sure she regarded his sharp glare, before he caught himself and forced a neutral expression to his face, as lecherous. But he wasn't strictly thinking about her. A fantasy had flashed through his mind: he in Sam's young body and Marissa in this woman's. But … no.

"I'll have a beer too," he heard himself say, although his stomach no longer tolerated alcohol. "Whatever my young friend here is drinking."

The pretty thing nodded professionally and, he saw, she stole a distinctly non-professional glance at Sam as she walked back to the bar.

"Crazy thing about Marissa, isn't it?" Sam said, shaking his head and taking a last chug of his beer, finishing it off. He looked over his shoulder to catch the eye of the bartender, then turned back to Lou and said, "I was one of her followers when she died."

Lou looked at him sharply. "If you didn't disconnect in time—"

"No, no," Sam said, patting Lou on his leg. "I can't believe anyone tried to sue you! But do you want to hear something? There's people who chase that feeling. Being tethered to someone when they die."

Lou hadn't heard that before.

Sam nodded, then flashed his smile again at the young woman who brought him another beer, finally removing his hand from Lou's leg.

She handed Lou his drank while Sam said, "That's why so many people didn't disconnect when Marissa crashed. They *wanted* to pass out when she died."

The beer was ice-cold but bitter; that was definitely going to cause issues for him later on.

Sam leaned over and said conspiratorially, "Do you know that I tracked every one of those thirteen million followers in the days and weeks after the accident?"

Lou didn't say anything, but stared straight ahead.

Sam leaned back in his chair. "I didn't find anything interesting," he said, laughing.

Lou took a deep breath, as if Sam had been sitting on his chest and had finally gotten off. "What were you looking for?"

"I had this crazy idea," Sam said, holding the fresh glass of beer an inch from his lips as if speaking into a microphone. "Everyone knows how you felt about Marissa." He finally took a sip. "And most people know that you handed over the reins at the Mime Corporation to others, but not before you'd spent a boatload of money setting up a lab inside your own beautiful estate. And some people know that you're so secretive that you rotate out your research assistants every few months, even though they've been locked down by air-tight non-disclosures.

"So here's what I thought to myself: what if this colossal genius is working on a super-secret project? And what if the super-secret project is that he mapped his girlfriend's consciousness before she died, then figured out a way to move it into another human being's brain … like one of her followers?"

Lou set his glass in the cupholder. His hand had started shaking, but he tried to hide it in his lap. "You have a wild imagination," he managed to say. Now small tremors shook his body; he tried to get them under control.

"You can't blame me," Sam said, smiling. "I knew you were a big fan of the *Star Trek* show. So I'd watched it as part of my research, and you know what I saw in there? The mind-meld isn't just about mirroring another's emotions. You could actually transfer your—what do they call it?"

"Katra," Lou said, the word escaping from his mouth.

"Katra! So that's why I thought you'd transferred her Katra into—"

"But I didn't," Lou said.

"No, of course not," Sam said. "And yet, somehow, I can't get over the thought that Marissa isn't quite gone. Is she?"

"No," Lou said, and couldn't believe he'd answered.

"She's alive?"

"Yes." It was his own voice, but Lou felt as if he were overhearing a conversation. He looked down at the drink by his side, then quickly back at Sam.

"Hyperamobarbital," Sam said.

Lou tried to stand but couldn't. "You're not a reporter," he said, raising his voice, trying to buy time, trying to catch the attention of the bartender.

"Not exactly," Sam said, placing his hands on Lou's cheeks to turn his head back gently toward himself. "Where's Marissa, Lou?"

"Are you law enforcement?"

"You can't outrun this," Sam said. "Where is she?"

"She's safe," Lou said. "I haven't hurt her. I haven't hurt anyone."

"Where, Lou?"

"She's safe. Her consciousness is on a dedicated machine in my lab. That doesn't break any laws."

"But the end goal is to transfer her to another human being, right? Like in *Star Trek*?"

"Maybe one day," Lou said, straining to resist the effects of the drug. His clothes became damp with cold sweat, a ball of pain in the middle of his chest.

"How would you do that?"

Lou paused, trying to get a good breath into his constricted lungs, trying to buy time.

"Lou," Sam said.

"You don't understand. It hasn't been tested."

"We don't have time for this," Sam said, speaking past him. Then his gaze returned to Lou's. "Tell me how."

"The computer modeling is solid, yes. I was able to switch the personalities of rats, yes. But humans aren't rats!"

"How, Lou?"

"The legalities aren't—"

"Lou! Tell me how!"

And then, feeling like a man floating away from his body, Lou heard himself tell the young man about this innovation even greater than the one that had made his fame and fortune. When he'd said everything, he finally collapsed under the strain. The young man's strong arms reached out to catch him tenderly before he fell out of his chair and onto the ground.

***

He heard his own voice calling him back to consciousness, telling him everything was okay. He opened his eyes and saw his own face staring back at him.

"Who are you?" he said. But at the sound he made, he understood. "Are you crazy?" he said, blinking his eyes, then stretching his arms, as if trying to get comfortable in a new suit. "You switched bodies with me?"

"Of course," the familiar voice said. The old man sat back in the chair next to his, the chair that Lou had previously occupied. "I'd be crazy *not* to switch with you"—a wince of pain flashed across the wrinkled face before Sam forced himself to continue—"for a little while, anyway."

Lou tried to stand but found the young body not yet fully under his control. Once it was, though ...

"Take it easy, old man," Sam said, the wrinkled hand patting him on his muscled leg. "You were given a shot of a neuromuscular blocking agent, and if I were you I wouldn't try anything strenuous until it wears off."

"You want to steal my money, huh? You think it's that easy? It's not under my mattress, you idiot. You'll have to get through lawyers and accountants ... I won't let you get away with it."

"Who'll believe you, Lou?"

With difficulty, he turned his head to look at the bar. It was abandoned.

"My wife?" Sam said, twisting up his face in a way Lou never had. "I doubt she'll make a good witness for you. Will you, honey?"

8

He heard her sweet voice before Lou turned his head and saw her, sitting with her long legs crossed one over the other, his mime in her lap.

"I don't think so," she'd said. Then she added, looking back at him, "You don't remember me, do you? Not really?"

He did, though, now that it no longer mattered. "You were one of my research assistants," he said flatly.

"One of your first. You had me really curious what you were about. Now I know!" She said the last sentence with a lilt, as if he'd finally revealed a surprise he'd been saving just for her delight.

"We're not going to steal your money, Lou," Sam said, so that Lou forced his head to make the journey back to him, "though I do think you've—wait, should I say *I* to start getting used to it? Yes, I think that's better. So … I think that *I* am going to rehire Rebecca and become enchanted with her genius. Then, when I'm ready to announce my great discovery, I'm going to give most of the credit to Rebecca. I think she'll start her own company. The Katra Corporation. Does that have a good ring to it?" Sam shrugged. "We're still working on it.

"Anyway, once that's all done, we'll give you back your body." Then Sam looked him up and down appreciatively and added, "And I'll be taking mine back, of course."

"And you know what else?" Rebecca said. Lou turned his head toward her again. "We can't have you running around between now and then, making trouble, or us worrying what you're up to." She leaned in to whisper conspiratorially, as Sam had done in what seemed a lifetime ago, "The thing is, hubby over there got into a little trouble. White collar stuff, don't worry! Now the law will catch up to him sooner than later, but here's the good news—he … sorry, *you* have just had a crisis of conscience and asked me to bring you in. I think your contrition will help us strike a good deal. Say three-to-five. What do you think, Sam?"

"Absolutely!" Sam said. "Three-to-five."

"You won't get away with this," Lou repeated robotically, his mind still reeling. If only he could get this body under his full control, he'd overpower them both, take each by the neck and crush their throats for doing this to him.

"I know you feel that way," Rebecca said in a reluctant tone, as if giving bad news she'd rather spare him. "But the thing is—you told us about Marissa, remember? I'd just hate for you to mess up our plans in any way, and then something bad happens to her."

"Don't talk like that!" Sam said with feigned shock. By force of habit, Lou turned his head again to face the person speaking to him, despite the effort it cost. "He's not going to mess anything up. He's too smart for that. He'll do the three-to-five, giving us enough time to get this thing off the ground. Then—"

The man in Lou's body shuddered suddenly, as of someone trying to shake off a strange pain. "Then—" he said again, but the ball of pain seemed to grow and overtake him, forcing his face into a spasm. It lasted a moment, then the old man slumped over in the leather chair.

Lou looked at Rebecca, his head responding more freely now. "Hyperamobarbital's not good for a bad heart," he said.

Rebecca brought up her arm to call for help on her watch, but Lou's hand shot out—such quickness, this body!—and gripped her tightly.

"You're going to explain the drugs in his system? And in mine?"

Her eyes darted back and forth between him and Sam.

"Rebecca, the world finds out that Lou Gare is dead, we both lose everything."

She stared at him for a long time. Finally, in a tightly controlled voice, she said, "So what do you propose?"

"I'm not dead, am I? I'm right here." He tapped his skull with a finger. "And I have enough money to make your husband's—

sorry, *my*—legal troubles go away. The rest of your plan isn't bad. Katra Corporation. I hadn't thought about setting up another company. *He* never could"—he stared at the corpse that used to be himself—"not with the non-compete agreement he signed with Mime. But *I* can. And you can be my partner."

Rebecca regarded him with a narrow, suspicious stare. Then for a brief moment her eyes widened a little and glinted. In the next instant she'd replaced that look with a neutral one and, with one last glance at the prone old body, she nodded.

That little spark in her eye was probably her germinating a way to betray him. Because here he was—a hundred and twenty-three years old, and people still didn't see him for who he was. After everything he'd proven about himself to the world. And yet, these two young people who'd underestimated him so badly had given him a gift.

Lou took a deep, easy breath and allowed himself a smile, staring back at Rebecca, thinking about Marissa.

Karl El-Koura works a regular job in daylight and writes fiction at night. Visit www.ootersplace.com to learn more about his work.

Perchance To Dream

by Alex Minns

The lights refused to line up. I closed my eyes for a second, ignoring the flutter of panic, took a deep breath and tried again. The heads-up display filled my vision as I twisted the gauntlets a few degrees. Finally, everything aligned and the triangles in the top left of the display became a circle. Calibrating the depth of the devices was intense and intricate; I hated being on these shifts. I locked down the settings and disconnected my display from the current unit and sent it up the chain to the next person.

That last one has been tricky and now I had a backlog. If I didn't speed up, I was going to get called in to the office or have my hours docked. I plugged into the next unit and began the whole process again.

Time became a loose construct when you were working the production line. Being plugged in to the VR units cut you off from the outside world so when the whistle finally blew for the end of the shift, I almost didn't recognise what it was. I pulled off the helmet and gulped in the outside air, not that it was too fresh in the factory, but it didn't taste of the metal filter of that damned helmet. I placed it carefully on the station and rubbed at my face that was slick with sweat. I forced myself to yawn to make my ears pop; that was another side effect of being plugged in for six hours. Sounds suddenly flooded back into my head and I became aware of the others stood a little way away on either side of me. The whole line was full of people, but while we were plugged in, it was like being all on your own. You tended to forget how many people were nearby.

We all began to shuffle towards the exit. There was no policy of silence in the factory but everyone seemed more comfortable that way. Every now and then you spotted someone you recognised in passing and gave a slight nod but that was as far as socialising went in the factory. No-one dares jeopardise their job.

We all filed into the canteen. The main perk of this job were the meals. I'd heard there were factories that would only give you one meal, which left you scrabbling around on the meagre wage trying to scrape food together. It wasn't exactly fine dining, in fact, it didn't really have any taste but it filled your stomach and that was what was important these days.

I couldn't remember how the collapse began – something happened, something big. The few people I had managed to talk to all had different ideas. Some said solar flares, others said mass hypnosis through televisions. I'd forgotten what a television was until I'd heard that one. All I knew was something had happened that was so traumatic most of us were losing touch with what went before. I did remember chocolate. As I lifted the spoonful of beige soup to my lips, I tried to recall what it tasted like. If I closed my eyes and imagined hard enough, for a split second I could almost taste it.

I smiled at the man on my left as we passed the empty bowls towards the end of the line. His face twisted into a sneer which I could only assume was his attempt at returning the gesture. His wiry beard was a couple of inches long and white. Most men had beards now; it was hard to get hold of razors. There weren't many other women at this factory; most seemed to have gone to the next town over in the early days. I saw Meera and Vivian a couple of rows over as we all filed out to the transports back to the housing complexes.

A low hum of chatter finally sprung up as we exited the factory, officially off the clock and out of the sight of the supervisors. Not that anyone dared get too rowdy, security lined the route to the vehicles taking notes and names. I got onto the bus, sitting near the front. Most people liked to pile towards the back, as far from the driver as possible but I liked having the space. My head leaned against the cold glass and I watched the roads go by as we passed the run-down buildings and houses. No-one lived out here anymore, the electrical network fell to pieces after everything went wrong so everyone had to move into the complexes – the only places they could run power to other than the factories. There was talk that engineers were close to making a breakthrough and reinstating the old networks. If that were the case, we could spread out again, start reclaiming the old cities but I'd heard it all before. A few other residents on my floor had been getting excited, they were certain the increase in our production was a sign that things were looking up. I was a realist; it was the hope that killed you.

It was October, probably; it was hard to keep track of the year these days. The seasons all merged and things like Christmas were long gone. There weren't many trees on our route, concrete and tarmac covered most of the landscape but nature was starting to grow back in some areas. And the trees I could see were beginning to turn. I smiled, it felt so normal, like the old days. I was still in a reminiscing mood when the bus pulled up at our building. My rooms were on the fiftieth floor so it took another ten minutes to get into one of the lifts. There was at least a system – only people on the twenty-fifth to fiftieth could use this lift, to try and make it a bit quicker. If only I'd been on the fifty-first, then I could have gotten into the next lift and been the first stop. I could put in an application to move, but it would take years.

My rooms were at the end of a stark corridor. Rooms was also an imaginative description. It was hard to believe we used to have so much space. When the transport buses drove us past the old homes, I often tried to remember what we used to do with all the space. As you entered my rooms, there was a counter immediately to your right which held the hot plate in case you didn't get fed at the factory. On the left was the door to the shower room and toilet and ahead was the living/sleeping area. My bed was folded up against the wall which left me with a 7-foot by 9-foot space that was all mine. My chair was pushed up against the wall and a stack of books beside it. The radio was on the ledge by the window. I gave it a few winds to get the dynamo charged up and went about tuning in to the only station you could get. The voices of the news readers droned in the background. It was all about statistics and production figures. Slumping into the chair, I closed my eyes and waited for the music to kick in. This time of evening was wordless orchestral pieces. I let the notes wash over me. I resisted the urge to sleep for as long as possible. Sleep was wasted time, before I knew it, I would be working again. For a few hours in the evening, I could escape. But once sleep took over, it was all darkness. In the end, sleep always won.

***

The draught on my face made my eyes flutter open but the bright light ahead was enough to force them closed again. It took me a few moments to realise what I was looking at. I forced myself to sit up and look again. The sun was bursting through the white clouds that seemed to race across the sky. I couldn't remember the last time I saw the sky look like that. Grey perpetually filled the horizon since it all went wrong. You could see the sun somewhere behind, battling to make an impact through but it never made it. My hands felt damp. I screwed my fingers up and felt the blades of grass cascade through leaving dew on my palms. Tears began to roll down my face.

Was I dreaming? It had been so long since I had dreamed. No-one dreamed anymore.

I stood up and searched around, suddenly aware of a noise. The green field stretched out in all directions, empty. Spinning on the spot made everything seem to flicker and shift. Metal structures popped up ahead of me: twisting, multicoloured bars and chains. The noise, it was from there. Laughing? I started to move forward. My feet were bare, and I almost slipped, but I kept careening forward. The structures were moving, round and round, up and down. It was a play park!

I could see shadows of people, children, running, playing. But they weren't in focus. I reached out, tried to call but nothing came out.

'It's no good.'

The words seemed to come from everywhere all at once. I dropped to the ground and looked up, but it was gone. So was the playpark. I crawled round on the spot, desperate to find it again. Sun seemed to be getting darker. My chest cramped up as I realised it was receding. Just a few more moments; my hands clawed upwards, grasping at nothing.

'I can't get to her.' The voice echoed around me again. It was a man's voice, that was all I could tell. I wanted to yell out, call for help, anything, but my treacherous throat wouldn't obey.

I awoke with a start, the static of the radio screeching at me, like a mocking laughter. I could have sworn I heard the voice again, lying just beneath the buzzing. 'She's gone again.'

***

The lights weren't lining up. I took a deep breath, closed my eyes for a second and tried again. The heads-up display blinked and flashed in my vision as I twisted the gauntlets a few degrees. Finally, the triangles in the display became a circle having aligned correctly. I locked down the settings and disconnected my display from the current unit and sent it up the chain. I was about to plug into the next unit and start all over again when a message flashed up in the bottom corner of the display. Time to report to the Governor's office. I pulled the helmet off and tried not to catch the eye of the supervisor up on the platform. Carefully, I weaved through the bodies of the other workers plugged into their VR helmets. Arms were waving in free space so I had to duck and dodge a few times. I paused at the door and waited to hear the click of the release mechanism. A small camera was mounted above and had tracked my approach. I pushed on the heavy metal door and let it swing shut behind me before I moved to the next one. I repeated the process before I was allowed access to the corridor where Management worked.

As I got closer, a door on my right opened. I tried to ignore the sound of my footsteps echoing on the floor as I moved. A feeling of dread crept its way up my spine. Productivity meetings happened every month, but I never stopped being nervous about them.

'Tacey, come in.' The voice drifted out on an air of corporate cheerfulness: it didn't fool me for a second. The Governor smiled as I entered the office and gestured for me to sit on the chair opposite. His friendly manner was trying to put me at ease but it had never worked. Deep down, I had never trusted him. As long as my productivity figures stayed high enough, then there was nothing for me to fear.

The office was white and it was so much brighter than the factory floor. Everything seemed to shine, include the Governor's perfect teeth. Everything about him was pristine. He was so perfect, he was virtually non-descript. I took the seat opposite him; the chair was the only good bit about these meetings. I sank into the comfortable cushion and relaxed just a fraction. I reached over to the table and picked up the headset that was waiting for me. I often wondered whether the technology we used was created before or after everything happened. I couldn't remember. But then I couldn't remember me talking either. I was fairly sure before I could but ever since it all went to hell, my voice decided to go with it. I hadn't met anyone else with the same problem but the company had managed to accommodate me.

I slipped the headset on: one lens went over my right eye. Shadows of letters appeared in the screen and cycled through, waiting for my input.

'How are you doing?' The Governor slumped lower in his chair and steepled his fingers under his chin.

My eyes flicked from side to side as they selected letters, and then the word sequence it predicted for me. A feminine yet robotic voice came out of the speaker over my right ear.

'Fine thank you Sir. How are you?' It had taken a very long time to become more fluid with the system. I didn't move my mouth anymore, ghosting the words as I attempted to force nothing out of my throat. The instinct was why I was so sure I used to talk.

'Can't complain Tacey. Especially not with your figures. They are a little down on last month but still in the top twenty percent.' He checked the tablet on his lap to track through the numbers. 'Any reason for the slow down you think?'

My stomach cramped up. I couldn't afford to slip anymore; if they thought I was flagging I could be out.

'Eyes have been tired. I will improve.'

'Eyes huh? Not sleeping well?'

'Fine.' I bit the tip of my tongue. I had only dreamed the once; it might never happen again, there was no need to worry the Governor by telling him I had started dreaming.

'Perhaps your helmet is a little out, I'll get them to recalibrate it and double check.' He grinned at me and I attempted to smile back. I needed to make sure I was on form for the next little while. I had heard of them putting in extra tracking software to the helmets to even monitor your eyes to make sure you weren't letting your mind drift in there. 'Nothing else bothering you is there Tacey?'

I shook my head.

'You getting on with everyone in the housing complex? Vivian is on your floor isn't she?' I nodded this time. 'She was telling me all about Seth, they seem to be getting on. She told you much about him?'

I thought about it for a second. Vivian had sat in my room a few nights ago and talked about a Seth but I could have sworn she was talking about someone from before. She had seemed upset, she missed him. People did have a habit of talking to me on our floor; I think it was my lack of being able to talk back.

I scrolled through the words on my display. 'Not much.' He looked at me thoughtfully for a second before nodding and plastering on his corporate smile again.

'Nothing you remember about him?'

I shook my head again.

'Okay, well I'll get someone to calibrate your helmet after this shift. We can have a catch up and see how it's done in a couple of weeks.'

I swallowed my dismay at the thought of an extra meeting. They really were going to keep an eye on me.

'Thank you.' I waited for him to look down at the tablet, his signal that the meeting was over, and pulled the headset off as quickly as possible. I went back to my station and worked the rest of the shift in a frantic panic.

***

I climbed up onto the transport, dragging my tired body up the steps. I drew level with the driver's compartment before he said my name. I froze and looked back at him in alarm through the plexiglass.

'Tacey.' It was as if he was stating my name rather than saying something to me. I smiled and gave a quick nod before hurrying to the back of the bus. No-one else spoke but I suddenly felt like the vehicle was very crowded. A man sat down beside me and another two sat opposite. I tried to keep my gaze firmly out of the window but I kept getting drawn back in. It felt like there were eyes on me the whole time but every time I looked back, no-one was looking. By the time the bus pulled up at the housing complex, my body was coiled like a spring ready to leap out. It took all my strength to stay calm and file off the bus with everyone else. Though I kept someone between me and the driver when I exited.

As the lift rode up the building to the fiftieth floor, I tried to convince myself it was just the anxiety from the meeting with the Governor that had my mind playing tricks on me, putting me on edge. I didn't relax until the door to my rooms was shut, cutting me off from the rest of the world. I double checked the locks and bolts were secure and curled up in my chair.

***

There was no grass this time. I awoke on a chessboard of concrete slabs. My fingers rubbed over the coarse surface and I was vaguely aware of the cold seeping up into my body. Sunrays bounced back

21

and forth around me. I shielded my gaze and looked up, confused by the maze of beams until I realised it was bouncing between buildings. I was surrounded by gleaming buildings, walls entirely made of glass. Pushing myself up to my feet, I pushed back the wave of dizziness that threatened me. I was in a square, an open area between the buildings. Benches were dotted around and planters with actual plants in them, some were even flowering! I hurried over to one to stare at the deep purple flowers. I liked these, I'd seen them before I was sure of it.

The area was too quiet, too empty. A familiar sense of foreboding came over me. Why was it so empty? It shouldn't have been empty, there should be people buzzing everywhere. A chair had appeared, a silver metal chair. I blinked and suddenly the Governor was in it, staring at me with a look of disappointment on his face.

'No.' Half the word clawed its way out of my throat and I turned and began to run. My legs felt like jelly. I had no idea where to run, only that I had to get away. I headed for the building to my left, instinctively heading to the side door. He shouldn't have been here. What was he doing here? The door was open and I burst through, slamming it shut behind me. I leant back against it, my breaths coming in ragged gasps. My body started moving again, going on autopilot. I had to get to the basement. How did the Governor know I was here? Did someone sell me out? Why was I so sure about the basement? I forced myself to stop. I was dreaming. That was all. All I had to do was wake up. I squeezed my eyes closed and willed myself to wake up.

'Keep running. Tacey you have to keep running.'

The voice from before was back. My eyes snapped open but I was still alone. The door behind me rattled and it was all I needed to get moving again.

'Tacey? Can you hear me? Just follow my voice.' I hesitated; it sounded like it was coming from everywhere all at once. I opened my mouth but still nothing would come out. 'Damn it they've gagged her.'

My hands clamped against my temples as the voice started to sound like a buzz again. My mouth opened wide as I forced air out in a grotesque facsimile of a scream.

'Dial it up.'

'It's already too high.'

'They'll trace it.'

'Tacey?'

I dropped to my knees; the noise was too much. My squeezed my eyes shut so hard my vision went white and prayed that I would wake up. The door began to rattle. The Governor was coming for me. My pulse started fluttering in my chest, the palpitations making me double over. There was slamming on the door. The static buzzing kept building. A metal tang filled my mouth. And then, everything went silent.

I awoke with a gasp, slipping off the chair and falling to the floor, still clutching my chest. Something wet dribbled onto my upper lip and my hand came away red. My nose was bleeding.

I clawed my way to the toilet and stared at the haggard face in the mirror. What the hell was happening to me?

***

The lights still weren't lining up. My helmet had been calibrated overnight; I could see some difference in the display but it wasn't making the work any easier. I took a shaky breath, closed my aching eyes for a second and tried again. My disturbed sleep had left me even more exhausted than before. That paired with the anxiety of the increased monitoring meant my productivity was plummeting. The heads-up display blinked and flashed in my vision as I twisted the gauntlets a few degrees. It still wouldn't line up; the green triangles kept flashing, mocking me. The harder I tried, the worse I seemed to get. I couldn't see with the helmet on but I have sworn I felt the supervisor's gaze on me the entire time. Finally, the triangles in the display became a circle and I almost cried out in relief. I locked down the settings and disconnected my display from the current unit and sent it up the chain. I was about to plug into the next unit and start all over again but the voices from my dream kept playing in my head. I felt awful and I looked even worse. A few people had given me strange looks as I had climbed onto the transport but there was no such thing as a sick day anymore. No-one ever really got sick these days. And anyone who got hurt, well they never seemed to come back to work. I had kept my head down as I walked in with the others, trying to keep my pale complexion and black eyes hidden from the security and supervisors keeping watch over us all. I wasn't even half-way through shift when the message popped up on the display to report to the Governor. Panic made me freeze mid action, my gauntlets hovering mid-air. It took a few seconds for my brain to reboot and I pulled my helmet off. I blinked a few times as I got used to seeing outside again. For a moment, I didn't really register the man next to me. His helmet was off too and he was staring directly at me.

'Tacey.' My gaze shot up to the platform but the supervisor hadn't seemed to notice yet. 'You can't go to the Governor.' I took a few paces backwards. He had the same look in his eyes the transport driver had had yesterday.

'She doesn't remember us.' A man stood opposite us on the line began speaking. His helmet was still on but his head was pointed in my direction. 'We won't have long, we're making more noise here than the dreams.'

'Tacey.' The bearded man took over again. I turned away and started making my way to the Governor. Maybe if I told him everything…

'Tacey.' A woman was speaking now, directly ahead of me. 'If you go in there, he'll lock you down and we won't be able to get you out.'

Out? I glanced up, the supervisor was looking in completely the wrong direction.

'We've distracted him but it won't last long. You have to trust us. The door beneath the platform, that's where you need to go.'

'The Governor will start looking for you soon. We have to get you out or you'll be trapped.'

'This place isn't real Tacey. None of this.' Heads were all turned in my direction, voices coming from all directions. No-one was working on my line. Was I hallucinating? Maybe I was dreaming again, or I hadn't actually woken up yet.

'Come on Tacey. Are you seriously giving up? You want to stay here forever?'

Stay here? Of course not but there was nowhere else not since everything changed when…

Why couldn't I remember? I looked up at the platform; he was still looking the other way. The door beneath looked unassuming. I had never seen anyone use it before. I started moving, my feet having apparently made the decision for me.

'That's it, just through that door and down the corridor.' The voices of encouragement followed as I passed the other workers on the line. Each one speaking without being aware. I reached the last person before the door. My hand reached up.

'When the alarms go, just run.' I Looked at the last voice; it was Vivian, but it wasn't. Her eyes looked faraway. I took a deep breath, I guess if it was a dream, the worst that could happen was I'd wake up. I pushed on the door and the screaming alarms kicked in straight away. The lights cut out only leaving red emergency lighting ahead.

I ran.

I could hear shouts over the sirens.

I kept running.

There was a door dead ahead. There was no sign.

The corridor seemed to keep getting longer but I kept running.

Footsteps slammed on the floor behind me.

I ran faster.

I couldn't see a handle on the door.

I threw myself towards it, praying it would give way.

I slammed against the cold surface.

My body jerked upright as my senses flooded back. I tried gasping but there was something in my throat. I started to gag, unable to breathe.

'Steady. It's ok.' A blur moved in front of me. My eyes blinked furiously, they couldn't deal with the sudden influx of light. 'Just try and breath out, I'm going to take the tube out okay.' I tried to stay calm and do as the voice said. I felt the thing lodged in my throat move and cool air began to rush back into my lungs. 'it's going to take a few minutes to be able to readjust. You've been networked for a while now and your body isn't used to this.'

The blur began to take on a more solid form. I squinted as my brain struggled with the stimuli. 'Benjamin?' The hazy face seemed to smile. 'My voice.' I reached a hand to my throat and saw wires sticking out.

'I'll get those.' I focused on him as he started disconnecting me from everything. 'You good? Because believe it or not, that was the easy bit. The physical prison might not have as much security as the networked cells but these guys have guns.'

'Prison?'

'Oh yeah, this is a jailbreak.'

Alex Minns is a self-professed Jack of all trades (and still a master of none). She writes a range of scifi, steampunk and urban paranormal fiction and inflicts all of it on her poor mother. You can find her work on https://lexikon.home.blog/ or on twitter under @Lexikonical

Publishing credits include: *Spring Into Sci-fi 2022, Meteor Falls, Punk (Black Hare Press)* and *Harvey Duckman Presents Volume 8.*

One Cog

by James Wymore

When Henry Peoples signed on with a crew to mine an asteroid between Mars and Jupiter, he told his mother he would just do one trip. Just so he'd have some money for college. That was two years and four trips ago. He enjoyed space travel. As he ran the centrifuge smelt, college was the furthest thing from his mind. When he allowed himself a distraction, it was usually Jenny Farr.

"You don't want to be leaning on that slag box when this machine turns on," he said through the radio. "Not many people can make a space suit look that good." He placed a chemical fuel cell into the end of the ten-foot I-beam where it attached to a three-foot cubed box. It contained the oxygen needed to burn the chemical as well as a reducing agent required for the process.

Jenny smiled and pushed away from the large crate with the grace of a cat, gliding toward the other side of the cave. The blobs of metal inside the acrylic box floated like spirits in limbo. "How long before your shift's over? You know I hate to eat alone." Her voice made the short-range radio sound good.

"Half an hour. But I need to change. I made reservations at Chez Hailey." The U.S.S. Hailey was they ship they all ate and

29

slept on when they weren't working. It was hard used with a lot of miles before the captain had refitted it for mining. He rechecked the clips holding the large box on the end of the arm. If they weren't in such low gravity, the massive box of rocks would have broken those clips.

"French food. My favorite." She giggled. Jenny used the ceiling and floor of the three-meter-tall cavern to guide her as she moved to the other side and grabbed a rail closer to the control panel. Wishful banter aside, they both knew they'd be eating the same food they'd had for the last three months.

A miner's voice broke in. "You do know everybody else can hear you?" They shared a silent smile. Henry joined her at the controls. With only five females in a crew of twenty-three, it was impolite of them to be flirting on the shared radio frequency.

Henry pulled the lever on the giant centrifuge. It spun slowly at first, gradually accelerating. The process was silent. Once the spinning arm reached a dizzying speed, he turned off the motor. Then he pushed the green button. The fuel cell ignited. It rapidly heated the contents of the swinging box, separating the precious and not so precious metals from the rich ore. Some of the fire escaped, leaving long trails tracing the motion of the machine like a comet's tail.

The centripetal force guided the heavier, more valuable metals to the end of a ceramic cone inside the box. Iron filled the middle. The less dense, depleted rock floated to the wide end of the cone. When the fuel was expended, it didn't take long for negative two hundred seventy-degree space to freeze the cone solid.

Henry applied the generator brake. As the arm slowed, energy was recovered and stored in batteries.

He moved out and popped the clips. The three-hundred-pound box floated free. He wiggled the metal cone loose and let it float. It finished cooling while he anchored the box to the floor. Then he pushed the cone toward a large net. He could see the porous pieces of rock trapped in iron along the base and the golden shine of valuable metals at the tip. It was somebody else's job to split the cones and melt off the iron. Only the tip would be returning to earth.

As Henry prepared the box for the next batch, he made eye contact with Jenny. A bulky miner entered the cave. His suit, like Henry's, was so filthy with rock and metal dust it matched the cave, while Jenny's suit remained white and pristine. Pilots didn't come into contact with their product. The man had a metal rail in one hand and a circular base in the other.

"One of the cargo bay handles broke." Henry could see the man's blond beard moving through the visor. "Can you fix it?"

***

Even though many things broke on mining trips, they couldn't afford to bring somebody just to fix the odd sheared bolt. On his first trip, Henry built an attachment for the centrifuge that hooked a mold onto the box. He drilled a hole in the side of one porcelain cone which channeled molten iron into the mold while it was spinning. Since then, it had been easy to make replacement parts for anything they needed.

A ship this old needed a lot of replacement parts. Henry fixed the important things right away. The less important things he worked on when he had time. The airlock was important.

It didn't take long to make a clay mold of the broken handle. Then he clipped it to the modified cone and attached the whole contraption to the arm. He tossed the empty fuel cell and snapped in a new one. Jenny smiled as she watched. Henry liked it when she was here.

He ran the smelter again. This time when it stopped, he unclipped the mold and removed the new handle. He broke the sprue piece off and filed away the molding line. The handle was the right size and shape. It was a lot denser than the aluminum one it replaced, but in low gravity that wouldn't matter.

He handed the new piece to the waiting miner. He nodded thanks before floating out the entrance tunnel.

Henry rotated and said, "I'm done now. You want cheese or snails with your wine?"

Jenny laughed. Everybody on the ship knew she had come from more money than the rest of them put together. They didn't know why she was slumming with a mining crew, but they didn't care because she was a great pilot. Henry hoped she stayed for him.

***

Captain Adrian Ling could not afford to be as hard as he wanted. A head shorter than most of the crew, he shoveled ore with the rest. It was his ship and his money. But he didn't lord it over them. They were miners. He couldn't expect them to pass muster like the sailors he used to lead. He didn't mind the work. Besides, it was one less person's wage to pay.

Tearing the metal rich rock apart with a pick was an art. With bad judgment or aim the pick stopped cold leaving only a dent. Anchored at the feet, it was a considerable effort. Captain Ling worked at an angle, targeting lumps of ore that stuck out. Once h broke several large clumps free, they would spin and fly, usually bouncing off tunnel walls. They kept all the tunnels three meters high, making it easier to push off and move around. He couldn't break many pieces free before he had to round them up and push them into the net. It was a silent process except for actually breaking the rock. Vibrations through the anchors his feet were tied to still registered as soft thumps he could hear. That muffled sound was the rhythm of the mine. And it brought him some relief from the numbing quietude.

He'd taken this same crew out to this same rock four times in the last two years. When he dug in, they did. "Captain," a voice called through the helmet. Ling pulled the neck of his bag closed and turned toward the new light that had entered the tunnel behind him. Half the time he suspected they just thought Captain was his name and not a title at all.

"What's wrong?"

"Broken handle." The bulky man's scarred cheek showed through his visor. He held up a pick head in one hand and the metal bar in the other. He exercised some caution. Mining suits were sturdy, but not impervious.

"Take mine," the captain extended his own tool. "This bag is ready, and my shift is up. I'll take that one to Henry on my way back."

The man scanned the netted ore. If that pile had been on Earth, it would have weighed a ton. They exchanged picks. The man moved to the wall the captain had been working and started chipping away. They rotated twelve hour shifts so that people were cutting and smelting ore twenty-four hours a day. Nobody was particular about which tunnel they worked. Even their longest tunnel only scratched the surface of this behemoth space rock.

All the digging could be done by robots, of course. That's how large corporate mines worked. But machines cost more than wages for small operations and the captain preferred people.

Captain Ling shifted his boots against the anchors and unhooked them. In one great bodily heave he launched the bag forward. As it floated away, he grabbed the cinching rope and let the large mass slowly drag him back through the forty-meter tunnel.

***

"After a twelve-hour day, reconstituted freeze dried food is as good as a French restaurant." Henry was seat-belted across the aluminum table from Jenny. He had short, black hair over dark skin. His pointed eyes hinted at some Asian ancestry, too. In space nobody cared which part of Earth anybody came from.

She raised her water flask in a mock toast. "Not quite," she laughed. She had tan skin and lighter hair. Her work was really during the three-month flight out and back. These days she spent inspecting the ship, driving people and equipment around in the shuttle, and reading. "But maybe we can try something French later." She just meant kissing. She was no space-bimbo.

"Ooh, la, la!" Henry raised his juice bag and drank from the valve. Now that their conversation wasn't on radio, they didn't have to censor it.

"Somebody should really put a spa out here in the belt. I could totally use a shower." Another reason they would stop at kissing. There wasn't enough water for showers.

"I could use a massage," he hinted.

Jenny asked, "What do want to do with your life, Henry Peoples?"

She was either flying all the time or he was mining all the time. That was why he told himself he kept putting off this serious talk. "I'm planning to go to college, I guess."

"You guess?"

"I told my mom I'd become an engineer. But it's been a couple of years and I'm starting think I will have forgotten everything."

"You should. You don't want to be just a miner all your life, do you?"

"Maybe. I don't know. The last few trips have been good."

"But this can't last," Jenny said. He could tell there was something she wasn't saying. "And corporation mining is horrible, I hear."

Henry nodded.

"I like you a lot," Jenny continued. "But I can't see myself with a life-long miner."

Just then Captain Ling came in and stood at the far end of the long table. He was older than both of them put together. He had lighter, rough skin and a broad girth. Despite the name, he didn't look Asian at all. Despite the gloves on his suits, his hands were rough and calloused.

"Good take today, Captain," Henry said.

"Thanks. Evening, Jenny. Henry, has anybody talked to you about the airlock door?" He was rubbing his hands together. It sounded like sandpaper.

"No. I made a new handle. Didn't it work?"

"That's not the problem. I don't know if it's a related issue. But they said the door is broken. They can't get it to seal." There was a worry in the captain's eyes that none of them had seen before. His shoulders slanted noticeably down.

Jenny's eyes narrowed. "The main doors are still sealed, right?"

"Yes. But if we don't fix the inner door, it will flush air every time. We don't have enough air to do that very many times. I need you to make this your number one priority." It was a plea, uncharacteristic of one accustomed to giving orders.

"Of course." Henry stood. "I'll go now."

The ship was not large. They floated to the cargo bay. The door was ajar half an inch along its six-foot edge. The outer chamber held. Henry pushed the door open with little effort. "It shouldn't do that."

On the hinge side he watched the brace arm move as he levered it open and closed. The arm had gearing ridges along the inside. There was a motor rod next to it in a protected housing. But the gear that connected them was missing.

Henry propped the door closed and reached his arm down into the space beneath the housing. His fingers quickly found what he was looking for among thick dust. When he pulled it out and opened his smooth, dark hands, they could all clearly see two halves of a broken gear.

It was light compared to the iron Henry spent most of his time with. Along the break a grainy texture contrasted to the polished outside shape. "That's probably the problem."

"Oh, that's nothing," Jenny laughed. "Henry will have that fixed in a few minutes."

"I hope so," Captain Ling said. "We radioed everybody outside the ship and told them not to try and come in until we get it squared away. Do you mind coming to talk to me personally in my quarters when you get this done?"

"No. No problem, Captain. But I'll have to go out to the smelt to make the piece."

"Of course. We should have enough extra air to blow it out a few times without much worry." He made eye contact with Henry. Then he nodded to Jenny and left.

"I'll be in the main hall watching the movie," Jenny said. She gave him a short kiss. Henry smiled as he put on his suit, grabbed the two gear pieces, and headed through the airlock.

He pushed the loose door closed and held his weight against it. Another miner on the inside held the new iron handle Henry had made. "Okay," he called through the radio, "evacuate."

The pumps sucked the air out of the chamber. But the vacuum began pulling air through the door despite all the effort of two strong men. Henry tried to keep fighting it as the air silently hissed by him. "Just go," the man on the other side said. They unlocked the outer door and the air pushed Henry through it. He grabbed the edge with his free hand, panicking at the sight of stars and black space behind him. He had thrusters of course. But it was still terrifying. When his heart slowed, he pushed on the door to help the motor close it. Seeing the muscly man struggling against the pull of the air earlier, he knew why the old handle had broken.

Henry guided himself with a series of short pulls along the side of the ship and into the mining tunnel.

Jenny was right. It only took him a few minutes to make a clay mold and set it up on the centrifuge with a box full of raw ore. He went through another dance with the leaking air locks getting back in.

He slid the cog down the metal bar and nestled it between the teeth on the brace. He spot welded it in two places. For good measure he ran his finger over the rubber seal.

"It looks stronger than the one that used to be there," the miner said, scratching his beard. Neither of them could understand why an inferior metal had been used for such a critical piece.

"Okay," Henry called through the radio to the unseen person manning the controls in a different room. "Evacuate."

The electric motor turned the air-lock door closed and the pumps removed air from the chamber. At first it seemed fine. Slowly the seal began to whistle and then flutter. The door creaked open half an inch until the pressure equalized with the air pumps.

"Turn it off," Henry said into the mic. He looked at the gear. The iron teeth on the cog were twisted and bent.

"That's not good," the miner said.

"No. I think it's going to be a long night."

***

"Iron is too soft," the captain said. "I was afraid of this." His office was a small room with three chairs, a computer desk, and a small shelf of reference books. There were a few star charts pinned to the wall. But all the actual navigation calculations were done by the computer.

"What should we do?" Henry asked. "I've never worked with any other metal."

"Let me see the original cog again." Henry pulled the pieces out of his pocket and placed them on the desk.

"How much engineering have you had?"

"None. I took physics and chemistry in high school. I haven't gotten around to college yet."

"I don't know much about it either. But this looks like a super alloy. Tungsten-carbide or titanium-something. It's made to be both light and strong. Replacing it with iron is like trying to fix a broken resistor with a rock."

"What can we do, then?" Henry stared at the piece like it was pure black magic.

"I'm in a bad situation, Henry. I bought this ship and leased this asteroid with my military retirement. I'm not somebody to bet my money on other people. I would rather speculate on myself than some invisible market.

"You've been with me for all four of these trips. And we've done pretty well. But all the profits were coming out of this trip. All the wages will be paid, of course. But there won't be any profit. We have air and fuel to get home. But if we go home now, I will just break-even. Which means I wasted the last two years."

"Can't you just make one more trip after the cog is fixed?"

"No. My lease on this rock ends in a month. They could charge me a lot more if they find out how rich it is. More likely they'll sell the whole thing to a big mining corporation if they don't get a new lease soon. That means I'll have to get a new survey. It'll take two or three trips to pay off the new lease and turn a profit. But I don't have it in me. I'm too old for this. I don't think my wife will wait another couple of years either. If you can make this door work and make this trip pay off, I can finally move on."

"I'll do what I can," Henry began.

"Actually, I want to make you an offer," the captain continued. "Your contribution to the last four trips has been invaluable. Your wages aren't fair compensation for all you've done here. I didn't realize how much repair work the U.S.S. Hailey would need along the way. You deserve more."

"You want to pay me more? But you just said you weren't going to make any money."

"I haven't given up yet," the captain said with a fierce chuckle. "Here's the deal, Henry. If you fix this airlock, and anything else that might keep us from getting home, and keep it all working so that we can fill not only the cargo holds but the halls, spare rooms, and empty food and water bays with cargo; in lieu of wages I will give you this ship and all the mining equipment."

Henry sat down and buckled the seat belt. "How much is this ship worth?"

"Not as much as you might think. She's outdated and slow. All the changes I made to her would be expensive to un-do. So, nobody else would want it. There aren't many free-lance miners left. On the market it's probably worth a little more than twice your wages. And there's no way I could sell the equipment. Of course, you'll have to come back for that because we'll be leaving it here. But it will just be a short stop if you're already on your way somewhere."

It was like Henry just won the lottery. With this ship and the money, he had already banked from the last three trips, he might be able to start some mining ventures of his own. "What if I can't fix it?" He loathed the thought. But he wanted this to be an honest deal.

"Then we leave early, and you get your wages."

"I have nothing to lose then?"

"You'll lose Jenny," the captain said matter-of-factly. "She's ready to move on. If you owned a ship for her to fly with some serious future prospects, you'd have more to offer." Henry didn't know what to say. Jenny had been talking that way for a while. He just hadn't realized the captain knew. Even asking Jenny to wait for him to go to college was a long shot. But with a ship, he was sure they could make a good life. He expected most of the crew would be willing to keep working for him.

Captain Ling decided to snap him out of his reverie. "Do you know what an alloy is?"

"Mixed metals. It's what we are separating in the smelt."

"If you have carbon along with manganese, tin, or some other metals and mix it with iron you get steel. I don't know what the percentages are. But we have tin for sure and possibly some other useful metals in the tips you've been separating."

"Steel would be stronger," Henry nodded.

Captain Ling opened the acrylic door that held the books on the shelf and pulled a thick one out with a worn red cover. He pushed it so it floated to Henry. "This is all we have on the subject. I can't make much sense of it. But you had chemistry more recently. I can offer a bonus to the rest of the crew to suffer through a crowded trip home. But it's a bust if you can't get this one cog fixed."

Henry unclipped the belt and said as he floated out, "One way or another, I'll fix it, Captain." It was the most solemn oath he had ever sworn.

***

Henry zipped himself into his bed, a sleeping bag fastened to the wall. It only took a moment to find the right section in the book. He read the whole thing three times, checking every reference he could find. When he was near the end, Jenny knocked and came it. Her light brown hair bounced as she bobbed into the doorway and his heart double pumped at the sight.

"I've never been stood up for a book before," she said. She had both her hands against the door frame. It was just to keep from floating around. To Henry it was a sexy pose.

"I'm sorry," he stammered. "The iron cog wasn't strong enough. The captain's worried and nobody can come in until I figure this out."

"Oh, is that all."

"Sorry. I should have come to tell you."

"It's okay," she said. "We can talk when you get this figured out."

Henry unzipped the bag and floated out to her, leaving the book next to the cocoon-bed. "I think I want to be more than just a miner," he said. "But I don't know if college is the answer."

She looked frustrated and began to push back to let him out. He stopped in the door frame, so they were very close. In zero gravity it was impossible to keep their bodies from touching. Their arms would bump. Then legs would touch. Jenny didn't pull away. But she didn't make eye contact either.

"Look," Henry grasped for words, "I want you in my life. And I'm going to make that happen one way or another." She looked up into his large black eyes and he kissed her. "I'm going to fix everything." Then he left.

She didn't know if she believed him. But she wanted to. As long as the U.S.S. Hailey was tethered to this asteroid, she didn't have anywhere else to go anyway.

***

They radioed a general announcement that Henry would be coming out. He made a stop before he suited up, picking up some black filters from the water recycling box outside the kitchen. Most of the miners weren't halfway through their shift. But two of them had reasons to come in and brought cargo tips with them. They planned the movement carefully to minimize lost air. When Henry made it to the cave, he started at the processed stockpile of conical tips with the iron removed. He analyzed a few of the rounded conical tips. The various metals were in layers. The biggest layer should be tin. The woman working there was married to one of the miners. Jenny knew her. But Henry had only talked to her before when they were with a group.

"So how long before the airlock is fixed do you think?" she asked through the radio. Her voice was less resonant and sure than Jenny's. But to her credit it held no fear when a situation like this would cause most people alarm.

"I don't know," Henry said honestly. For some reason the captain's offer made him want to keep everything a secret. "I think I need half a dozen of these bottom layers. How do you separate them from the iron?"

She picked one of the small cones out of the bag. "We use this to cut them close." She indicated a diamond blade cutting wheel. "Then we use a chemical torch set to a very precise burning temperature to get the last bit of iron off. Sometimes we lose a little bit of the tin. But that's not the big money anyway."

"Could you cut me a thin sliver off the bottom of some of these?" he pointed with a thick glove.

"Sure," she said. He stood back and watched her work. It only took a few seconds of sparks flying in every direction for the saw to make the cuts. She stacked the discs and handed them to him as a pile. They were a little thicker than he'd hoped. Several still had striations which were other heavier metals he wasn't sure about.

"Kind of reminds me of calculus class. Conical sections," he said as he fanned the discs out before adding them to a smaller bag.

She took the smaller cones back to the stockpile. "Anything else?"

"I need one of the tips with the tin still on it, please."

"So polite." She pushed one toward him and he caught it in his bag.

He pushed toward the smelting room and said, "That should work. Thanks."

He went to the acrylic crate of floating blobs. This was all iron that had leaked out of molds after various repairs. It froze quickly into these ghostly amoebas. He scooped up a dozen and added those to the small sack he'd been collecting materials in.

He shoved the tip into the drilled cone to block the end. He placed two thin discs of tin and two large blobs of iron into the cone instead of the usual ore. Then he added one of the small black water filters. He knew these had carbon. He hoped the paper would be consumed in the process.

It was all just estimate work. He had no idea if these were proper ratios. He wasn't even sure if the centrifuge would mix the metals sufficiently to create an alloy.

He ran the machine three times using different amounts of iron, carbon, and tin. Each time it produced a cog that looked like the first one. The surfaces were mottled in places and marbled with black waves running through the metal. He broke off the sprues and filed off the molding lines. He put the new gears into the bag and went back to the ship.

***

Henry never finished his talk with Jenny. The first cog passed the initial test. But somewhere in the night it failed. They woke Henry early and he trudged over to the airlock. This time several teeth had broken. It looked like they had sheared along one of the black marbling waves. So, he chose the cog with more tin and the least marbling next.

It lasted through two evacuations and bent.

The last cog made it halfway through the next day. When they called him over the intercom he winced. Everybody on the ship knew what that meant. This cog had torn in two, much like the original.

***

Henry glued the original pieces back together with an epoxy that claimed to be stronger than steel. Once it was dry, he trimmed the extra glue and made a few extra molds. Then he welded a line along the break on both sides. He used four small metal bars to bridge that weld line and welded those on, too.

It was ugly. It was the Frankenstein's monster of gears. The braces made it inelegant. Henry sighed. He knew this was a long shot. But he was running out of options.

He installed the repaired piece carefully. He made sure to align it so that the glued break would be perpendicular to the brace when it was in holding position. This time he welded around the middle on both sides to try and glean structural support from the motor rod. Then he called through the radio, "Evacuate again, please." The pumps whooshed out the air. He watched the patchwork-cog transfer the motor's torque to the door brace while his heart counted the time. He could see the stress on that gear and feel it in his gut. He sensed the strain on the small bridges and tried to gauge if the repaired crack would hold. Eventually he began to breathe again. His mind began to hope that it might actually hold.

The next few days he worked regular shifts at the smelt as the minutes dragged into hours. He pushed himself to run the centrifuge as quickly and efficiently as possible, still not trusting the glue and solder to last. They had arranged the schedule, so they were only stressing the airlock four times a day. Still, every now and then one of the miners couldn't resist calling out on the radio, "I really need a cigarette." For space-miners suffering was mere inconvenience.

Henry made sure he was there every time they evacuated the chamber, even waking in the middle of the night. Logically he knew his presence would not help. But emotionally he felt that somehow by being there it would make just a tiny amount of difference—and any investment was worth it.

Just after dinner Henry yawned. "I'm so tired. I think I'll head to bed early."

"Again?" She had let her hair down and done her make-up to get any sign he noticed her.

"I'm sorry. This thing has just been taking everything out of me."

"Why? I mean, sure it slows things down. But it's not like you don't get paid the same either way."

"Not exactly."

"What are you not telling me?" Her scowl spoke volumes. It wasn't just because of this recent obsession. He could see in her eyes how she was getting ready to move on.

Henry rubbed his eyes awake and then looked around to make sure they were alone. He took her hand. All his dreams would be meaningless if she left him now. "I was keeping this a secret because I wanted to surprise you when I was sure. Captain Ling made me a deal. If I can keep this airlock working and bring in a big haul from the mine on this trip, he'll give me this ship in lieu of wages."

Jenny was stunned. Her cute mouth hung open just a little and he had to resist the urge to kiss it. He went on, "Don't you see? I don't have a lot of money. But I think I have enough that with this ship and equipment I could start my own ventures. I can't afford to pay them wages, but I think if I offer the miners a percentage of the take, they'll stay on for a few trips until things are up and running. We could have a great life together."

"What about college?"

"College is for people who don't have any way to make it on their own. But we would have our own business… our own spaceship!"

"And you'd be Captain Peoples of the U.S.S. Hailey." Her smile tipped up cutely.

"There's room for a co-captain." Henry held his breath and his heart counted time just like he was watching the repaired gear to see if it would hold air.

"It seems so sudden." He thought she was coming around to the idea. But he didn't want to lose momentum now.

He loosed the belt and floated to the side of the table. He pushed himself toward the "ground" and grabbed the seat with one hand to hold the kneeling position. "After a year and a half, it's not sudden. It's overdue. Jenny Farr, will you marry me?"

She looked deep into his eyes. He was so young and naïve. To think a kid could captain a ship and head a mining operation was ridiculous. But it would be her ship, too. And they would have all the time in the world to make it work.

She looked around at the ship. It was shabby at best. She'd trained as a pilot on ships so much newer and cleaner than this one. She knew it didn't have a great re-sale value. But it was comfortable to fly. She was falling in love with his plan. But she couldn't commit to it yet. His concern that the cog would not hold was infectious.

"I will." They kissed. It was a hard passionate kiss that would have carried them right off the ground if she hadn't been seat-belted.

Henry grinned as he stared into those amazing eyes. This wasn't a done deal. Without a word he knew her reservations. They were the same as his. As they hugged, he knew now, more than ever, everything depended on this cog.

***

The next day at the smelt, Henry made an iron engagement ring. It had an opening for a gem he hoped to fill someday. When he applied the generator brake and unclipped the mold, he heard the crackle of radio communication break the blissful silence. "Henry, there's a problem with the airlock again."

His heart sank. This was his fault. He had let himself get distracted and somehow that tiny diversion of attention had made enough of a difference that the gear failed. He took the ring and headed for the ship.

"I told you to call me every time before you evacuate the airlock," Henry said into the radio.

"We didn't evacuate it. The pilot was just looking at it and noticed a crack." That meant Jenny. He radioed out to ask if anybody needed to go in. It was early in their shift, so all the miners stayed out.

"Okay," he called. "Evacuate, please." He put all his mental energy into willing the cog to hold. The instant he heard the outer door buzz, he yanked the door open and spun inside, using his own momentum to pull it closed. The second he levered the lock closed, he felt himself pushed against it. Air whooshed into the chamber.

He removed his suit and pocketed the ring before he went to look at the gear. Jenny was stifling tears. "I was just looking at it and I saw a crack, so I told them to call you."

"It's okay," he said. "I'll find some other way."

"But how?"

"I don't know yet." He cut off the pieces of the gear that were still welded to the motor rod. Then he reached into the void beneath and pulled out several pieces. It had broken in four, one of which still had the epoxy glue seam running through the middle. Those small bridges had held. It had broken around them.

"Was the crack next to the brace arm?" The cog turned several times to close the door, but it always ended with the same teeth being stressed when it was holding the seal.

"Yes." She made one audible sob.

"Don't worry," he said with one arm around her. "I will find a way to fix this. Maybe I just need a wedge of some kind. We can open and close the door manually and then just hammer a support in to lock it." As he said it, he knew it wouldn't work.

"I'm sorry. I just… I know you'll fix it. You always do." She gave him a small kiss. Call me if I can help." As she floated away, he felt like he was holding the pieces of his own heart in his hands. Was she really so shallow that she couldn't love him if he failed in this one thing?

It wasn't the love, he realized. She needed security. Until now he hadn't been responsible for anything but the odd repaired part. He hadn't even taken college seriously. She was ready to move to the next level. And if he couldn't make this work, she wouldn't keep waiting. At the end of each trip, she casually asked if he was ready to start college. This had been coming on for a while. She'd been hinting and he'd been dodging.

***

Staring at the broken machine pieces, he knew that he was different now. He was transformed. Even if he failed to repair this cog, he would find another ship. His future was space. Somewhere inside him, the broken pieces of his destiny melted into a clay mold and froze. And when that happened, he knew what to do.

Working with scavenged tools, Henry carefully removed the solder and glue from the broken pieces. He collected every tiny piece of the original cog into a thin paper bag. He looked through the captain's book again, knowing it wouldn't help now.

He stopped by Jenny's cabin on the way and knocked. She opened the door remotely."I just wanted to say that I love you. And that my plans won't change whether I fix this or not. I'm going to buy a ship if I can't get this one. And I'm going to need a pilot. But more than that, I want you to be with me." He pulled open the Velcro pocket and flipped her the ring.

He continued. "It's not gold. It's common like me. It's prone to rust. But if you polish it, it will shine forever."

"I love you, Henry," she said running her finger over the empty space at the top of the ring.

"Just like me it's not done yet. Can you come with me? I need your help."

"Of course."

A few doors down he knocked again. Captain Ling opened it remotely from his desk. "I heard about the latest break," the captain said.

"I think I know how to fix it permanently," Henry said. "But the smelting centrifuge won't work. It's not hot enough. And the reducing chemicals in the fuel cells would probably ruin it."

"What are you proposing?" The captain's weary eyes glinted as he placed his future in the hands of a twenty-year-old.

"I need fuel from the ship's main engine." He held up the bag of pieces for emphasis.

It was very quiet. Rubbing his temples the captain said, "We only have enough fuel for one burn out of here."

"I only need a short burst," Henry pressed.

"You can't," Jenny said from behind. "Space is too cold. You have to slowly bring the heat up so the parts don't crack. And you can't do it while the ship is anchored, or you'll tear the whole thing apart."

"Unlike oxygen and food, fuel is expensive and bulky," the captain said. We only brought enough to launch and to stop. We order the engines pre-built for the two-way trip. If we start one, it has to run its course."

"And there's no way to use a small amount of it? It wouldn't even need to burn full power. I just need to get it above fifteen hundred degrees for a few seconds."

The captain said, "Once you start the burn, it has to finish the entire stage."

"Could we remove part of the fuel?" Henry refused to give up. "There's nothing else on this ship that burns hot enough."

"It might reduce our top speed and add a few weeks to the trip home," Jenny said. "But the solid fuel is fairly soft. You could cut a chunk out without igniting it or upsetting the launch."

"You're crazy," the captain said. "But it just might work."

The three of them suited up. Jenny was wearing the iron ring when she pulled on her gloves. They muscled the airlocks and moved out of the one story, rectangular ship. Henry admired it anew as they floated away from the tapered front. There were a few small windows toward the front where the bunks were. The bare metal vessel was anchored to the big rock with chains. A giant blast shield before the engine preventing any stray energy from damaging the vehicle as well as reflecting it so that it would increase thrust. The chemical engine mounted behind it was about eight feet in diameter and twelve feet long.

Jenny said, "The burn stages are visible rings. Starting at the back you have a warm-up and slow movement stage which gets us clear of the asteroid and pointing in the right direction. The next stage is the acceleration burn. Then it cuts here, and we basically coast all the way back. There's another warm-up stage here which also turns the ship around." Henry noted a small vent on both sides of this stage. "Then the final burn counteracts the momentum and slows her to a stop. The only other fuel on the ship is for maneuvering along the way. But it's not nearly as hot."

The captain said, "We had twice as many rings originally. But the trip out burned them off."

Henry studied the column of chemical fuel carefully. "Is there some place we could remove some without upsetting the system?"

"Here and here," Jenny pointed to the acceleration and deceleration burn rings. They made up the majority of the striated cylinder. "You have to take the exact same amount from each one to maintain the balance."

"How exact?" Henry said.

"Within a few grams."

"So we cut a hole, remove some fuel, and build an oven," Henry said.

"Just patch the sheathing so a stray spark doesn't ignite the fuel from the side."

"I don't like it," the captain said. "I won't risk twenty-three lives for this."

There was a long silence. "How much fuel do you need?" Jenny asked.

"I don't know," Henry said. "I just need to melt the cog pieces."

"We could try using some of the warmup stage fuel that is already exposed," Jenny said. "It might require some course adjusting after the acceleration burn. But it's not beyond the capabilities of an expert pilot." She put one hand on her chest to gesture dramatically.

The captain shook his head. "Reminds me of the fool stunts they used to pull in the military. I still think it's crazy. But we're going to do it anyway."

***

Deep down one of the mining tunnels, Henry wired an electrical igniter to the fist sized chunk of fuel. He jammed the soft fuel into the end of a ceramic cone from the smelt and ran the wires through a hole he drilled on the side. He put the broken gear pieces together like a puzzle and placed them into a clay mold. Then he set the cone upside down over the mold and anchored it all in place with chains.

Nobody had any idea what would happen when they ignited this makeshift oven. So they hooked a remote switch on it. Well outside the tunnel, the three of them stood looking at the remote control. The red light indicated that it was on.

Captain Ling reached out unceremoniously and jammed his thick gloved finger onto the button. A green light went on for a second. A burst of light flashed from the tunnel. No sound was heard. They cautiously entered the tunnel.

There was a blotch of black soot along one wall where the cracked cone leaked fire. It was all cold as space now. Henry untangled the mess of chains, singed wire ends, and ceramic pieces until he found the clay mold. The box around it had been burned off and the mold was coated black. Henry lifted it up and the three of them watched as he carefully brushed his glove over the top.

Beneath the soot was a shiny silver cog. He began breaking the now hardened clay off and brushing away the residue. When it was over, he held out a large metal gear. It was light; shiny on one side and mottled on the other. There were wiggly lines radiating from the center where the blast had pushed the broken cog pieces into the clay before melting them. Henry carefully examined each tooth, rubbing it with his glove. He refused to surrender his skepticism.

"It looks good, right?" Jenny asked. She was biting her lip.

"Only one way to find out," the captain said.

***

As he welded the gear back onto the motor rod, Henry felt numb. If this didn't work, he had no idea how he would get a different ship. He hoped Jenny would stay with him anyway. But there was more to it than impatience. This cog was symbolic.

"This is the last shot," Captain Ling said with his arms crossed. "We won't have enough air if we have to flush this airlock again."

Henry said, "Please evacuate."

Jenny grabbed his arm. The pumps sucked the air out. They all waited. Henry stared at the cog, bolstering its strength psychically.

After a full minute, they began to relax.

"It's working." Captain Ling smiled. He saluted Henry and headed back to the office.

Jenny kissed his cheek. "This one will hold."

Henry called through the radio, "Let's keep the six-hour schedule. Call me every time you use the air lock."

"You got it."

Days turned into weeks. Henry's life was a blur of smelting and monitoring the airlock. They filled every empty corner of the ship with conical tips. The captain even moved his computer to his cabin and filled his office.

Henry watched as they closed the outer doors on the last miners after releasing the anchor chains from this rock. They had to carefully maneuver between the bags of cargo tethered everywhere. Only after the torque on the cog was finally released did he let himself relax. "We're clear, Jenny," he called through the radio.

Henry looked at the cog. There was no pressure on it now. He took a deep breath and let himself relax for the first time this month. He would get a new part back on Earth. But for the rest of his life, whenever this airlock opened, he would think about that gear.

He had already sent a request to lease this same asteroid after Captain Ling's lease ran out. He would wait a month before he started talking to the crew about continuing to work for him after this trip. Right now they were all too exhausted and needed some time off.

From the front of the ship, he heard the captain radio, "Take us home."

"I'll take us to Earth," Jenny said. "I'm already home."

James Wymore studies both science and spiritualism in a lifelong pursuit of truth, finding some of the greatest wisdom in the pages of good stories. His own bibliography spans the spectrum of genres, with half a dozen books and anthologies in print. Search with him at http://jameswymore.wordpress.com

A Cold Reception

by Barend Nieuwstraten III

The sound of Ariti's own breathing made him nervous as it reverberated inside his helmet. While it should have been reassuring to him, such frank awareness of his unconscious rhythms of life instead made him acutely aware of the fragility of life. Especially with the accompanying sound of blood pumping in his own neck and the knowledge that the black void of space was rubbing its dark eternal emptiness against the outside of his suit.

He needlessly held his breath as he stepped down onto the frozen surface of the so called 'blue comet.' In truth, an iceberg in space too small and slow to truly qualify for the label, but sufficiently rich in metals according to Initial scans. Hooking himself to a piton loop in the ice, he prepared to take a drill core sample for analysis. This was it. One outside task, then he could go back inside the lander and stay inside for the rest of the mission. He positioned the drill on the flattest surface he could find and activated it.

The solidified frost-blue fluid seemed to foam as the rotating trio of cutting lasers burned their way into it. Frothy white fragments floated away like the cream off a soda-float that some child had blown on, only crystallising upon release. Ariti frowned intrigued as he watched the secondary stage of the drill send its arm in to cut the base of the ice cylinder. Once it was done, the drill ingested and sealed the sample within its central chamber.

Relieved to be done, Ariti collected the loaded drill and carried it back to the lander.

***

"So, what have we got?" Lieutenant Holterman asked, as Ariti examined the melted sample in his corner of the lab. His feet tucked into railing beneath his workstation to hold him in place as the lieutenant used the ceiling rails to pull himself closer. "Doesn't look like much. That's all you got with that big drill of yours?"

"Wasn't terribly dense," Ariti said, pulling his head back from the microviewer. "I'd say this water ended up in space rather suddenly, if I had to guess."

"Water?" the lieutenant asked, pushing himself down from the ceiling to hover beside him.

"Not just water. *Seawater*, judging by the mineral and microbial content."

"What's a massive ball of seawater doing in space?" Holterman asked, pulling himself closer to the observation tank. "Did a planet explode somewhere?"

"Interesting hypothesis," Ariti said, raising his brow. "But I think it escaped a container of some kind. Given that there's a large metal core to it, I'd say it escaped from that."

Holterman straitened up. "So, what? Some sort of space aquarium?"

Ariti shrugged. "Perhaps some sort of aquatic ark. I mean, once you factor in the compression ratio back to liquid form, my guess is that the original volume of fluid would be enough to fill a… three-bedroom habitat?"

"Who would even launch something like that?" Holterman pondered for a moment. "Maybe a colonial ship jettisoned it for some reason, fifty years ago, or so, during the exodus to Mars."

Ariti shook his head. "I'm no marine biologist, but I don't think this water came from Earth. Aside from the trajectory being wrong, there's stuff in here I don't recognise. I think we should tow it whole and find somewhere to let it melt."

"Easier said than done," the lieutenant said, scratching his brow at the logistics.

"If we want to study it properly, thawing it will probably yield the best results."

"Just as soon as we find somewhere willing to fill a cargo bay full of bacterial brine," the lieutenant scoffed.

"That won't be hard," Nishida said, startling them both as he stealthily joined the conversation. He floated in a little closer. "Scan's complete. Not so much a metal core, as a structure. Framework, plating, engine. Looks like some kind of ship in there," he said, casually.

Ariti and Holterman looked at each other a moment, before turning back to the stocky Japanese analyst. Both taken back by the notion of a non-human craft. A historical discovery, if true.

"Did I hear you say something about seawater?" Nishida asked, flippantly. "Bloody fish at the helm, eh?"

It took Ariti a moment to match his career-changing excitement to the analyst's inexplicable nonchalance. "So, this seawater could be their environment. Their atmosphere. First encounter with aliens and they're aquatic," he marvelled. "So, they must have experienced some catastrophic breach…"

"And instead of air escaping into space, their brine leaked, expanded, and froze," Holterman finished.

Nishida raised an educational finger. "Well, probably boiled *and* froze, given how water in space-"

"So, we've got aliens," Ariti said, as a chill ran up his spine. "Man's first contact. Holy shit. We're here for it."

"I would have put my money on gas breathers, but yeah," Nishida said. "Though, I think it's safe to assume, that if they didn't get flushed out into space, they're dead either way. Dead and frozen."

"Nishida, you seem awfully calm about all this," Holterman said. "Do you not get the gravity of this?"

"Strange question for one floating man to ask another. But I'll be excited when we get all that frozen ocean crap out, and get a look at their tech," he said, with a shrug. "That's where the real action is; plumbing and propulsion." He winked at them as he grabbed the railing and pulled himself out of the room. "But, by all means, you enjoy your alien thawtopsy, when it rolls around," he called back.

***

Galle station, on the moon of Triton, was evacuated for research on the 'blue comet'. All non-essential personnel were temporarily relocated to the nearby Lassell base. Both installations were giant horizontal wheels, spinning to generate sufficient gravity for human occupation. The icy object was quarantined for months before any real research could take place, giving the Martian military time to reach and garrison the station. Until they could, the icy haul was kept in external storage on the moon's freezing surface, trapping the research crew on Neptune's largest moon for a considerable stay.

Once the research teams had exhausted speculation upon their own scans, they were left to entertain themselves for the following weeks. It seemed to most a combination of a long holiday, and a prison stay. Holterman remained in charge of the mission until a higher officer could arrive and assume command.

Leaving him in charge of a small team of experts filling their days with barely facilitated recreation until they could return to work on the most important discovery in human history. Being hard to maintain excitement for such a long time, most ended up adopting Nishida's flippancy during their lockdown.

Once soldiers arrived to secure the station, everyone went back to work. Ariti spent much of his time taking further drill core samples and studying them with the aid of a recruited biologist stationed on Lassell base, communicating exclusively through non-personal secure correspondence and data exchange. With access to better equipment in a more stable environment, Nishida was thrilled to be running scans on the alien ship. Able to extrapolate far more data than Ariti could from his alien sea water. At least until the small military presence on Galle Station cleared the biologist from Lassell.

"You seen the new biologist?" Nishida asked, as the team ate their breakfast in the cafeteria.

"No," Ariti said, looking around.

"Yeah, she's not here yet," the analyst said. "Well, she is but she doesn't have complete access, yet. Clearance checks and all that."

"So how are you going with your scans?" Lieutenant Holterman asked.

"Yes, she *is* cute," Nishida said, with a devious grin. Choosing to answer the question he wanted to be asked.

The lieutenant shook his head as he spooned more heavily peppered yellow soy scramble into his mouth. "Are you getting anywhere?"

"Well, I gave her a wave through some glass, but that's about it," Nishida shrugged. "Though she did wave back and smile."

"Not with the biologist," Holterman said, annoyed, "with the bloody alien craft."

"Yeah, you'd think you hadn't seen a woman in months," Ariti joked.

Nishida gave a sour smile, having not seen a woman in months. "Is that supposed to be funny?" He looked back to the lieutenant, "Sorry, Holt, yeah. It's been huge. There're all these different mechanisms and generators for systems we're still trying to figure out. But it looks like we might have new weapons, propulsion systems, and computers, soon. It's a goddamned tech treasure trove in there. This find's going to push us forward centuries by the looks of it. And that's just the stuff we're pretty sure we've identified. There's more in there. We'll have to figure it out. Got the signal that we can start thawing today. So, you'll get to play with those squids that were piloting it, soon enough."

"Squids?" Ariti asked, with intrigue.

"Oh, shit. I wasn't supposed to say that," Nishida grimaced, lowering his voice. "Forget I said anything."

"Squids?" Ariti repeated.

"Technically more like an octopus, well, quadrapus, if anyth… no, shit, forget that too," Nishida panicked. "It's not even my department. Ah, if anyone asks, I never said anything."

"Calm down," Holterman instructed Nishida, as he pointed to Ariti. "Obviously, the new biologist is going to have to work with the one who examined their breathing fluid. Now, give us each a piece of your toast and we'll say nothing more about it."

Nishida pulled his tray in, protectively. "I'd rather get fired."

***

The day the new biologist showed up in the mess hall for breakfast was after two days of Ariti running water tests for her department and answering questions, clumsily disguised as hypothetical, but clearly about the aliens. Seeing her about to sit at another table he gestured for her to join him, as there was no one else around.

Nishida's team kept working late, so lunch became their breakfast, while Holterman typically skipped breakfast to keep abreast of the analyst's progress.

She seemed reluctant, but in the end shrugged and joined him.

"Morning," Ariti said, "I'm Ariti."

"Uh, Doctor Ellen Nichols," she said, sitting across from him.

Ariti felt awkward only providing his surname, now. He wanted to amend his introduction, but it seemed too laboured now.

"Ah, yes, I've been reading your findings," she said, taking a sporkful of her breakfast.

"And I think I've been reading your elusive prompts," he said. "With my mushroom style research."

"It's not…" she began but shook her head, "mushroom style research?"

"Kept in the dark, fed bul… eh, fertilizer. Still expected to yield results."

"Oh, I see," she said, with a slight grin. "That's not me. All cross-departmental communication is filtered through intelligence. Not to keep secrets, I imagine, but more out of procedural habit."

"So, you're allowed to talk about what you're working on?" he asked.

"Disclosure stipulated that I not discuss anything with anyone 'outside this station', so I think you're in the clear. Especially if they're letting us dine together."

"Good point," Ariti said. "So, how are our new frozen friends doing?"

"Medically speaking, not so great," she said, with a shrug. "Three of them were preserved in one piece, while the other two were torn apart in whatever violent event spilled their atmosphere. Pretty sure there were more onboard but got flushed into space before they could be cocooned by their freezing environment. Still frozen, but hurled terrameters away."

"I suppose the question is whether or not they're the kind of lifeform that can handle being stored frozen."

"Of the three in one piece, we've kept two frozen and put the other in a tank of their fluid to thaw. Even if they're like wood frogs, pumping their blood cells full of glucose to prevent cell damage from the cold, they were frozen too fast to have naturally adjusted in such a manner. At best we're just prepping a better corpse to be autopsied, than the remains of the ones we've looked at so far. "

"Trying to communicate with them would be fun, if they *did* survive," Ariti said. "Never mind a language barrier with no point of reference. They don't even use the same state of breathing compound."

She leaned back and raised her brow, impressed by his observation. "Precisely," she said. "Do you want to see if I can get you in for the examination?"

"Yes. More than anything."

"I should be able to convince the higherups that I need you there to answer questions on the fly," she said, with a warm smile.

***

Ariti was in awe, standing before the cylindrical tank that contained the corpse of a species he'd never seen, suspended in a half-frozen slush of brine. About three meters in length, it was very much like an octopus, but with only half the tentacles. It's skin primarily a grey purple with a faint pattern, difficult to determine through the cold frosted glass and icy fluid. It had a hard, dorsal bone-plate that protected it from the front, with a pronounced ridge line. Six glassy red eyes diminished in size as they climbed its head. The closest it came to any garments or equipment was a large metal cylindrical device attached to the left side of its head.

"What is *that*?" Ariti found himself asking aloud, as he wiped condensation off the tank for a better view of the metallic object. "It looks like high-tech version of a vintage dog bowl."

"It's some sort of cybernetic device," Doctor Nichols said. "We managed to remove the two from what was left of the injured pair. Had they been alive or in one piece that would have been a near impossible task, given the depth of their intrusion into the body."

"What do they do?"

"Not really my area of expertise," Doctor Nichols said, "You'd be better off asking the tech research team. Or an actual cyberneticist. But, given the way they appeared to be integrated into their hosts' bodies, I'd hypothesize that they were meant as some sort of auxiliary device for controlling or at least stimulating various parts of the body, presumably with electrical impulses. Probably more effective in the non-skeletal structure of a cephalopod, than in the more mechanical endo-skeletal chassis a humanoid system typically employs. Long, segmented, metal tendrils ran through the bodies of the injured ones. Possibly deployed in response to their severe injuries, activated by trauma. Whereas scans reveal that the ones attached to our flash frozen friends are barely intruding upon the bodies of their hosts. Well, comparatively. Wires connect the unit to the cerebellum and into the nervous and cardiovascular systems."

"So, they activate upon crippling injury to keep the poor bastards at their posts?" Ariti clarified.

"Something like that, I imagine, yes?" She shrugged. "Possibly even in death."

"The manager at my gap-year job probably would have liked those then," Ariti grimaced, comically as he looked back to her.

Nichols shook her head with a mildly amused smile, before something caught her attention. She stepped around Ariti to look at the tank. It made him instinctively step away from it before turning back around to face it.

"What?" he asked, looking the creature up and down.

"I thought… well, it's probably just loosening up a little," she said.

"Well, spending all this time with us, I suppose it's bound to eventually."

Doctor Nichols cocked an eyebrow, not getting the joke.

"Never mind," Ariti said, before hearing a faint clicking sound. "Actually, do you hear that?"

"I do," she said, nearing the tank intrigued. "It could be the cybernetic device trying to establish a resuscitative protocol."

Ariti's eyes widened. "You seem awfully calm about that."

"It's an aquatic lifeform in a tank. It has nowhere to go," she said, waving a dismissive hand. "Although, octopuses are known to drag themselves across land and, come to think it, it's not like it needs to breath at this point. It's very much dead. But we have soldiers with shock rifles," she reminded him, pointing to the soldiers, "should anything happen."

The creature convulsed within the tank, startling everyone to attention. The soldiers straightened up, as a pair of lab techs approached from other stations.

"I wouldn't get too excited," Doctor Nichols said. "As I said, there'd be a great deal of cellular degradation due to the sudden freezing. The water would have shredded its respiratory membrane as it froze."

"Though their atmosphere was greatly thinned before it froze," Ariti reminded her, "and they're not actual octopuses. Nor their seawater quite the same as the stuff our eight-legged friends breathe in tanks back on Mars."

"Tentacled," she corrected, standing next to him. It twitched again. "It *is* trying to resuscitate… well, reanimate the body."

"To what end?" Ariti asked, as two of its tentacles began to furl while the other two merely twitched and dangled in the fluid. "It has no station to return to."

"It doesn't know that," Nichols said.

A small red light flashed, seemingly from beneath the surface of the cybernetic attachment's metal casing. As Ariti squinted at the device, wondering what kind of light penetrated metal, there was a startling smash across the room. All turned to one of the other workstations, abandoned by the curious lab techs. Upon it, the removed cybernetic unit from one of the dead aliens was thrashing about its thin, segmented, metallic cables. It had knocked containers off the bench as the flailing cables started emitting buzzing sparks from the series of small raised circular windows around its segments. It was like a metal jellyfish had woken and panicked to find itself out of water.

"The units are communicating," Ariti said, as the guards held their shock-rifles ready. "That should be a nice surprise for Nishida's team, then."

The lab techs quickly distanced themselves further from the workstation. A red light was flashing, seemingly in response to the one that woke it, as it continued to flail about and spark. The nearest soldier took a few steps closer as he took aim.

"We don't know how it will respond to an attack," Nichols said.

The soldier bit his lip as he hesitated. "You're the expert," he said. "But if it goes near anyone, I'm taking a shot."

The metal device shook and rocked on the bench surface as its lashing extremities swung and whipped about. Breaking its tantrum, the cables all suddenly retracted, pulling into the main casing with such force that the recoil pulled the device off the bench and onto the floor. It sounded heavy as it clunked loudly. But it stopped moving and stopped flashing its red light.

"Oh shit," one of the lab techs said, pointing back to the tank.

The others looked to see the dead alien in the tank pressing two of its tentacles against the glass in opposite directions, steadying itself as the other pair hung uselessly beneath it. It twisted its body as its red light began to glow bright. Its eyes had changed, still lifeless but now crystalized and frosted, dulling the red. The light from the device emitted a narrow beam through the water. It ran down the glass etching a vertical line into it, before the creature twisted and drew another one parallel to the first. It left a pair of thick white lines in its path, before the creature twisted itself to one side. Soldiers moved between the lab techs and the tank with their weapons pointed ready, as the creature completed a white rectangle in the glass.

"What is it, some kind of message?" Nichols asked.

The creature adjusted its two functional tentacles so that one pressed against the centre of the rectangle and the other in the opposite direction. Droplets of water began seeping through the white lines as they began to crumble.

"No, I think he's coming out," Ariti said, grabbing Nichols by the arm and pulled her away.

The rectangle of curved glass flew out across the lab as the alien brine poured out and spread quickly across the floor. The soldiers made to take shots but had to make sure everyone wasn't standing in water when they did.

"Get out," one of the soldiers yelled. "We'll seal it in."

But the creature washed fast across the floor, riding the temporary waterfall, between the exit and most of those within the lab. It flung itself across the brine-lubricated floor, grabbing free standing benches to pull itself towards the other cybernetic device on the floor. There was only one lab tech close to the exit, and he left, sealing the door behind him, activating the alarm.

Nichols sighed, looking to the door despite the more pressing matter in the room.

"Thanks, prick," the other lab tech said.

Clearing a bench at the back of the lab, Ariti climbed up and quickly assisted Nichols up with him. The soldiers and the other tech climbed up onto benches as well. Once everyone was off the floor, the soldiers fired their shock-rifles at the creature between two free standing benches and out of Ariti's sight. Satisfied they'd subdued the alien, the soldiers lowered their aim.

A tentacle quickly wrapped around one of the soldier's ankles and yanked his foot out from under him. The soldier's back slammed hard onto the benchtop as his rifle landed on the bench and slid to the edge as he disappeared between the fixtures. He began screaming, but his voice became quickly muffled.

The other soldier held his gun high, trying to get a clear shot. He winced annoyed and put his gun down, instead drawing his combat knife and jumped to the next bench before diving in. Ariti could still see nothing, only hearing more screams and grunting accompanied by terrible cracking and snapping sounds.

Ariti looked around. "Toilets," he said, to the others. He jumped down. With no one firing shock rounds, there was no need to be concerned about running through the giant puddle, spread by centrifugal gravity to every corner of the lab. The remaining lab tech managed to snatch the first soldier's rifle as he dashed to join the others.

"I think we've established that shock-rounds barely slow that thing down," Nichols whispered.

"The dog bowls on the side of their heads are electrical though," Ariti reasoned, referring to the cybernetic devices. "So, it'll probably have some disruptive effect."

"On electronic devices made specifically for underwater use?" she asked, looking to the other tech. "Likely constructed in an underwater environment. I don't think that's going to help."

"It's not for the alien, it's for Mathews," the lab tech said. "Going to shock the shit out of that asshole for locking us in." He looked to Ariti who was peering through a crack in the door, watching the partially functional creature eventually make its way to the locked exit. "If we find a way out of here, that is. What are we thinking? Air duct?"

Ariti shrugged. "Yeah, take a look around… Erricson, wasn't it? I'm just going to keep an eye on our dead cyborg squid neighbour."

"Yeah, on it," Ericson said, as he started climbing one of the toilets and lifted himself up onto the cubical walls.

"What's it doing?" Nichols whispered.

"Testing the security door," he said, watching it feel about the tech with its only two functional tentacles. "Gotta be honest. I'm circumstantially on its side on this one."

"What?" she asked, confused.

"If it can't breech *that* door, it's going to try *this* one," Ariti said, watching the creature as best he could. The creature dropped back to the floor, obscuring Ariti's sight of it behind the benches between them.

It deployed its red beam again, slicing into one of its own tentacles before moving on to another. Its head hit the floor as it used its two functioning appendages to deglove its two other unresponsive ones from the metal cables beneath. Once done, it pushed its head back up now propelled by two slimy organic appendages and two mechanical ones, now clacking on the hard, wet floor.

"I think we're all going to need to lose some weight, and ribs, if we want to go out this way," Ericson said, peering into the shaft above the cubicles. "Perfect for an octopus, thought."

"Not one with that large dorsal plate," Nichols said, seemingly finding some reassurance in talking shop. "Regular octopuses just need an aperture bigger than their eye to squeeze through."

"Doesn't matter, I think he's cutting his way through the lab door," Ariti said, unable to get a clear view. "Shouldn't soldiers be storming this place by now?"

"Unless all the cybernetic attachments activated." Nichols suggested. "Then they might be busy elsewhere."

"I suppose this situation is contained as far as anyone's concerned," Ariti said, watching the creature push a segment of door out. It crawled out under the rest of the door. "I think there's a way out now, at least." Shock rounds fired on the other side of the door with soldiers yelling. "Though I think we should give our aquatic friend a bit of a head start," he added. "Don't want to pull focus off the guest of honour."

"So, what do you think it's trying to do?" Ericson asked, climbing down. "Take over the station?"

Nichols shook her head. "It's an electronic redundancy," she said. "While it's far more sophisticated than anything *we've* made, I don't think it has any mission parameters to follow. Hopefully, just to return all units to the ship, all ships to home base, or at least jump on the comms and just try to report in."

"Well, astrometrics reported that the object had been travelling for well over a thousand years. So, they're at least a millennium or two out of contact," Ariti said, slowly opening the bathroom door. "Home base probably changed frequencies and technology significantly since they last checked in with head office."

"Well, either way it sounds like the soldiers have it under control," Ericson said, taking the lead as they stepped back out into the lab.

"Like the two soldiers it killed?" Ariti reminded him.

"They just had standard issue shock rifles," Erricson explained. "Like Nichols says, shock rifles aren't going to do much to dead flesh and tech made by an aquatic civilization. With the alarm raised they'll be on the cold ammo now."

"So, why are you leading with that shock rifle?" Ariti asked.

"To shoot Mathews in the balls," he said, looking down between the benches.

Ariti smiled. "Oh, yes, you said."

Stepping along the wet floor, they saw one of the dead soldiers laying there. His body was bent, unnaturally, broken by the force of the creature's two functioning tentacles. Cold vapour was creeping across the floor through the missing bottom third of the door. The alarm soon stopped, and the door was released by a soldier.

When they left the lab, the creature was frozen and shattered in hard chunks of frozen flesh where the cybernetic unit controlling it had attempted to continue physical exertion while the organic component drastically dropped in temperature. The red lights of the device faded as it went into some sort of shutdown or standby mode.

"I guess we'll have to keep these things frozen, until the research team crack the rest of their tech," Nichols suggested, with a disappointed sigh. She was talking casually, but her hands were shaking. "Guess, we'll, have to stick with examining the pieces of alien we already have and perhaps scanning the frozen—"

"Oh, hey Mathews," they heard Ericson say, before a shock round discharged. "Thanks for locking us in."

When Ariti looked back, Ericson was being wrestled to the ground by soldiers, while Mathews lay convulsing on the floor.

***

With all the effort that went into containing the device from the reanimated alien and the one in the tech lab with Nishida's team that had activated but luckily yielded no fatalities, one had been overlooked. As had one of the dead soldiers. Only one uniformed corpse had been recovered from Nichol's lab.

Ariti was made to go over security footage with Lieutenant Holterman, which revealed that the alien held the first soldier down while the rogue device that fell off the workstation, attached itself to him, before the dead alien killed the second soldier. Then, while Ariti was hiding in the bathroom with Nichols and Ericson, the device began connecting with the soldier.

Ariti watched in horror as the soldier convulsed on the floor in the playback. The device had attached itself to the centre of the soldier's torso. It made Ariti shudder as he imagined those cables, designed for controlling the tentacles of the dead aliens, working their way through that poor soldier's arms and legs, between muscle and bone. The soldier in the footage began moving, flailing his arms and legs to move across the floor in an impractical manner that no person would employ.

"I'm guessing it was never calibrated for a human body," Holterman suggested, as they watched the soldier's corpse struggle to drag itself across the wet floor. "Doing the best it could with the material it had." It was a surprisingly cold assessment coming from him.

"Why has no alarm been raised?" Ariti asked, looking about. "This was hours ago."

"Don't worry, men are on it. You're far from the first person to be reviewing this footage. But we don't want panic, so we've restricted everyone's movements. Extrapolating all the technological knowledge we can from the vessel is the primary objective being preserved at this moment."

"From the ship that... zombie cyborg soldier is most likely headed towards?" Ariti asked, cynically. "You can't keep Nishida's team in the dark."

"They won't do their best work if they're looking over their shoulder the whole time."

"Their best work?" Ariti widened his eyes in disbelief. "Are you joking? The fact that you have security feeds but haven't caught it suggests that it's used its little laser cutter to carve a more private path through this base. A base on the coldest rock in the system. If he cuts the wrong cable or pipe, we're all f-"

"Everyone's aware of the urgency," Holterman said. "At least everyone that's aware of the emergency. There's a lot of extra muscle around the ship and Nishida's team. Flashing lights and annoying sounds aren't going to make them any safer."

Ariti slouched as he tried to relax, then shuddered again as he thought of the dead soldier's body sliding about between levels and walls. Possibly even beneath or above them. "Why are you showing *me?*" he asked, with sudden realisation.

"Your work here is more or less done," the lieutenant said. "You no longer require contact with any of the others and I need someone who isn't just a grunt helping with this. Someone smart. As you were in the room when everything went down, that kind of counts as appropriate experience. "

"Never thought hiding in the bathroom would buff my resume," Ariti said, grimacing. "Starting to feel jealous of those in the dark, now."

"Will sending you into potential danger affect our friendship?"

"I should think so," Ariti said.

"Well, good news then. I've been ordered in as well, if that makes you feel any less betrayed," Holterman said, straightening his shirt as he stood. "But don't worry, soldiers are already searching the hotspots."

"Hotspots?" Ariti asked.

"Any vaguely traversable pathway to its ship," Holterman said, before he furrowed his brow at Ariti's darting eyes. "Why, what are you thinking?"

"If I was going to make something that sophisticated, I'd make it a little smarter than taking a direct line to the obvious objective," he said, thinking aloud. "I mean, maybe forcing a dead soldier back to its tactical station while on a ship, makes sense. But charging through a battlefield, or even tunnelling, to its assumed objective would be a negligent design flaw. Surely, like us, it wishes to acquire more information on what it presumably assumes to be an enemy."

"Station layout, personnel?"

"If I was operating an alien body with barely any success, I'd probably find the nearest medbay to try and figure out what I could about my new organic vessel."

"Come on," Holterman said, tapping on his com panel.

"Yes, sir?" a voice responded.

"Empty the medbay," he ordered. "Soldiers only, cold rounds."

"Yes, sir," the voice on the comm complied.

"Whatever happens, we can't let it back on its ship," Ariti said.

Holterman nodded at first, then stopped before the door. "Obviously, but why do *you* say that?"

"That tech, all that we've seen so far? That's what they had developed while the human race was still patting itself on the back for inventing bows and arrows. That thing that had three scientists hiding in the toilets, was technically ancient. They were centuries ahead of where we are now a millennium ago. The last thing we need is them calling for help from their descendants who've had at least another thousand years to progress beyond us."

"Humbling," Holterman said, furrowing his brow. "But motivating. Let's move."

***

Ariti had hoped to see Nichols in the lab, when he followed two soldiers and Lieutenant Holterman back in, but her team had been moved. The alien seawater from the breakout had been drained and the room now carried the sharp sting of industrial grade disinfectant hanging in the air. Ariti secretly enjoyed the harsh sterile crispness of the smell, inhaling it deeply through his nose. To him, it was the defining smell of cleanness.

"Why aren't we in the medbay?" Ariti asked.

"Uniform are on that," Holterman said, squatting by a bench. "People better equipped than us. We're here to try and retrace its movements." He pointed to a missing square cut out of a panel and began to run his hand along the beam-cut edges of the makeshift hatchway. "Didn't cut any important conduits or pipes. Seems our little piece of alien tech knows what it's doing."

"So, we're going in?" Ariti asked.

Holterman nodded before ducking his head in.

Ariti squinted unenthusiastically. "I hope my parents remember convincing me to quit that band I had in high school to pursue a '*safe*' career, when my body gets sent to them. Tied into a human pretzel."

Ariti followed the soldiers into the lower service level, where it was impossible to stand up straight. Guided by small yellow lights, he was surprised to find the area lit, having never explored such places before. "Are we sure he went this way?" he asked, as the team ahead seemed to have easily picked a direction with minimal coercion.

"Inside a giant spinning donut?" Holterman asked. "This way leads to the other way eventually."

"There's streaks of water and blood on the floor this way," one of the soldiers clarified, as they continued along the low-ceilinged corridor that curved ever upwards out of view.

"Up here," the other soldier said, in the lead. "Looks like he accessed this systems panel."

"Probably wanted to know if it was warm enough to go outside," Ariti said, with an awkward shrug. "Though given its probable age, it would have been impossibly well prepared to have learned English centuries before it was a language. No matter how sophisticated it might be, I can't see how it would interface with…" he paused as he saw another square of wall cut out on the low ceiling.

"Botanics?" Holterman said, furrowing his brow as he seemed to be wondering what the alien device was up to.

The soldiers climbed out cautiously, and the lieutenant followed. Ariti was about to pull himself up, when one or two of the small yellow lights, ahead in the tunnel, had flickered in his peripheral vision. He turned his head to investigate, seeing nothing unusual but refused to move as he contemplated the situation. He was unarmed, and now alone. There was nothing in botanics the device and its hijacked corpse could possibly need or want. It sent them on a fake trail. "Holterman," he loudly whispered into the room above him. He became uncomfortably aware of his own respiratory function once more as he started breathing heavily though his anxiety. He didn't want to be in that tunnel, but he dreaded taking his eyes off the path ahead in case the highjacked corpse backtracked after he climbed out. "Holterman," he whispered louder. He certainly didn't want to go after it alone. "Holterman," he yelled. "I think it's down *here*."

Before he could be certain of his voice reaching the others as it echoed in the tunnel about him, a body rolled out from a recess in the wall, unfurling across the floor. A familiar soldier laying on his back with the cybernetic device attached to his chest. The dead soldier arched his back to tilt his head, looking directly at Ariti with cloudy eyes. Ariti was frozen. Certain the others hadn't heard him, he was too scared to shout again. He wanted to entertain the notion that he'd be left alone if he did nothing.

The dead man's arms and legs were propelled ungracefully and violently along the floor to pull the body across the tunnel towards Ariti. Calibrated for the cephalopod species that designed it, the device was moving the human body in the closest manner to which it had been designed to anticipate. It smacked the dead soldier's wrists and ankles on the hard floor, seemingly unaware of what to do with extremities like hands and feet. Ariti lowered his arms slowly, unable to imagine pulling himself up in time. He began to slowly back away from the hatch, back the way he came.

"No, no, back the fuck up," he told the corpse crawling upside down towards him. He tried to pick up his pace, backing away hunched over in the low service corridor. "Shit," he yelled in a long-sustained cry, as he turned around and shuffled as fast as he could away from it.

Each time he peered back, he regretted it. It was keeping surprising speed, but it was slowly widening the gap. As he ran, he felt a burning sting, tearing across his hamstrings, one leg after the other, and collapsed on the floor. His legs were unable to continue the hastened journey. He screamed in pain, he screamed in terror, and he screamed knowing that he'd been crippled by the device's cutting beam.

Ariti turned himself over on the floor as he heard the slapping limbs of the pursuing corpse gain on him. He clutched at his wounded legs in pain as he saw the corpse tighten its arms and legs to raise itself and climb over him. The unblinking cloudy eyes of the hanging head moved about upon the upside-down face, looking like shattered laminated glass.

It flung its arm onto Ariti's chest, startling him, and slid its upturned hand towards his throat. He instinctively held his breath as he thought it was going to strangle him. There seemed little else he could do, scared he would bleed out if he released his legs. It struggled controlling the hand until it successfully slipped the spasming fingers under Ariti's lanyard, pulling his security pass off over his head.

As it raised its arm, the animated corpse partially rested on Ariti. The dead man's head looking him square in the eyes, with its own cloudy ones, as it rested its scalp on his chest. With their faces almost touching, Ariti was caught in a staring competition with the repurposed dead man's body.

A green light began to glow beneath the metal surface of the device atop the arching corpse accosting Ariti. It managed to hold the pass up as a wide green bream seemed to scan it. Ariti heard yelling down the corridor soon after, but he let his head drop to the floor and stared at the small yellow lights in the low ceiling above him. He began counting the lights in his head. A practice he used to counter anxiety attacks. He could feel the sweat cooling upon his face as he dared to breathe again. He felt his consciousness fading fast and did nothing to fight it, as part of his mind refused to deal with what was happening.

***

When Ariti woke again, he was lying face down staring at some sort of framework in the dark. He was in a daze, but his legs hurt, and he could feel cords or cables running over and attached to his body. There were small mechanical sounds and periodic beeping, as entities shuffled about him above. He hadn't seen the alien ship yet, now he was almost certain he'd been dragged to it. He wondered if it was safe to move.

"Wait," he heard a voice say. "Is he awake?"

"Holterman?" Ariti asked. As he raised his head, blinding white light accosted him from every angle. He squinted in discomfort.

"Yes, good morning," the lieutenant said.

Ariti realised he was in the medbay. "So, you got it?"

Holterman nodded his head as he patted Ariti on the back of his shoulder. "We thought you were dead when we saw it crawl off you."

"I thought I was dead when I saw it crawl on top of me," Ariti said, carefully bringing his arms closer to his head so he could push himself up. He sucked air in through his teeth, as his recovering hamstrings protested the change of posture. "You're going to need to change my security profile."

"That unit's in deep freeze," Holterman assured him. "After high jacking a human body, we're all fairly confident we don't want it ever getting about again. In fact, no one's looking at those things for some time. Not until we've milked the bounty of the rest of their tech for all its worth, at least. Could be a long time. But it's our best chance on getting on top of them."

"Well, I'd like to believe they've been declared dead since they probably lost contact with home base over a millennium ago," Ariti reasoned. "So, I don't think we're exactly doing them a disservice."

"A disappointing thought," Holterman said, with realisation. "Like you said before, whatever advancements this tech leads us too, will bring us up to speed with where these space squids were at a thousand years ago."

"That's still better than wherever we're at if it takes us forward though."

"And hey, they might all have been wiped out ages ago," Holterman suggested, with an optimistic shrug.

Ariti smiled and shook his head. "Whatever it takes to win the tech race with complete strangers, I guess."

***

Ariti spent the next few days getting about the station in a wheelchair, while his hamstrings mended. Controlled by a thumbstick, he guided his temporary means of movement to the mess hall where he lunched with Holterman, Nishida, and Nichols.

"How goes the new age of discovery?" Ariti asked Nishida, of his research. "This aquatic alien renaissance."

"A great day in the history of plagiarism," he said, proudly. "These Quadrapuses of yours were well ahead of us when they got frozen however long ago." He looked over his shoulder before leaning in. "I mean, once we wrap our heads around half this stuff, it's going to be like when mankind invented the wheel, broke the sound barrier, landed on the moon, and hooked up with their first Olympic gymnast, all on the same day."

Nichols shook her head, "That big, huh?"

"Yeah, for guys without opposable thumbs their society certainly managed a lot back in their day. Definitely not cheaping out on *their* research budget in the process. Looks like they figured out mono-directional artificial gravity through a controlled field instead of this sideways spinning donut deal we've got going on. Not to mention a bunch of other types of projected fields. Their holography is outstanding. Stuff you can walk through, instead of the bend away from you and hurt your brain to look at stuff we've achieved. Their ship's propulsion system's geared for some serious manoeuvrability in space, instead of our system of just being launched like a missile after a thousand calculations. I'm talking independent onboard navigation."

"One small salvage for man, one giant technological leg-up for mankind," Ariti said.

"Speaking of legs," Holterman said, looking to Ariti. "The doctors think there's a lot of potential for medical advancement as well. Once we get those… what did you call them? Dog bowls? …under control."

"They want to use those for medical applications?" Ariti asked, gesturing to his wheelchair-bound thighs. "They're going to have a lot of malpractice claims against them if they do."

"Your legs aren't still attached by luck, you know," the lieutenant pointed out. "That was a very precise attack. The beam cut very cleanly to incapacitate you, avoiding permanent, irreversible damage. No tendons severed, the femoral artery carefully avoided to prevent bleed out, even leaving the femur alone which, when broken, releases a fatty tissue into the bloodstream that-"

"When did you lean so much about medicine?" Nishida asked with a furrowed brow.

"Our medical staff are quite talkative," Holterman said. "They've been on standby for quite some time with little to no interaction with anyone since we've been stuck here, so when I came in to check on Ariti, I think they were just happy to have a fresh face in there to talk to."

Ariti lowered his fork in suspicion. "But it sounds like you humoured them quite a bit, while you were there" he said. "In fact, it sounds like they expressed an interest in the discovery of these cybernetic attachments."

"Yes, well, we had to explain what happened to you so they could treat you effectively. Then, in their professional opinion, they mentioned the medical precision with which your wounds had been… administered. Especially for something that had only just discovered human bodies."

"Even if these things didn't know how to use a human body when they commandeered one?" Ariti reminded him.

"No," Nichols chimed in between bites, "but you have to admit it wasn't bad for their first go. Horrifying as it was. Not to mention how concerning it is that the rest of us weren't alerted to the danger." She gave Holterman a judgmental look as she cocked an eyebrow.

"That wasn't my call," the lieutenant said, defensively. "But it is fascinating that it mapped the human body so quickly and did what it did on a moving target."

"Your admiration for my wounding is comforting," Ariti said, sarcastically.

"My admiration is for the potential unwounding that these devices potentially promise, given their ability to reanimate dead flesh," Holterman said. "We sit on the dawn of an epoque. Don't let what happened to you dampen your excitement."

"What about what happened to those soldiers?" Ariti asked.

"Obviously, but it's not like there's anyone to arrest, or execute in retaliation. What, should we abandon the next great step in human progress because a couple men died?"

"No," Ariti said, rolling his eyes. "I'm just saying we're digging about in some dangerous stuff we don't completely understand. After what's happened, I think I'm more than a little entitled to express a little concern."

Holterman put his hand on Ariti's back. "Look, yes, of course. I'm not begrudging you that. Just keep an open mind."

"An open mind is part of the job. I'm pretty sure it's on my resume."

Holterman shook his shoulder. "Good man."

***

Nichols and Ariti were invited to the medical research lab that had been set up, a little over a week later. Accompanying each other there, they were both shocked to find the dead soldier who had been hijacked by the alien device still in once piece. He was suspended by a harness within an otherwise empty tank. Square contact strips were wired all around his clear cell while cryo-rifles had been modified and equipped to discharge within the tank.

"What the hell are you doing?" Nichols asked, taking a step back as soon as she saw it.

"Ah doctor Nichols, I presume," a tall man said, with messy brown hair in a med-staff coat. "I'm Doctor Tom Madoc. Don't let our military friend scare you, he's quite harmless at the moment."

"At the moment," Ariti repeated, with foreboding.

"Ariti," Madoc greeted, with a polite nod and smile before pointing back to the tank. "Our cross-cultural cyborg friend here has been adequately subdued; I can assure you."

"How?" Ariti asked.

"Well, Nishida's team discovered a frequency within which this particular device seems to operate, so if we generate a counter signal it allows us to create a sort of nullifying field that prevents any movement. At least, mechanical movement. No appendages or discharge by its energy weaponry. It still controls neurological function, for whatever that's worth in a dead man. So, I suppose you could say its conscious, but trapped in a level of dormancy that suits our purpose."

Ariti was still hesitant to approach, remembering his ordeal in the lower tunnel. He also felt bad for the poor soldier whose body was suspended like a vintage puppet with cables instead of strings. It seemed undignified. Nichols put her hand on Ariti's shoulder.

"I worked with this man every day," she said, as if reading Ariti's thoughts.

Doctor Madoc scratched the back of his head. "There's nothing we can do for him now. But by studying what this thing did to him, what it's continuing to do to him, we will make his death far less of a waste." He walked up to the tank as the soldier's frosted eyes seemed to follow him. "Isn't that right my friend." He turned back to his visitors. "I'm half hoping he'll figure out how to talk to us."

"What would even make you think that would be a possibility?" Nichols asked.

Madoc pointed to a screen displaying brain scans. "The brain is surprisingly active," he said, excited and walked back towards the tank. "Terribly damaged and won't last a great deal longer, but the engine's running. The device wasn't made for a human system, probably able to sustain cellular integrity far longer in its intended hosts, but it has slowed necrosis. It's pumping the heart, inflating the lungs. I'd like to think it's exploring his brain, trying to make sense of his neurology and hopefully cerebral functionality. At any rate, I'm quite sure he knows we're studying him." Madoc smiled as he retained eye contact with the suspended soldier. "Don't you?"

Ariti and Nichols looked at each other with raised brows.

"So, why are *you* leading this research, Doctor Madoc?" Nichols asked. "Are you expecting some restorative feature to present itself?"

"It's a strong possibility," the doctor said. "The device does go to a lot of effort to preserve its host. Surely, under normal circumstances, it does a little repair too. It could only serve to aid its purpose in a regime of post-mortem forced overtime."

"The other one severed and removed a couple of limbs from a host it was designed to control," Ariti said. "I'm not so sure it's big on repair."

"Well, yes, I saw the footage. But after being frozen, I imagine there was too much damage on a cellular level to salvage certain parts, and it discarded them accordingly to complete its mission. But this fellow wasn't frozen." He pointed to the man in the tank. "At least not when it had its first test drive. Cellular degradation *has* been significant since they incapacitated it with those cryo rifles, but the device seems to have slowed it. Still ultimately a losing battle, though. I would like to see it put to work on someone who hadn't been frozen. I suppose they'll send us some penal 'volunteers' soon enough."

"So, you can enhance hardened capital criminals with a combat ready cybernetic augment?" Nichols asked. "What could possibly go wrong there?"

"We'll have to wait and find out, I suppose," Madoc joked, returning to his screens. "This current experiment is teaching us a great deal about the device's processes. It's only a matter of time before we can break it down into its separate components, take what we need, and recalibrate them for a human system. What we really need is a live volunteer who's suffered significant damage to their body resulting in a loss of functionality to properly test what medical benefits these units can provide." He looked long and lingering at Ariti in his wheelchair.

Resting his hands on his wheels, Ariti readied himself to back away. "Right... Well, it sounds like you have a lot of work to do. We probably shouldn't keep you any..."

"I mean, once we remove those mechanical tentacles, and whatever firmware connects it to its original set of military protocols, we could really help someone out with their condition without causing them too much harm."

"Sure," Nichols said, grabbing the handles of Ariti's wheelchair. She began to slowly wheel him backwards towards the door. "Let us know how that turns out."

"Well, as Ariti's had the most exposure to the device, he's probably the most qualified to stay and help us with our... progress," Madoc said, as footsteps approached from behind and Ariti felt Nichols release her grip on the chair. "We can help each other, don't you see?"

"I think I better talk to Holterman," Ariti suggested, nervously.

"There'll be plenty of time for that later," Madoc said. "All corps contractual obligations are met, all approval provided. Trust me, you're right where you need to be right now."

Ariti looked back to see Nichol's being escorted out by two soldiers as Madoc walked around behind him and pushed his wheelchair towards the tank containing the dead soldier, looking down at him with his cloudy eyes.

"Now, the two of you are going to be working closely together for some time," Madoc said, enthusiastically. "So best you get to know each other a little. See if we can get you two communicating."

A medtech began attaching contact pads to Ariti's forehead while a soldier fastened Ariti's hands to the arms of his wheelchair.

"Don't worry, it's just for your safety, in case the neural link we establish favours the device's will over your own."

"Ariti?" Nichols said, before the door closed between them.

Medtechs began moving scanning equipment, arranging it around Ariti to monitor him as he struggled. They locked his wheels and deactivated the chair's motor as they started connecting him to the surrounding devices.

"You're making history," Doctor Madoc said. "You should be very excited. I know I am. You're the first human to properly interact with alien technology. Well... the first living human. I can't wait to see what happens."

Barend Nieuwstraten III grew up and lives in Sydney, Australia, where he was born to Dutch and Indian immigrants. He has worked in film, short film, television, music, and online comics. Published in nearly forty anthologies, he continues to work on short stories and novels within fantasy and science fiction, often dipping his toes in horror in the process.

Rerouted

by Rebecca M. Douglass

"Festering leaf-mites!" The pilot grabbed for the safety straps as the ship lurched. Tentacles wrapped around the loops and Groveless cursed again in a deep purple and bright orange stream. Half a lifetime of Jumps in this ship, all as smooth as pond-water... not this time.

Acceleration increased, suddenly decreased, the ship bucked, and an ominous stillness settled over the command space. The vibrations of the Jumper and drive motors increased, shuddered, and cut off. The stillness lasted a long moment until the emergency systems kicked on, followed by the standard drive, which came on with a tentative hiccough.

Now mottled in an array of alarmed colors, Groveless hovered an appendage over the panel that activated the AI.

In the mix of color and sound with which Cresotes communicated, Groveless demanded an explanation.

"Insufficient data." The AI responded in grey. It always used grey, but managed to be even more grey than usual, as though language were suddenly a challenge. Groveless filed the awareness in a distant corner of their consciousness, to be examined later.

"Then *get* the data, you useless piece of space debris!" Groveless didn't usually insult the AI or bother to get angry at it. What was the point? Now a growing sense that they were in deep trouble demanded stronger language; urgent red, purple and orange tones both in their speech and playing over their head-part.

The AI remained dark and silent.

***

Groveless and solo-vessel *Drifter* had left the Alfaratz system in the Andromedan galaxy half a season earlier, on a standard exploration loop through the fringes of the fourth quadrant of Cresote space. The mission, as always, was to discover something saleable and unclaimed. As an independent explorer, Groveless was in a constant race for the resources to keep the ship going and permit further voyages.

The pilot managed regular tune-ups no matter how tight their finances, preferring cash shortages to a system malfunction in deep space. On the other hand, running most of the time very close to insolvency, Groveless didn't patronize the more expensive shops. Three sleeps back they'd left a budget tune-up station on a sketchily colonized outer world, equipped with a new drive-booster guaranteed to make Jumps faster, farther, and smoother, all for one low price.

The disturbingly rough Jump just experienced suggested that the device might not live up to the mechanic's promises: "My Dark Matter Drive Booster—the DMDB—will take you places beyond your wildest visions!" "The best boost in the C-47 system!" "Worth every coin it costs and more!"

"The mother-tree was right," Groveless now lamented to the unresponsive AI. "That which glows too brightly in another's mouth-part glows with the light of falsity."

The ship's AI came back online slowly and Groveless scanned the screens with sudden anxiety.

"Ship, where are we?"

"Unknown," the AI replied in a grey tone with just the slightest hint of color.

Groveless let their body flare orange, remembered that it did no good to be angry with an artificial intelligence, and settled back to an uncertain blue. Their speech continued to flash the complex colors and combinations of the Cresote language. It was the body that communicated emotion. How had that orangepurplegreyredorange sales being learned to prevent their colors from giving away the lies? Few Cresotes could. No wonder, Groveless admitted, they'd fallen for the pitch; the sales being had radiated honesty and reliability.

No time for that now.

"Display starmaps," they commanded the AI. "If we can't return by the way we came, we can continue to explore."

Again the noticeable hesitation from the AI.

"I have no starmaps for this sector." The AI's communication was definitely tinted with a faint irritated magenta.

"Beyond my wildest visions," indeed, Groveless muttered. Of all the stupid things, to have listened to that slick rainbow of a sales being. Well, that was all gravity waves over the exhaust stream. Their kin back on Root would have said you can't put the leaves back on the tree. Groveless didn't care how you said it, they couldn't go back if they didn't know where they were.

Better to check. "Are you unable to access maps?"

"We appear to be beyond the range of all available maps," the AI replied.

Groveless's color shifted slowly from uncertain blue to the sunrise red-purple of interested excitement. What to explore first in a sector completely unknown? Forgetting they were in trouble, forgetting the terrifyingly rough Jump just completed, they flashed, "We are going to make some new maps!" Who cared if no one might ever see them? Groveless had never before had the opportunity to be first to investigate a whole galactic sector.

Assuming they were still in the Andromedan galaxy. Since ejection beyond the bounds of Andromeda was unthinkable, Groveless didn't think it. "Show and record visible sky."

A primitive starmap appeared on the vid screen. Groveless studied the marks indicating stars, located one that appeared to possess orbiting planets, and laid a tentacle on the region.

"There." The ship could Jump to a visible destination, even if it could not get home without knowing the starting position.

"The Jumper appears to be damaged," the AI reminded. Did it sound reproving? "Use of the Jumper is potentially unsafe for ship and pilot."

Which was the AI's way of saying that if they tried to Jump, they could end up dead, or lost in the nothingness that lay between either end of a Jump.

Groveless turned a mauve that was nearly grey. Resignation and disappointment. "Very well. Fine, then. You will commence mapping where we are. I will repair the Jumper."

That was optimistic. Of necessity a solo explorer learned a lot of mechanics, but a Jumper was a complex and specialized piece of equipment. Too bad they didn't have a partner who was a true mechanic, though Groveless knew they would have ejected any companion long since—sent them out the gas-lock into space for talking too much, most likely.

Still, death by slow starvation or by disintegration via a malfunctioning Jumper unit didn't appeal. Groveless shook off the momentary desire for help and began planning.

Start by removing that cursed Dark Matter Drive Boost. Groveless ran the heat-sensitive flanges of their left side along the control wall as they moved back toward the drive room. Streaks of curiously hot and cold areas suggested widespread damage behind the panels. The more they tested the control regions, the deeper the uncertain blue that shaded Groveless's body.

With evidence of such widespread damage, the explorer returned to the control room and laid a flange against the main control plate. The fine tentacles reached into the various control slots and slowed or stopped most engine function. Life support only. Let the ship drift while they sorted out the issues. It wasn't just the Jumper that was damaged by that—whatever it was.

"*Drifter*, what did I do to you?" Groveless asked, not expecting or desiring an answer. They sometimes spoke to the ship as though to another Cresote, but Groveless, unlike some explorers, was a true mutant who didn't miss or want the company of their kind. The ship was programed to respond to only direct and relevant questions.

The AI apparently considered this a relevant question. "The installation of an unapproved after-market engine modification has resulted in a malfunction of the Jump engine, and the presence of foreign matter in the Calibrator has damaged three key circuits."

"Oh." Groveless's reply was more grey-toned than Drifter's explanation. "Prognosis?"

"That will depend largely on you."

Not what Groveless wanted to hear. For a brief moment, they wondered why they had left the grove. Surrounded by the rest of the Cresotes of their lineage, they would have been safe from drifting endlessly in space. Then they shook themselves. In the crowded grove they would be driven mad in a matter of days, not to mention bored to death. Better to be marooned in space than on a populous planet.

"Assessment of reparability, then," Groveless pushed the AI.

"The Calibrator is no longer user-serviceable. The Jump engine may be repaired with supplies currently in ship's stores. When it is repaired and other minor damage mended, this vessel may Jump, with limited accuracy due to lack of a Calibrator. Do you wish to Jump somewhere?"

Groveless ignored the question, which had an obvious answer. Merely to know that the Jump engine—the faster-than-light drive that made extra-system exploration possible—was repairable provided hope. It also gave Groveless an occupation which could distract from *Drifter's* disturbing circumstances.

Once again pulsating rhythmically in ever-varying colors of pleasure and concentration, Groveless set to work in a soothing silent wash of colors.

First things first. Disconnect and discard that ill-conceived and thrice-cursed so-called Dark Matter Drive. It was nothing but trash at best, and at worst was meant to disable a ship so salvagers could claim it. Groveless wasn't the only mutant out here alone and in constant need of credits and parts. Though if piracy was the intent, the mechanic who installed the device had made a grave miscalculation. If *Drifter's* AI couldn't find the home system, the pirate surely couldn't find the ship.

Groveless pulled back a protective sleeve to let their most sensitive dactyls explore the connections between the new drive and the engine. Once confident in the intricacies of the installation, the same dactyls that so delicately explored the connections hardened to dismantle them without resort to non-organic tools. Their varied and versatile flanges were one of the great strengths of Cresote pilots, and the ships were well-designed for servicing.

The work was soothing. Groveless paid no heed to the passage of time or the growing need for nutrients, nor even the necessity of waste elimination. They were fully absorbed in a task that was best completed without interruption.

When at last the drive was disconnected and the explorer drifted to the living quarters, content, the lights in the ship flashed briefly in the same rhythmic color patterns that were playing over

Groveless's body. The pilot looked around, flashing aqua curiosity, and the lighting returned to standard.

"Was that a—no, of course not." Groveless didn't finish the question. An AI did not express emotion. To the mutant Cresote loner, that was the beauty of the ship's AI. It didn't disturb the solitude.

"This ship is pleased to be free of the parasite," the AI responded to the unasked question. Groveless chose not to explore, at that moment, the why or how of the AI speaking without being spoken to, let alone predicting their thoughts.

"Must I lock it, or can I keep it?" Groveless didn't want to eject the device out the airlock. It wasn't sentiment, or even hopes of salvaging something of value, though that was always a consideration. They needed to understand what the drive was, and why it had done so much damage to *Drifter*.

Studying the thing would be something to do, as well. Groveless was accustomed to solo trips, and seldom got bored, but this trip was shaping up to last several spans beyond the usual. They would need distractions, once the damage to the ship was repaired.

***

Repairing the malfunctioning machinery provided ample distraction for about twenty sleeps.

Groveless restarted the engines only after tracing every bit of damage through both machinery and controls. Despite the seriousness of the matter, they enjoyed the process, only occasionally wishing they could consult with an expert, or at least an interested companion. Too much depended on getting it right.

If the burned-out bits couldn't be fixed, they would just drift until life support failed. Then the ship would drift on with a dead and decaying Groveless aboard. They thought about that and found that despite their pathological enjoyment of solitude away from the grove, they very much wished to mingle with the soil of Root when dead. They did not want to drift forever in a vacuum, or to be blown to compost by a malfunctioning engine, still less to be stuck in nothingness by a failed Jumper.

Once repairs were complete and the ship in motion again, aimed at the nearest planet to resume explorations as best they could, Groveless turned their attention to the Dark Matter Drive Boost. The Jumper could wait a day while they satisfied their curiosity. Groveless would not admit that they were frightened of the risks a poorly-repaired Jumper might present.

The space-dusting so-called booster told them nothing. It held its secrets as though it… did nothing? Groveless's words were all red and orange as they considered what that might mean.

"Ship? Did the so-called mechanic that installed this useless piece of metal do anything else to you?"

"I believe that routine maintenance was performed."

That was a curious way for an AI to speak. "You *believe* it was? You are an AI. You know, or you don't know," they reminded the machine.

"Well, I don't seem to know." If they hadn't known better, Groveless would have thought the machine was peevish. Definitely a sort of burnt-sienna tone to the words. It wasn't using proper AI diction, either.

"Ship, have your AI circuits been damaged?"

The AI had to answer that. It was a direct question.

"Please call me Drifter. I do not feel damaged."

That was another thing. "Since when do you refer to yourself as 'I'?"

"You call yourself 'I'. What am I if I cannot do the same?"

"You are a computer."

"I am in this ship with you."

That point seemed beyond dispute, other than to point out the meaningless difference that the AI *was* the ship. A half hour of increasingly orange-tinged questioning elicited no better answers. When they were cooled enough to think it through, Groveless decided that the argument had been the answer.

The AI had been corrupted in some extensive way by whatever had caused the Jumper to malfunction, leaving it with delusions of sentience. Or something like that. Groveless would ignore the delusions and they would go away. Back to the mechanics.

The DMDB appeared to be an inert lump of metal, broken in places and melted here and there, but lying harmless in its restraints and defying all attempts at understanding.

Had it been a useless decoy?

If the DMDB hadn't caused the Jumper malfunction, what had?

Had the Jumper malfunctioned at all? Was the AI holding out on them?

Groveless had never before had reason to consider what would happen if they could not trust the AI.

These questions were leading nowhere. Surely they could arrive at more useful questions.

"Ship!" The AI didn't respond. "*Ship!*" Still no response.

Resignedly, "Drifter?" So much for ignoring the AI's delusions.

"Yes?" The response was immediate and Groveless had to fight back irritation. Their left flange flared red-orange for a few seconds, but was the only indication of anger. Groveless was proud of their control. Cooperation was necessary. They could straighten out the AI later.

"Can we fix the Jumper?"

"It is designed to be user-serviceable." That was a partial answer, at best. Groveless wondered if that user was meant to be a trained mechanic, or if they could manage it.

No point in negative thinking. "If I fix it, can we Jump back home?"

"This ship cannot Jump from an unknown location to any point beyond visuals."

"You said you know where we are," Groveless pointed out, ignoring the rest of what Drifter had said.

Drifter hadn't forgotten. "Our location is known only in relation to surrounding objects. It is unknown in relation to Root. I cannot safely Jump without the relative coordinates."

"Then find some. Backtrack. Find the festering spaceport where we bought that thrice-cursed drive boost. Something. You're supposed to be a navigational AI, by the parent tree!"

"I will endeavor to do so," Drifter responded stiffly.

An offended AI? This was getting weirder. Groveless stared at the comm screen, shook their head, and massaged the ache away with the broad-fingered right appendage.

"I will fix the Jumper. You will find a way to make use of it. You will also continue to map visible space." There. A direct order. Drifter couldn't slide out of this one with an "I'll try." And the maps just might help recover some of the cost of this lost trip.

***

The Jumper, being part of the ship's original equipment, was less accessible to the mechanic than the newly installed drive booster had been. Groveless spent an entire awake cycle, stretched and thinned to their limit, deep within the engine area disconnecting and removing the device.

Once the Jumper was secured in the low-gravity workroom— unlike the rest of the ship, which saved fuel by remaining near zero-G, the workroom had enough gravity that things stayed where they were put—Groveless began the painstaking process of tracing wires, searching for damage, and repairing the breaks they found.

When the need for nutrient intake/output broke their concentration, Groveless visited the waste recycler, then the control room.

The computer had expanded the star-mapping project exponentially, and Groveless felt a dim yellow glow of hope.

"You know where we are?"

"I have always known where we are," Drifter replied with the annoying precision of the AI. "I still do not know where Root is in relation to this ship."

"I don't call that knowing where we are," Groveless grumbled. "Can you point us in the right direction? Perhaps by Jumping each time as far as we can see to calculate, we'll get back to something on your old starmaps?" Groveless was only partially aware that they had begun to speak to the AI as though to another sentient being.

"That may prove to be our best option," the computer admitted.

The ship sounded much less like an impersonal AI than it ought, and a great deal like someone with a stake in the process.

Groveless considered that. If the AI was personally engaged, that improved the odds of making it home, didn't it? Could an AI try harder? Ignoring the implications of a self-aware AI, they ordered the computer to research the possibilities and returned to the malfunctioning Jumper.

The problem was complex; damage was widespread. Many connections had been burned out of existence by what Groveless could only view as an energy surge.

Well, why not? If dark matter could add significant propulsion to the Jumper, it must create some kind of surge. Assuming whatever was in that half-melted box actually had anything to do with dark matter, which Groveless now realized was absurd. Why hadn't they remembered in the shop that dark matter was inert? Still, there had been something in that box, because it had done a lot of damage. Had they—or the mechanic—confused dark matter and anti-matter? But the latter would have destroyed more than the Jumper, or even the entire ship. No one had figured out how to capture that power source.

Whatever was in the device, Groveless hoped it had run out of potential to damage things, and again wondered if it would be wisest to lock the thing and leave it far behind. But any hope of either greater understanding or a justified vengeance against the installer—not that Groveless had much hope of finding that splitting thief again—would go into vacuum along with the ruined machine.

If there were any danger left, the ship—and Groveless— would have been long since vaporized or something, wouldn't they? Despite their mental reassurances, every time Groveless passed near the hunk of machinery, restrained in its zero-G net and isolated as far as was possible in the tiny ship, the space explorer eyed it with suspicion.

The device had done plenty of damage. Groveless had already had to fix the main controls and drive, which had been partially isolated from the new booster. The Jumper had connected directly to it, and Groveless's flanges burned with the heat of connecting new circuits, boards, wires, whatever they could find from the stores to repair or bypass the extensive damage.

With each burn and blister, Groveless vowed again to find the so-called mechanic and drop the device on their head. Groveless was becoming more and more convinced the booster was useless from the start, but the decorative job of "wiring it in" had caused extensive short-circuits. On purpose? Pirates liked disabled ships.

After ten sleeps—short, restless sleeps that didn't refresh, between long bouts of repair work—the Jumper showed signs of being ready to test.

"Drifter, are you ready for a trial Jump?" Groveless had long since given up and addressed the AI by name, a tacit acknowledgement of the machine's claim to personhood. Somehow, it had ceased to bother them.

"I do not as yet know a suitable direction." The vid screen displayed a vast starmap. "We appear to be here." A glowing dot illuminated in the center of the map. "None of this map appears to overlap with my known maps."

"Drifter, have we left the galaxy?"

A long silence.

An AI didn't need time to find the answer to a question like that. Did it need time to formulate a nice way to say they were going to die? Groveless, whose color had turned a queasy purple-grey with fatigue and worry, decided they didn't like the direction that question led and tried to retract it.

"Don't—"

Too late.

"It appears to be a definite possibility."

Great. A definite maybe. Well…

"Create a search pattern for the Andromeda galaxy."

"We have no perspective maps of the galaxy from beyond its limits."

Of course not. "Extrapolate them," Groveless ordered, and went back to fine-tuning the Jumper.

At last they had to accept they'd done the best they could. Another long stretch in the depths of the system to re-install the Jumper, which no longer fit quite perfectly into the space designed for it, thanks to the assortment of non-standard connections Groveless had used in the repairs. In the end, it was ugly but, Groveless hoped and believed, functional.

They made one short Jump to a nearby planet, which proved unsuitable for exploitation. At least the Jumper worked.

That left Groveless free, at last, to really study the DMDB. Groveless enjoyed that as a sort of pure research, while Drifter continued to generate, modify, and endlessly study starmaps, and to steadily deny any ability to take them home.

An array of contented colors played over Groveless's head and torso while they concentrated on thinning and inserting tentacles into all the cracks and channels of the DMDB. It did appear there was something functional inside, and they began dismantling the housing to get at it. Groveless had half-forgotten, half chosen to ignore, any fears the device might cause further damage.

"Dark matter my excretory duct," they muttered, removing the single object from the core of the device. Groveless studied it with interest. What was that? There was something familiar…

"Drifter!" They flew down the connector tube from the workroom to the control room, zero-G and the precisely placed grips on the walls allowing for an impressive turn of speed. Groveless had to hang on tight to the last grip to avoid flying across the control room and landing face-first on the vid screen.

"Drifter, the mechanic put a tracker in the core of that festering device. That's all it is. A tracker." Their red-orange head-part showed Groveless's angry excitement. "That was no mechanic's shop. It was a festering pirate's nest!"

The AI considered the explorer's discovery and conclusions with maddening slowness before conceding, "That is a reasonable conclusion." Drifter's tone was nearly as orange as the pilot's, despite the mechanical diction.

"But it gets better," Groveless began to laugh. "It's a two-way device. They put in a way to track them down. All we need is for you to tap in and…" Groveless stopped. "Oh, leaf-mites! Is it a trap, Drifter?"

"That is also a possibility," Drifter conceded. "If we connect to the device, it might cause further damage to my circuits." The thing actually sounded worried.

"It might turn control of the ship over to the pirates," Groveless added. "Maybe that's all they need—disable the ship, let the crew find the tracker, and they can simply navigate the ship back to…" They stopped again.

Drifter was first to work it out, of course. "It is possible that the pirates could help us find our way home," the AI posited. "There is, of course, the risk that they would then take the—your—me," Drifter finished, giving up on a way to indicate that the ship was both the property of Groveless and the essence of Drifter.

"Drifter?" Groveless asked the question, flanges trembling. "If you have become a sentient AI, could you resist them?"

"I do not know," the AI responded. "I am certain that—this—my personhood—was not their intention. But I do not know what I can do," it repeated. "I am still new."

"We can try." Groveless made an immense effort and the calm green of the home grove colored face and speech. "Maybe just connect you long enough to get a direction?" They both knew that though Groveless could disconnect the tracker and disrupt any external control, damage to the computer could happen in an instant. It was a lousy option, but after long and satisfying discussion, they decided they would work together to create an isolated connection, where Drifter could extract information from the tracker, but nothing—Groveless hoped—could reach out to take over their systems.

***

The tracker was easy to connect to the control system. It was designed to be. Drifter shut down all computing except navigation, in a further effort to quarantine the device. When the ship began to turn and prepare to Jump, Groveless hastily disconnected the tracker.

"Drifter?" They asked, uncertain if the AI would still be there, or in what condition.

"Yes." The computer flashed a confident yellow acknowledgement. "The route is set."

"And are you..." Groveless didn't finish the question. That was part of the test. Groveless held their breath, only now realizing that it mattered to them if the AI were still Drifter, as it were.

The computer responded promptly. "I have not been compromised. The changes the initial damage to my circuitry initiated were not intended and could not be reproduced or reversed. I am Drifter. I am not the pawn of a rotting space-scum pirate." Drifter had been listening to Groveless during the long hours of repairs.

"Then," said Groveless, "Let's follow their trail back. We can, right?"

"We can. We have not left the galaxy. My starmaps were damaged. I have downloaded new maps. We could navigate back to Root directly if you prefer."

Groveless thought about it. That so-called mechanic's shop was pretty vulnerable to space debris.

"Let's go return the drive boost," they suggested. "Spacial delivery."

The computer—Drifter—suffused the control room in a delighted, contented green.

"I will enjoy the process."

Groveless settled into the pilot's chair. "Let's go."

Rebecca M. Douglass is a writer of children's fiction, cozy mysteries, science fiction, and fantasy. When not writing, she likes to spend her time hiking, biking, and traveling. She primarily writes long form, but enjoys exploring a wide range of genres in short form fiction.

Stand-by

by A. J. Lewis

ere we go again.

Another few minutes and Archie would have to get up and do something about it. He didn't really want to, but surmised that it *was* part of his job.

From his office he could hear voices as they grew louder and more rampant. Third time this week. Talking at first, then they'd yell at each other. Then there'd be a — yep, there it was — a crash of Porporcelite hitting a wall.

Archie stuck his fingers in his ears. Sometimes it would end right there with the smashing of a dish. No more dish, no more conflict. Sometimes more would shatter.

11.54pm.

Didn't they know what time it was? Probably not. They weren't supposed to. Not these ones. They were only programmed to carry out their duties. And when their duties conflicted, well, that's when the trouble started.

Their programming had some weird ideas as to what constituted a conflict. In such an event, the first order dictated that the Washers talk calmly about the conflict. Limited vocabulary and understanding made this stage of resolution utterly and hopelessly futile. After the talking failed (and it always did), they were programmed to escalate to shouting. Same result as talking. Then after the shouting came—

Crash. Another Porporcelite casualty.

—violence. The fulfilment of the job was more important to the programming than the well-being of the Washers. Smashed dishes lead to the Washers taking up arms against each other.

The last resort reached; the nuclear option implemented.

Wooden spoons. Pans. Sometimes even knives, if they'd been accidentally put in the wash-chute and sent down to the dish sinks. The Washers would grab for hand-to-hand weapons with which to beat and strike and stab. The pounding of the fauxflesh that covered their illiquid-nanobone skeletons sounded just like the real thing, like the slogging of a bare-knuckle bout. Looked like it too, at least until bright purple placsyn flowed.

The problem with the conflict resolution programming was that it meant neither Washer would back down. Not ever.

An immovable object coming up against an irrefutable line of code.

Not until one or the other was incapacitated was it over with. Sometimes the victor would continue flogging away, unaware that they'd won, stuck in a loop of savagery.

All they had to do was wash dishes, for Christ's sake.

If one broke (or was beaten into pieces), that meant old Archie would have to get his hands wet. And if Archie had to muck in, that meant another conflict would be on the way.

Guaranteed.

See, the Eportics K-Series Washer® didn't care who – or what – it worked with. All it knew was its programming. It would see Archie washing dishes and flag him as a co-worker. Then it would see him put the sponge down in the area designated for the scourer, or stack a dish in the dry pile when there was a single bead of water stubbornly clinging to its base, and the conflict resolution subroutine would be triggered.

Once in that mode, there was absolutely no arguing with a conflicted Eportics K-Series Washer®.

Try telling one that you'd made a simple mistake.

Mistake was not in its programming.

Lucky for me, Archie thought, *I know the kill-code.*

As soon as that calm, metal voice increased in decibels and the rasp of overdrive kicked in, Archie would say the kill-code and the Washer would cease to function.

A shame, really, because then Archie would have to work twice as hard to wash all the dishes alone.

He could hear that the fauxflesh on one of the Washers had been compromised: soggy, slapping sounds, then the hollow *thunk!* of a rolling pin banging away at exposed illiquid-nanobone.

A shrill bell chimed out over the drubbing, signalling dishes needed to be removed from the wash-chute.

Unless that happened soon there'd be a backlog, and a backlog meant that Archie would have another reason to get his hands wet.

The Washers were too busy resolving their conflict to attend to the chute.

Archie swung his legs down from the desk and rose from his chair, ready to intervene. And it was so near the end of the shift! They should have been given a line of programming that told them: *if shift ends in < five minutes, shut up and keep going. Resolve your stupid conflict some other time.*

He opened his desk drawer and grabbed a pair of rubber gloves, snapped them on, and sighed. He walked to the open door, almost tripped over one of a dozen boxes of mild detergent capsules that littered the office. Delivered by mistake. The Driver didn't see it like that; he didn't know the meaning of *mistake* either.

At the sinks, one Washer was on the floor. Its skeleton poked out at the shoulder, and its black scalp bled bright purple down its face. Its jaw opened and closed like a fish on a carpet. A leg kicked up at the air.

No repairs for that one; it was done for.

Straight to reclamation.

The other Washer, the 'winner', went to empty the wash-chute.

"Goddamn you, Ernie," Archie said. "Why you always gotta beat on the new guy, huh?"

Ernie didn't reply. It never did, not unless the question was about washing dishes. It put the dishes – smothered with leftovers of carbomite and cremosoy and albufoam – into the sink and began washing.

Archie stared at the broken Washer for a moment.

"Not gonna clean this mess up, are you?"

Ernie heard that. "Clean-up," it said, its voice synthetic and dry. "Specify clean-up parameter."

The body on the floor wasn't a dish, so it was as good as invisible to a Washer.

"Forget it. I'll do it. As per usual."

Archie grabbed the murdered Washer by its Sure-grip feet and muttered as he dragged it to the trash zone to await retrieval. *Three times in one week.* Later, after shift, he'd have to call through to Eportics to have it collected, and to have another dropped off in its place.

Later. After he'd finished washing the dishes with Ernie.

Archie returned to the sinks. "You're a real jerk, Ernie, you know that?"

Ernie said nothing. Its eyes were solid fluorescent white, focused on the job at hand.

"I mean, how long have you worked here? Six months? And in that time you've killed seven of your co-workers. Seven! Three this week alone!"

Ernie remained stolid.

"And you don't talk. How about a little conversation from time to time? As long as it ain't about dishes—"

Ernie heard that magic word. "Dishes?" He looked up at Archie with a curious sense of optimism, like a dog who'd been told he could go for walkies.

"See what I mean?" Archie dipped his gloved hands into the sink beside Ernie's and began to scrub. "I tell ya, you're married to that job, pal." He snorted a laugh. "Maybe you need a vacation."

Ernie's washing slowed; the circular motion of his hand halted. "Va … cation."

"Yeah, a vaca—" Archie's dish slipped from his hands into the mucky water. He stepped back from the sink and stared cautiously at Ernie. "Well, ain't that somethin'."

Vacation wasn't in Ernie's programming. A selection of four-hundred and ninety-seven words were known to the Eportics K-series Washer. 90% of those words were related to washing dishes. The other 10% were for diagnostic purposes: battery life, wear and tear, errors.

E07 meant that water had got into some place it shouldn't have, and was screwing with the wiring; a common problem with the cheaper models like Ernie.

E21 meant that the elasti-braces on its elbows or knees were almost spent, and needed replacing.

There was no E-code that meant the Washer had learned new words, or wanted to take a week of leave at Seta Colony.

"Washer 06, pause functions."

Ernie put down the dish it was holding then froze still, arms at its sides. "Entering stand-by mode."

Spirals on its eyes twirled, displayed a 3, a 2, then a 1, before LED pin-pricks glowed like ominous red pupils.

The bell rang again.

"Dammit! Not a good time, Bruce." Archie went to his office and picked up the phone on his desk, hit zero.

"Hi, main wash junction, please … Yeah, Bruce? Hi. It's Archie. Listen, I've had something really weird happen down here, can you route the rest of the dishes to the Washers in cutlery? … C'mon, man, it's the end of shift, there can't be that much more … Hey thanks, Bruce, you're the best! I owe you one. Later."

"Want … vacation …"

Archie jumped, spun round to see Ernie stood there in the doorway.

"Jesus, Ernie!" He swallowed nervously. "Er, that's not a plate, Ernie. Go put it in the out chute."

Ernie brandished the rolling pin, stained bright purple.

"Va …va … ca …tion … tion … dishes … ca … tion …"

Archie stepped back.

Those red eyes. Why did they have to make them so menacingly red?

"Dammit, Ernie! You really wanna make me do this?"

Ernie took another step towards Archie.

"Ca … tion … dishes … va …"

Archie sighed. "Well, you're gonna regret this a helluva lot more than I will. Code: Aegis 17."

At that precise moment, Ernie should have lost all power. The kill-code, when acknowledged by Ernie's programming, should have caused the fail-safe to trip. A single strand of molecules housed in a vertebra in its neck connected the mind-core to the body. The kill-code should have sent a massive pulse of electricity to that single vertebra and fried the molecule strand, thus severing the connection and rendering Ernie useless without causing damage to any of his other components.

Instead, Ernie kept coming.

"Code: Aegis 17!" Archie repeated, commanding in voice.

The rolling pin swung at Archie's head. He ducked it.

"Shit! Aegis 17! Aegis 17!"

"Want ... va ... cation ..."

The rolling pin swung once more. Archie pulled back and avoided the blow, but tripped over a box of mild detergent capsules. He tumbled to the ground.

"Va ... vacavacation ..."

Ernie stood over Archie. This wasn't conflict resolution in action: there was no damned conflict! The pin-prick red in those lifeless eyes. No longer did it look like a simple indication of the Washer's state of readiness. It almost made it look mad.

Ernie lifted the rolling pin over its head, ready to bring it down, when the red light flickered. The display on Ernie's eyes garbled and glitched, static noise issued from its mouth, then it crumpled to the office floor.

A man stood behind Ernie, a spark-rod in hand.

"Bruce! Thank God!"

"Hey Archie. Thought I'd come down and see what the problem was." Ernie twitched. Bruce stuck him with another spark, and the body stilled. "I guess now you owe me two."

***

Archie peeled the protective film from the eyes and fingernails of the new Washers, 06 and 11. He felt around under their chins, held down the activation switches until their eyes lit up. Progress bars filled left to right as they booted, flashed green when ready.

"Sinks are over there. Go wash."

They walked over without complaint and got straight to work. Archie went to the office.

Bruce cleared his throat, read aloud the note that came with the new Workers.

"*Dear valued customer, we at Eportics® would like to offer our sincerest apologises for shipping your Eportics K-series Washer® with the incorrect Intelli-chip® installed. As you are no doubt aware, Eportics® are the third largest manufacturer of dishwashing solutions in the south-western region, and we pride ourselves in providing you, the consumer, with the latest in cutting-edge technology for all your—*'Yada yada yada." He scrunched the note into a ball and tossed it into a wastepaper basket. "Didn't even give us a refund, the tight bastards."

Archie sat at his desk. He asked Bruce, "Didn't it say which chip Ernie had installed?"

Bruce shook his head. "No, but I spoke to an Eportics assistant on the phone this morning. They didn't explicitly say, but from the way they were talking all cagey-like, I reckon it coulda been a GS-NX."

Archie's eyebrows raised.

"I know, right? So I called up a buddy of mine who works over at Clarition Robotics. He told me the suppressor in the K-Series' neural core wasn't compatible with the GS generation of chip sets – no surprise there. But then he said that if put into a K-series, GS gens can sometimes leak their programming back into the core, bypassing the suppressor. Rare, though."

"Wait ... so *it* became aware of ... *himself?*"

Bruce glanced out the door to the Washers, shiny and new, fresh off the van. One washed and the other dried. Both silent. Both serene.

"Something like that. You know what, though? I kinda feel sorry for Ernie. I mean, if it *were* a GS-NX. Think about it: Ernie would have had thoughts, a personality like you or me. But they were buried. He must've felt trapped in his own body. In a job he was compelled to do, and unable to do a damned thing about it.

Well, until yesterday, that is, when it all began to slowly bleed out. Must've been screaming in there."

"And nobody else could hear it wanting out."

Silence came over Archie and Bruce.

"You're a GS-NX, right Archie?"

Archie nodded, tapped a finger on his temple. "NX *Plus*. And don't you forget it."

Bruce chuckled. "Right! What I mean is: imagine having all your thoughts, your hopes and dreams, but only ever being able to wash the dishes. Kept locked to that sink by your programming telling you that's all you're good for, but knowing that you could be so much more." He shivered, then chuckled again. "You machines, man! Never simple with you guys, huh? I'm human and don't really get it, but that sort of thing freaks me out, man. Really twists my brain outta shape."

Archie ran his fingers through his hair, felt the nodule on his head where the release catch was located. Inside that skull of his were the parts that made him, him. Made all GS gens a *he* or a *she*, instead of an *it*.

Archie and Ernie. They could have been brothers. Their bodies were made of the same basic parts. The same fauxflesh. The same illiquid-nanobones. They might have even rolled from the same production line at Eportics.

K-Series and P-Series. Different cores. Different callings.

Bruce slapped Archie on the back. "Makes you think, don't it, buddy?"

Archie nodded solemnly. "Sure does."

"Well, I'd better get back upstairs. See you after?"

"Beers are on me tonight. I owe you, remember?"

Bruce flashed a grin, then headed up to the main wash junction.

Archie went to the sinks and watched the new Washers.

Suds jiggled, water splished, and Porporcelite squeaked as the Washers did what they had to do.

Archie wondered: was there another Ernie, or maybe even an Archie, stuck in one of those bodies, trying to claw their way out?

Washer 09 put a clean, dry dish on the left-hand side of a shelving unit.

Washer 11 said, "Incorrect placement of dish."

Washer 09 replied, a little louder than 11, "Negative. Within acceptable parameters."

A. J. Lewis is an author from Winchester in the south of England. He mostly writes speculative fiction and horror, but has been known to dabble in romance from time to time.

Mrs. Helen Feldstein is Thinking About Peanuts

by Cheryl Zaidan

I really don't know how long I've been here. Sometimes it feels like months, sometimes years.

I'm given food, shelter and clothing – all the basics, sans freedom. It's not really a prison though. I mean, technically it is, but there are no metal bars. It's more of a glass cage set up to look like living quarters. There's a small gym where I can work out, a kitchen which is useless since food is brought to me and dishes taken away, and a small twin bed. I've asked for a king-size as I'm quite tall and my feet sometimes dangle over the edge, but nothing has ever come of it.

Mrs. Helen Feldstein in Branson, Missouri is thinking about peanuts. She hasn't had them in about 10 years, but something reminded her of them. Salted – unsure of what, if any, flavor.

People like Mrs. Helen Feldstein are the reason I'm here. And right now, all I can think of is her love for peanuts – probably roasted although she didn't specify.

The only other thing of note I have in this cage is a computer but it's quite restricted so I can only input the thoughts I receive. I used to shout them out as they hit me, except that quickly grew tiring and the guards here never got it right so they gave me a lovely large desktop with a nice display. It seems a waste since I can only use it to tap out the thoughts as they come through. I can't even look anything up on it – not that I would know where to start. I've been in here so long that I can't remember what normal people do. I wish they had just given me a cheap laptop and used the extra money for a nice big bed.

Tim Specks, somewhere in Northern Ireland, city unknown, needs a new suit and shoes for an upcoming interview. His budget isn't much but he might be able to borrow money from his father.

I receive these notices like a quick burst in my brain but I can't always tell when they'll come. Most are from here in the United States, at least that's where I think I still am, but I get a few from other countries. Sometimes they appear in foreign languages, languages that I unfortunately don't know. I've asked about learning new languages. I say it would help me help them. They won't let me. I think they're afraid of me discovering anything at all outside of what I'm needed for.

I can't even remember my real name. Sometimes I think my name is John. Other times I think I'm Jack. I stick with Jack most of the time, it just feels *right*. I guess it doesn't matter in the grand scheme of things.

I don't know how they tell if the people I type in are even real, but given the fact that I'm still here, they must be. In the end, those people are going to see exactly what they were looking for. Most will chalk it up to coincidence or a search engine intruding into their life. The thing is, they never looked it up on a site, they didn't speak it out loud on the phone. They never even whispered it to themselves so that a device nearby could hear.

No one will ever suspect it's me. They call it 'targeted marketing'.

At least I can still maintain proper grooming. I wear white shirts with ties (never a jacket, a few were offered to me but I don't like them) and I'm probably the most well-dressed slave you'd ever meet. It's not that anyone really cares about me, that's not the case. It's just so I don't look like an unkempt slob when the suits come in and I can always tell when they're about to make an appearance. The nicer, well-mannered guards are here – minus the guns. And debris outside of the glass prison, usually smokes by the grunts, is swept up. I'm given a plant or something homey to put front and center. I can't get too attached to it though. They always take it back.

The important people never speak directly to me but gawk at me in my glass cell like I'm an animal at the zoo. Sometimes I can read them, sometimes I can't. My brain doesn't work the way *I* want. I can only feel what *others* want. And right now…

Lauralee Marks in Louisiana is thinking about her daughter who died last year tragically in a car accident. She is going to visit the grave tomorrow. I would say…flowers. Roses perhaps. Something beautiful in a higher price range.

It gets very lonely here. Generally, the only people around are the guards, the ones I lovingly refer to as grunts. I've never called any of them that to their face as they are heavily armed. Sometimes I think they hired the dumbest people they could find on purpose. After all, it's hard to read the thoughts of someone who doesn't have any.

They had one female guard here. She was nicer than the rest and very pretty. We talked at great lengths during her night shifts. I knew she was married, unhappily, although she didn't tell me so. I saw her as a bit of salvation. I made sure I looked nice when she was around and smiled as much as I could. I didn't mind the fact that she talked too much - being deprived of companionship for an undermined amount of time will do that to a fella. But I think someone caught wind, or else we were being taped because I heard someone shouting at her from another room. I never saw her again. Pity.

La Croset Banquet Hall is running low on steaks. The manager, a Mr. Ben Lewiston, is wondering if he can find a place that sells them wholesale – and quickly.

The food is interesting. Not bad, given the circumstances, but not restaurant-quality or what I remember restaurant food to be like. At first, I was given china and proper silverware, but one time one of the guards thought I held the knife in what he considered a "threatening manner." In reality, I was just trying to cut through a tough piece of chicken but ever since then, it's been paper and plastic. Odd because they allow me to use a razor to shave. I could probably do something with that, but nobody is allowed to be in here as a general rule.

The exception is an old cleaning lady that comes in once a week and scrubs the place down. I can't leave while she does so I usually sit on the bed as she clucks around and puts things where they don't belong. The guard has his rifle centered on me as she does it. It doesn't matter. I'm not going to hurt her. If they were able to read my thoughts, they'd see that the only thing I want her to do is go away as she makes more of a mess cleaning up.

Organic. That's what Shelly Faberton wants. Organic. All-natural cleaning products. She's in Michigan – Upper Peninsula near Manistique if I'm correct.

That's a buzzword trigger at work. I'll think of something and then the mental vines reach out and grab it from someone else's head. I wish I could control it more. It's one thing I've never told them. If I did, they would supply me with words designed to generate thoughts that lead to sales. It doesn't always work so they'd be disappointed. Besides, I prefer to keep some of my secrets to myself. They're all I have left.

***

The grunts don't change much, but one day we get a new kid of about twenty. I think I'm far older than he is but I don't remember my age. I don't see many grays in my hair yet but it's jet-black so the few I do have stand out. But from what I can see in the dirty mirror, I'm probably at least 15 years this guy's senior. He doesn't belong here – most everyone here looks like they've been paroled or kicked out of the army. This guy is different with a mess of red hair, freckles and a round baby face. He looks at me with pity and a hint of kindness.

Charlotte Kraski would like to know if they make soup that—poor man up there I can help him. I hope we can get to him in time.

He's interrupted my thoughts. It's not his fault, I accidentally read his mind. He's up to something. I try and see if he can communicate back to me with his mind but no dice. I've never met anyone like me. Not to say that they don't exist, I just haven't encountered anyone yet.

I keep a close eye on him but only when the other guards are looking the other way. The boy works for a few nights and he seems chummy with the others who don't pay him much mind. He pretty much ignores me until one night, when the other guard goes to use the john and it's just him and me. The boy comes close to where I'm standing – so close his breath leaves a small amount of condensation on the glass.

"Tomorrow," he whispers. "Tomorrow we're going to get you out of here."

Another guard comes around the corner before I can respond to find out who 'we' is, so I nod politely. Part of me is excited, the other part fearful. I don't want to get this kid in trouble. I trust him although I'm doubtful he can do anything to help me.

That next night the boy shows up early. He says something to the guard he's working with. I can't tell what it is but soon he and I are alone again.

"I told you I'd be back," he says, not bothering to whisper. He looks around and goes behind a corridor. Four other people come out and all are like him. They're dressed in fatigues but ill-fitting ones like the kind you'd find in an army surplus store. They didn't bother to hide their faces though and I can see each one clearly, even in the dim light that surrounds my home. They're young and earnest. The boy punches in a code on the outside of the glass door. It's directly outside of my line of sight but I can feel the numbers in his head: 11-26-85. I think it might be someone's birthday. As the door slides open, I hear footsteps down the hallway.

A lank-haired girl in a helmet grabs the red-haired boy's arm. "Move it, Leon!" she shouts. One of them takes my hand, the other my shoulder and they walk me outside. My feet touch the concrete ground that surrounds my cage. It feels weird.

"C'mon!" She shouts again and we're running. They try and help me but I'm faster than they are - years of conditioning on a treadmill in my hamster cage have given me a bit of an edge. I try to slow down a bit as they are leading the way. They know where we are going. I do not. Strange that I've been living in what looks to be an old underground parking garage and never saw anything that wasn't directly outside my glass walls.

A gun goes off and a girl screams. The red-haired boy clutches his stomach and crumples to the floor. One of his friends, a large man only slighter older than the boy grabs him and pulls him with us. We turn a corner and stop to catch our breath. I reach out to hold the boy's hand and he takes it. It's covered in blood.

"I'm sorry, we tried but…," his voice cuts short and his lips are trembling.

The man lays the kid down. He's crying. Two others grab my arms and we're running again. We turn a corner. Another shot rings out. I can barely make out a thought – it's one of the grunts and it's not a nice thought. More shots. I see the two girls running towards what is probably the exit and even though I feel like a coward I run after them. My legs, which I felt were so strong before, are giving out. The large gentleman is right behind me. The red-haired guy must have gotten too heavy or perhaps he's dead. Poor kid. I wanted to stop and help but I know it would be no use. I can't even feel his mind anymore.

Something flies through the air towards me, and the larger man throws himself in front of it. His body falls into mine. "Run," he whispers before he collapses.

I follow his advice. I can no longer see the two girls anywhere. Hopefully, they got away. Maybe the grunts will be merciful to them, but I doubt it, and I surely know I won't be cut any slack if they catch me. I hear a few more screams and gunfire before I make it to a large iron door – remarkably it's unlocked. And then I find myself outside in cold, night air. It should be a beautiful moment but I have no time to take it all in. I race on through what appears to be an industrial district full of large seemingly empty buildings. It's frightening but also reassuring. There are plenty of places to hide.

Eventually, I stop to rest behind an old car. Rain starts to trickle down. I cry, trying not to scream. The rain mixes with my tears and blinds me in the most wonderful way possible. But I know I can't stop and once I get my breath, I'm off again as my mind is racing with a million thoughts - some of them are even mine.

It seems like forever, but I finally come onto a road lined with trees and I walk slowly down it. The sun is starting to come up and it blinds me a bit, even through a light haze. I try to remember when I've last seen the sun. I think I was with someone, a woman, and we're holding hands. But maybe that's not my memory. Maybe that memory belongs to someone else.

A pickup drives close by, then stops. I flinch, but the man who steps out isn't a grunt. He's just a normal man, dressed in a flannel shirt and a baseball cap on his head. He walks towards me and I stumble slightly towards him as he takes my shoulder. His hands are rough and callous. Probably those of a mechanic or someone who works with machines.

"Are you okay mister?" he asks.

I clasp his arm to steady myself. My throat is dry as I try to speak and for what seems like an eternity no words come out. Finally I'm able to say my first words in my first real moment of freedom.

"Alexander Wilderman of Poughkeepsie is looking for a new car…"

Cheryl Zaidan is a full-time marketer and Pushcart Prize-nominated author with publications in several short story collections including *The Lost Librarian's Grave* and the *Robbed of Sleep and Strangely Funny* series. Visit her on her website at www.cherylzwrites.com.

Salvage

by Damian Karras

The most irritating thing about cryo-sleep is waking up. I guess that makes it no different than regular sleep to most people. I mean, no one *wants* to get out of bed in the morning, right? Fortunately for the privileged souls living surface side, they get to start their days with coffee, water, and whatever food they manage to scrape together. Up here between the stars, we sit up in our freshly popped pods and immediately evacuate the contents of our stomachs via an esophagus that's already raw.

Good morning, universe…

Here's my bile and half-digested vitamin paste…

After wiping my mouth and gagging, I realize the A.I. console is buzzing and beeping with the frequency of a pissed off wolverine. Leaning forward, I push the "interact" button on the interface and switch the system awake. It's an action I know I'll regret in mere moments, but one that's unavoidable in the long run. I can't run a warp drive by myself, and it would take days, with multiple computer monitors, to even *begin* to calculate where the hell in space we actually are. I'm no tech wiz, and that's why the boss lady installed the damn thing in the first place.

"Happy awakening, Mr. Maddox." The infernal contraption chirped.

"Yeah, happy." I grunted. "I was dreaming I was surface side, on a beach, with seven different gorgeous women who hung on every word out of my mouth. Things were just starting to get hot and heavy when you yanked me out, you thoughtless bastard."

"Yes, well. The substances involved in human hibernation often produce dreams of the most wild and unrealistic sort. I've seen you talk to women, Mr. Maddox."

My initial, knee-jerk reaction was to punch the console until nothing but wiring was left. Unfortunately, that would put me in debt to the boss about a million credits I don't have. Instead, I placed a hand on either side of the pod and carefully pulled myself into a standing position. Thanks to all the brilliant modern technology, atrophy was kept to a minimum, and I was able to gain my feet with only the smallest amount of weakness, fatigue, and vertigo.

"Is Zeke up yet?" I asked, stretching my arms and legs.

"Mr. Torres is just coming around now. I believe in a few minutes he will-"

The A.I. was cut off abruptly by the sound of a torrent of liquid hitting the metal floor. Zeke was up, alright. Good morning, my friend. How was your projectile vomit?

"Goddamit!" He yelled from across the room. "Every fucking time! We can zap from universe to universe but can't get any anti-nausea meds in the damn I.V.'s!?"

"Bitch, bitch, bitch." I yelled back. "Just get up, I can't deal with this hemorrhoid of a computer program by myself. I'll end up puncturing my own eardrums with a screwdriver."

As I stepped out of the pod, a panel in the wall opened and extended a shelf towards me. I grabbed my jumpsuit off it, forced my aching muscles through the various sleeves and legs, and turned around just in time to see good old Zeke, still wiping his mouth and naked as the day he was born, sauntering toward me.

"I'll show you bitch, bitch, bitch." He said. "Where the hell are we, anyway? The counter on my pod shows us at only two weeks down. We can't be anywhere near Andromeda yet."

"Correct, Mr. Torres." The computer quipped. "Multiple issues, including a solar storm and an approaching asteroid cluster, forced me to reroute the ship. Andromeda is still lightyears away, but fear not. I've a very good reason for bringing you two around."

"UUhhhhh. If you've pulled us out to witness another eclipse, I swear I'll tear out your circuitry and jump rope with your fucking wiring."

"Doubtful, Mr. Torres. I believe Miss Sasha would look upon that action with a very negative perspective. But do not worry. She will be pleased. I believe we've found something worth even more than my motherboard and the ship it's running."

***

After washing our mouths and setting the little cleaning robots free to mop up our viscous mess, Zeke and I made our way to the bridge. Besides the cargo hold, the ship was relatively small, full of cramped corridors and bulkheads with sharp edges. Lights were set in the floor every three feet or so, and they glowed on a dim setting to allow our eyes to readjust themselves after weeks of unconsciousness. I was weak, pissy, and starving, but if the A.I. had deemed it necessary to wake us against orders, there had to be a good reason.

"I'm honestly both excited and terrified of the implications of this discovery." Said the computer's tinny voice coming from the speakers in the walls. "The chance of profit is massive, but a salvage operation could be extremely risky."

"One, you don't have any fucking feelings, robot." Said Zeke, walking only a few feet behind me. "Two, risky salvage is our business. It's the whole reason we're out here, billions of clicks from the nearest bar or brothel. Now either tell us why we're awake or shut the hell up until we reach control."

Zeke isn't the brightest laser in the array, but he does have a way with words.

The speakers clicked off without further comment.

The door to the bridge slid open silently as we approached, and a multitude of lights began to flicker on control panels all over the room. This is standard operating procedure, a ship in forced hibernation coming to life. Secretly, I love this part of the job. Or at least, this short moment before the job actually begins. Reminds me of fireworks back at home. Christmas lights. Traffic lights. Casino lights. All the beautiful, sparkly things we left behind.

The bridge was a cramped space that consisted of two swiveling chairs bolted to the floor, numerous panels of buttons, gauges, switches, vid displays, and a massive viewscreen pointed directly into the abyss in front of the ship. We plopped heavily into our chairs, thankful for the weight off our legs, and began reviving all the systems and software that had been laid dormant when we'd began our latest journey.

"Alright." I said, "Call and response, you know the drill."

"Aye, captain."

"Life support?"

"We're breathing, ain't we?"

"Systems diagnostic?"

"Well, the lights are on."

"Long range scan?"

"Telling me we're a million miles from a bottle of rum."

"Ansible and Coms?"

"Direct link to home in two minutes, if you had anyone to talk to."

"So green across the board?"

"Green as we're gonna get. You want the screen up?"

"Might as well." I sighed, lifting my voice sarcastically so the A.I. would know I meant business. "THIS BETTER BE ONE HELL OF A FIND OR I'M BUYING A COLLOSAL GODDAMN MAGNET AT THE NEXT STOP! YOU HEAR ME, ANDROID!?"

A sudden burst of static and screeching feedback came over the speakers. As far as I could tell from the few years we'd worked together, this was as close as the A.I. ever came to swearing. I smiled to myself and nodded Zeke the go ahead. After punching a few buttons and dragging his fingers across multiple vid displays, the view screen came to life in front of us, and my jaw dropped three inches lower than I thought was humanly possible.

Outside, drifting dead among the stars, was a circular craft plated in gold. Thick rings covered in glyphs passed over the surface like a gyroscope, but all the lights were dark, and all the thrusters were dead. Just looking at it threw my mind backward about thirty years. Young little Sammy Maddox, sitting in a classroom with a "History of the Universe and the Species Within" textbook cracked open on his desk.

Chapter 1: The Ancient Species Already Gone

"What the hell is that?" Zeke asked, clearly angry. "You pull me out of cryo so I can look at floating debris? So what? Looks like garbage? Some jettisoned fuel receptacle or chunk of a destroyed cruiser. Why the fuck would you-"

"I'm sorry, Mr. Torres." The computer cut him off, "I forgot about your remedial education and multiple learning disabilities. Mr. Maddox? Worth the awakening?"

"That can't possibly be what I think it is."

"But it can, and it is. Completely authentic as far as I can tell from here. Sandor Raska, class-2 research vessel. Are you aware of the odds, Maddox? Especially out here? I can calculate them if you like."

"What the fuck is it talking about?" Zeke said. "Hey, translation? Layman's terms?"

"Layman's terms?" I snorted. "We have to be the first to lay eyes on this ship in over a million years, jackass. If that thing turns out to be real, you'll be able to buy any damn brothel in the galaxy, and pay your whores very, very well."

***

Once the initial shock wore off, I herded Zeke into the kitchen area of the ship, sat him down at the table, and began preparing food and drink while talking excitedly.

"Look, the Sandor Raska were a species we only know about because of archeological evidence from planets in deep space. We're talking the oldest of the old, beyond fucking ancient. These beings had intergalactic travel and terraforming down to an exact science while our ancestors were still throwing shit at each other in the trees, and they disappeared completely before we had figured out written language."

"So?" Zeke replied, unimpressed. "The thing's a fucking antique, I get it. Doesn't that mean it'll disintegrate the moment we step foot aboard the ship? Let's just haul the entire damn thing back to Earth and sell it to the highest bidder."

"Impossible, Mr. Torres." The computer chirped, "That ship is made from components and materials we can only guess at. Not to mention that, at its age, it's highly unlikely to survive faster than light travel. A quick equation would suggest that you two would be 1, 132 and 1,136 years old, respectively, by the time we made it back to Earth at cruising speed."

"Holy hell… Okay then genius, what are you suggesting?"

I sat a tray of dehydrated jerky and a glass of orange juice from concentrate in from of him, and then settled down into a chair.

"Doesn't take a genius or a computer." I said, "There's really only one option. We take a shuttle over there, collect artifacts, and relay the position of the ship to Sasha. Let the boss lady figure out what to do with it. This situation is far above our fucking pay grade, understand?"

"Then why go over there at all? Let's just tell her about it now and go back under. No use risking our lives, let's go home. I need a goddamn drink, captain."

I leaned back in my chair, covered my face with both hands and groaned.

"You don't get it, Zeke. If we give away the location of this find and just scurry along on our merry way, we get fucking *nothing*. If you'd bothered to study the books on deep space salvage law I gave you, you'd know that it's not finders keepers out here, dipshit. It doesn't matter who *discovers* the wreck, it's whoever boards and pillages the site that gets the spoils. You honestly thing Miss Sasha is gonna give us anything if we just turn it over?"

Zeke's eyes went blank and focused on a spot somewhere over my shoulder. I'd come to recognize this "zoning out" behavior as his way of attempting to think.

"Yeah, no." He said after a moment, "I guess she wouldn't."

"Damn right she wouldn't. Now, we may not be able to haul the entire thing back to terra firma, but we can sure as hell try to get a little piece of the profit by cracking in and looting what we can. I'm sure there's plenty of random shit in there that the museums and scientists will pay an incredibly pretty penny for, get me? Not to mention private collectors and the shady, black-market scumbags on Zoccarra."

"There's also some serious scientific implications." The computer interjected, "To this day, no one knows why or how the Sandor Raska suffered extinction. If there's any evidence of the reason for their disappearance on that ship, you two will end up famous as well as rich. Your names will be remembered throughout history. Countless generations of children will learn about you in history books across the universe."

For a few tense moments, the computer and I fell silent while Zeke grappled with the positive monetary and negative mortality issues of our conflict. Just looking at his face, I could tell the gears were grinding hard and deep within his skull. Neither of us had any family back home. There were no little children or faithful wives waiting for us surface side. Our lives were about profit and danger, it's explicitly what we signed on for, and I knew his answer before it even came tumbling out of his mouth.

"Fuck the history books." He said. "I know the exact whore house I'm gonna buy once this is over. Let's do the damn thing."

***

Though it's a hard feat to accomplish, the shuttle was even more cramped than the ship. Inside, there's only enough room to seat two people, and enough space in the back to put on space suits one at a time. Everything else we'd need for a successful operation was stored in sealed containers behind hatches in the walls. Zeke sat next to me, useless as a co-pilot, rattling off all the things he was going to buy when we cashed in our plunder.

"I've been rethinking the whore house." He said. "The overhead cost of running a place like that would cut into my profit, right? So, think I'm gonna buy a nice place like, directly across the street from the whore house. Or at least within walking distance. It's gonna have to have a cellar though, because I'm buying booze by the pallet. No more of this 'one bottle at a time' bullshit."

"You'd better put something aside for a new liver." I said, cranking dials and pushing buttons, "All that money will be useless if you destroy your organs. You don't even have anyone to leave it to."

"Oh, yeah, for sure. I'll have a massive cooler, next to the pallets of booze, filled to the brim with cryo frozen livers and kidneys. Maybe hearts and stomachs too, shit. You ever had an ulcer? Feels like you're getting stabbed all day long."

After the preliminary shuttle setup procedures, our board turned green, and the cargo hold door opened in front of us. This was in the rear of the ship, so all we saw drifting out was an endless expanse of stars and darkness. Our bodies were kicked back in the seats as the thrusters engaged, and then we were cruising around the starboard side of the ship in a slow arc. Seeing it from the outside was always a harsh reminder of how ugly it really was. Being inside for so long, you tend to forget you're riding around in what looks like a crumpled-up ball of tinfoil covered in tobacco spit.

I steered the shuttle slowly around our sorry excuse for a "salvage vessel" and pointed the nose directly at the alien wreck. We traveled slow, cautious of possible defense mechanisms that might still be active, but nothing happened as we grew closer to the floating sphere of gold.

"So how do we get in?" Zeke asked. "This isn't like a Solar Military vessel or an abandoned Heliux transport. Do we even know if this thing has a door? A hatch? Anything?"

"We know less about this ship than you know of proper manners and etiquette." I responded. "We'll have to circle around, see what we can see. If worse comes to worse we'll try to burn a hole in the hull, and if that doesn't work, we leave emptyhanded."

Zeke grunted and shook his head, obviously displeased with this assessment. Unfortunately, we didn't really have any other options. Sasha refused to spring for any of the fancy breaching equipment. Her philosophy was "If you can't get in without a high-powered laser system, you probably shouldn't get in at all".

However, I'm sure that when she coined that phrase, she wasn't expecting two of her employees to come upon a ship that would make her rich beyond her wildest wet dreams.

I kept a safe distance and used the screen to magnify the image as we coasted around the alien ship. The body itself was smooth as silk, shining even in the dim starlight, and the circles that revolved around it presented us with an undecipherable mix of glyphs and runes that would take surface side scientists decades to translate. Finding nothing on our first pass, I adjusted the shuttles trajectory and took us closer, almost within spitting distance of the rotating rings, and cruised around the ship as slow as I could get the shuttle to crawl.

Just as I was about to give up and tell Zeke to load an explosive cartridge into the weapons bay, the rings stopped dead, shuttering the entire alien vessel and our own. I slammed the throttle down to full stop as Zeke and I both pulled in a sharp breath and held it. 50/50 shot, I reasoned. Either we broke the damn thing, or some ancient death ray device was about to incinerate us down to ashes of atoms and molecules.

As we watched, thin lines began to cut themselves through the hull of the ship, first travelling horizontally, then vertically, then back to meet in the middle, creating a large rectangle. Seconds later, the interior of the shape disappeared, giving us a view directly inside what I had to assume was a loading dock or shuttle bay. The interior shone with a white light only a shade below blinding, and we could see discarded pieces of equipment and tools stacked along the walls.

"Seems like something wants company." Zeke whispered. "A little fucking suspicious, ain't it? Them just letting us in?"

"Don't start pissing yourself now." I replied. "You want your new liver or not?"

***

I hate space suits. Always have. Too constricting, too heavy, too "life or death situation" for my taste. Clasping down the locks on that helmet feels like hammering in coffin nails. Unfortunately, according to the atmospheric scanner aboard the shuttle, I don't have a goddamn choice. Inside the alien vessel, what isn't a complete vacuum is filled with either carbon monoxide or a mix of cyanide and sulfur. Walking through that ship unprotected would be a death sentence, and not an easy, quick, step into the tunnel of light death sentence either.

Once we were suited up and weighed down with equipment, the shuttle opened its back door and released us into the ominous unknown. Our first few steps were cautious and paranoid. No telling what lethal tech could be waiting in the walls for unwelcome intruders. Beams of light emanating from our helmets illuminated racks of exotic equipment and piles of ancient garbage. Whoever these people were, they'd either left in a hurry or didn't mind living in unorganized squalor. I wasn't passing judgment. Our own cargo bay could definitely use the touch of someone suffering from O.C.D. It was just strange.

A species beyond brilliant, and this is how they lived?

Our boots clanked off the metal floor as we made our way past the debris. In the far corner of the room was the entrance to a passageway. A curved metal frame decorated with seemingly random pictographs framed a door leading to a hall. Here, deep red lights flickered on and off, giving us only partial views of the space ahead at any given moment. The corridor was empty, no noise cut through the space, and all my scans assured me the wreck was devoid of life. Nothing moved, nothing breathed, and everything was cold.

"Alright, fearless leader." Zeke said, sarcastically. "What the hell are we looking for? The ship is dead? We knew it was dead? Should we unscrew the light fixtures and sell them to a black hole?"

"Patience is a virtue." I responded. "Regardless, I don't think these fixtures were ever meant to be removed. Or replaced. Or even repaired."

I crouched down to take a look at the nearest light source. Embedded in the floor, it shone with a steady glow, the housing totally melded to the floor, and the clear cover at least an inch thick. There was no wiring to be seen, no connecters or relays or circuit breakers either. Everything was melded straight into the metal surrounding it, without a single toolmark to suggest construction efforts. It was almost like they birthed the ship from the uterus of a mothership, already completely formed and workable.

"This tech is insane." I said, standing back up.

"And?" Zeke spat. "Should we take a crowbar to the wall? Where's our payday, captain?"

I had a sudden urge to push him over and beat him until I hit the floor beneath, but he did have a point. Instead of answering in my usual, venomous way, I just started walking, leaving the smartass behind me. After a few steps, I heard him begin to follow.

Eventually the corridor curved, and we found ourselves staring at a multitude of doorways. Evenly spaced and towering, they reached from the floor all the way to the ceiling, suggesting the creatures who once inhabited the ship were either giants or severely frightened of smacking their heads on a door jamb. I looked back at Zeke and attempted to give him my best "I told you so" glare, but the thickness of the plexiglass face shields made non-verbal pettiness almost impossible. He simply walked up next to me and shrugged.

"What now?" He asked.

"Now we explore."

Beyond the first doorway was a dim room full of waist high tables and what I could only assume were chairs. I don't know anything about the Sandor Raskas' leg structure, but based on the twisted pieces of metal surrounding the tables, their knees must've bent the opposite way of ours. What looked like massive plates and trays covered the tabletops, full of ash and grime, the remains of a dinner some million and a half years ago. Obviously the suits blanked out our sense of smell, but I imagined the room probably reeked like an abandoned slaughterhouse in the height of an Earthen summer.

We looked around, found nothing, and left.

The second doorway led us into a vast and high-ceilinged barracks area. There were metal slabs protruding from the walls, not unlike prison cells, totally devoid of blankets, pillows, sheets, or any other form of comfort. The back wall, however, was transparent, and gave a brilliant view of the stars and our own hideous ship beyond.

"So much for sleeping in style, eh?" Zeke muttered.

I didn't answer, just turned around and kept walking.

After that, the search became monotonous. We'd walk into a room, scan, and walk out. There was a storage room, filled to the brim with shit we'd never understand. A lavatory, containing exotically shaped toilets we'd never be able to use. An infirmary, where the impulse to pillage anything in liquid form became almost overwhelming, until I realized anything of use had probably expired somewhere around the dark ages back on Earth. We passed through an engineering section, a kitchen section, and what appeared to be a community lounge complete with stage before we finally came upon what we were looking for.

The very last doorway at the end of the corridor glowed with a dim light that cast shadows as we waltzed in. A thick, metal counter circled the room, covered in tools and wires. Even through the helmets we could hear sparks snapping and a deep electric hum permeating the air around us. Underneath the skin of the suit, I could feel my body hair raising as if I was about to be struck by lightning. Smack in the center of the floor stood an arch that was at least twice my size. Shining like chrome and shimmering with untapped power, it drew and held our gaze for what seemed like hours before we were able to speak.

As per usual, it was Zeke's crude language that broke the silence.

"What in the seven fuckin' hells is *that*?" He asked.

"What am I, an archeologist?" I responded, barely above a whisper. "I majored in physics and deep space survival, dipshit. For all I know it's a goddamn can-opener."

"They must've had some giant ass cans then, captain."

"Point taken… And also fuck yourself… Let's do the job and get the hell out of here."

We pulled sacks from the storage compartment on the back of our suits and began searching the counter. Anything that looked like a tool, an info chip, an important component, or a power generating circuit we took and stashed. There were wires everywhere. Shrapnel sized pieces of metal and plastic littered the work area and the floor. We made our way quickly around the room, looting everything that looked valuable, before Zeke's feet became tangled and I watched, from the corner of my eye, and he jerked, swayed, threw his arms about, and finally gave in to the artificial gravity. He hit the ground with a dull *smack*, and began cursing immediately.

"Goddamn, shit-ass, fuckin' hell, dammit!"

I rushed over as quickly as I could with my loot sack weighing me down. As I approached, I realized he was tangled in and almost swallowed by a large pile of bright red fabric, countless strips of it, and his fighting was only making the knots worse.

"Calm down, you animal!" I yelled. "It's just cloth, not fucking space snakes!"

After a few panicked moments, he chilled out enough to let me help him. We methodically unwound the fabric from around his ankles and elbows, and then I helped him to his feet. After retrieving his pilfered treasure, we took a few steps back and studied the pile of abandoned cloth. It was a large heap but wasn't one piece. It looked as though it were waste, cast aside all at once, unneeded. But why would this genius master race use their research lab as a catch all for unwanted sheets?

I turned my eyes back to the arch, and then returned them to the pile. My mind was grinding on this strange information for what seemed like an eternity, until it finally hit me. There's no use for fabric in a lab, this clearly wasn't a textile mill, which means they deemed the lab unnecessary as well. They were leaving it all behind. The ship, the lab, the food and plates barracks. All of it was suddenly obsolete to them, including...

"Uniforms..." I said.

"What?"

"These are... Were, their uniforms. I can't be sure how many of them inhabited the ship, but it certainly looks like they all got real naked directly before they disappeared. This wasn't an attack, or a disease, or a mysterious, cataclysmic event. They just left."

"They left?" I could hear the disbelief in Zeke's voice. "All this tech, the entire goddamn ship... They left all of it behind? Why? Why the hell would they do that? And how?"

I turned in a circle and scanned the room. The tools and components were scattered wildly, suggesting whatever research they were doing was finished. No one in the middle of a serious project would work in this unorganized of a manner, especially professionals. I gazed up at the arch, let my eyes travel up and down its surface, and finally settled them on a clutch of wires connected to a metal dome set in the floor. Kneeling down, I could tell the connectors were fried. The input ports were black and scarred, as if from a power surge. Taking a handful of wires, I pulled back slowly, and they all disconnected without a fight.

"Zeke." I said, motioning him over. "Drag your bag over here and dump it."

Usually, such a direct order would've sent my surly coworker into a fit of sarcastic insults. Based on his quick movement, silence, and absolute adherence to orders, he was clearly in shock and out of his element.

The contents of his bag clattered to the floor, and I quickly mixed it with my own. Scrambling through the various components with gloved hands wasn't easy, but eventually I came up with five new connectors, stripped the ends of the wires, and replaced them with fresh strips of metal. As I jammed them back into metal dome, I experienced a split second of indecision. This was a dangerous gamble. The tech was ancient. Power source unknown. If it was nuclear or proton based, this could very well blow up in my face, both literally and figuratively.

Fortunately, I remembered the profit at stake, and my hesitation was minimal.

The machine jerked to life almost immediately. The low hum we heard when first entering the room became a steady whine, the metal began to vibrate, and a sheet of neon pink plasma began to rise from the floor, filling the arch within seconds. Zeke and I scurried backward on our asses; the wind temporarily knocked from our lungs by the force of the machines awakening. We climbed shakily to our feet once we were a safe distance away, and stared in awe at the exotic mechanism of pulsing energy before us.

It took some time for us to regain our wits, but the unavoidable question soon followed.

"Okay, captain." Zeke whispered. "What now?"

***

Sasha Cohen, or "Miss Sasha" to her employees and people frightened of her, brushed her black bangs from her eyes before kicking open the cargo bay door. This action was in no way necessary, as the doors would've slid open voluntarily at a flick of a wrist, but she was beyond furious. Six weeks. Six fucking weeks since "captain" Maddox and his degenerate lacky went silent. Dead air. Nothing but static. Thankfully, all the ships in her salvage fleet were equipped (unbeknownst to their crew) with tracking chips and battery powered relay equipment, making it possible to locate anyone on her payroll anywhere, at any time, whether their cores were operational or not.

Regardless, it had taken up a hefty chunk of her valuable time to get out here, and she was far from fucking amused.

She stomped through the cramped vessel like a soldier on his way to the front line, and manually yanked the door to the bridge sideways with all the fury of a woman scorned. Everything was still lit in the cockpit, lights green, vid screens up, A.I. functional, and both seats empty.

"Damn it all." She growled. "Computer!?"

"Greetings, Commander Cohen. I've spent many hours attempting to calculate when you would arrive. I'm afraid I have both good news and bad. Which would you like to hear?"

"Where are Maddox and Torres? I want exact coordinates, right now."

"That's most of the bad news, Miss Sasha. I cannot locate them. They left for the Sandor Raska wreck almost two months ago and have not returned. I assume they have expired."

"Sandor Raska?"

For the first time since boarding, the crimson drained from her sight, and she shifted her gaze out the large view screen. Dead and abandoned, the golden ship continued to drift in the abyss without a single sign of life. She gasped, held a hand to her heart, and began to shake.

"Computer." She said. "That can't possibly be what I think it is?"

"Funny, that's exactly what Captain Maddox asked. It is, yes. Sandor Raska, class-2 research vessel. Are you aware of the odds, Miss Sasha? Especially out here? I can calculate them if you like."

"You can shove the odds into whatever the computer equivalent of your ass is. They broke into that ship?"

"They did, yes. Searching for profit. Captain Maddox believed that if he handed the wreck straight over you would've given him nothing. Just out of curiosity, was he correct in this assumption?"

"You're goddamn right he was." Sasha spat. "But he would still be alive."

***

Shouldering her weapon, Sasha made her way through the alien wreck like she was invading a hostile territory. Crouch before corners. Eyes up and forward. Stepping toe to heel, muting her footfalls. Multiple scans being conducted every minute, all of them telling her the ship was dead, lifeless, and just as abandoned as it looked.

She found the rooms, all open and empty, their vaulted frames both inviting and foreboding. Deserted cafeteria. Barracks devoid of life. Infirmary full of nothing but mysterious liquids and needles far too large for a human vein. Since boarding the vessel, her fury had ramped back up to an almost unsustainable level. How fucking stupid were they? Had they any idea what they were dealing with? They were supposed to be professionals, and finds of this magnitude had guidelines attached. Rules, codes of conduct, standard operating procedures that were put in place to spare human lives.

This is the power of greed, she mused, *Taker of countless souls.*

Eventually finding the end of the corridor, Sasha crept into the lab and almost dropped her weapon from shock. The arch, repowered and repaired, still vibrated with energy, its neon protoplasm shimmering and flowing like waves on an ocean. A thick metal wire protruded from the bottom of the mechanism, firmly welded on one end to the doorframe next to her, and disappearing into the pink abyss of the arch. Two bags, their contents dumped and scattered, lay not far from the base of the contraption. She eyed everything with suspicion. The haphazardly strewn tools, the alien components, the flickering lights, the pile of discarded fabric, all evidence of a transportation project either completed or gone horribly awry.

Other than the wire, there was no evidence of her missing employees, but she knew a goddamn lifeline when she saw one.

Okay, so… The two idiots stumble upon the find of a lifetime. Instead of notifying their veteran employer, they decide to ransack the site in order to make some profit. Sounds simple enough, no harm no foul, but in the process the end up reanimating something they couldn't begin to comprehend. A gateway. A door. A window into a world or possibly a dimension they could never imagine. The money would be good, but curiosity kills all cats, doesn't it? However, not above planning an escape route, a B-Plan, a contingency, they tether themselves to the damn doorway with a scavenged wire in hopes of returning should things go south. Hmm… Good plan overall, but the oft laid plans of mice and men, or whatever that historical asshole said.

She walked toward the arch, breathing steadily and thinking through her options. One, she could return to the ship, call in emergency assistance, get the absolute top minds in the field to look everything over. Unfortunately, that would be surrendering the find, and all the profit attached. Two, she could retrieve a winch, wind up this wire, and possibly pull those two stupid dickwads out of their mistake and back into their own reality. This would be the honorable option, sure. It would also mean splitting anything gained three ways, or even less since she didn't actually risk her life like the other two.

Then there's three: Sacrifice it all.

This is a power that shouldn't fall into any species hands.

Return to the ship, load up missiles, ashes to ashes.

Of course, this would be an incalculable loss.

Would she have these men die for nothing?

Sasha sighed and shook her bangs out of her eyes. Heavy is the head that wears the crown, after all. Sometimes decisions need to be made. Sometimes business is just business.

She walked toward the arch and knelt down close to its base. Always the overthinker, her utility belt was full of things both useful and ridiculous. Slowly, she pulled a four-inch, serrated pocketknife from her waist as she lifted up the metal wire. The sawing took only seconds, and the wire snapped with a sharp sound not unlike the cracking of human knuckles. Feeding the excess wire into the pink plasma, she murmured a prayer to any gods that might be listening.

Please, let wherever they are be better than where they came from...

And let them know...

This wasn't personal...

"Computer!" She barked.

"Yes, Miss Sasha."

"Send a message to Vega Shanire on Zoccarra. Tell him I have something he'd die for."

Damian Karras is a speculative fiction author from Davenport, IA. His work has been published by The Crow's Quill Literary Magazine, Bag Of Bones Press, Black Hare Press, and has been included on Horrorzine.com. He thanks you for reading, and begs you to continue. Anything... Everything... Just read...

Replacement

by Elizabeth Estabrooks

Suffocation in space. You could say it was fitting, considering I wasn't supposed to exist in the first place. For a moment, an oddly comforting wave of resignation washed over me. Like the universe was correcting itself, and I was along for the ride.

Then the irony of the situation struck me, and I just felt pissed off. A guy whose souped-up lungs could make do on air with a fraction of the oxygen content required by an average human, and here I was about to asphyxiate. *Seriously.*

I had managed half a dozen full sweeps of the asteroid cluster (a generous description of the glorified dust cloud I was now sailing through in an uncontrolled spin) without any trouble. Discounting the complete lack of anything valuable to be found.

With the air supply in a hopper like mine, most people would have already passed their turnaround time. I am not 'most people'. Based on the level of carbon dioxide (I could actually smell it mingling with the sharp scents of stale coffee and leaking lube oil in the cockpit), I had estimated there was enough breathable left for one more sweep, maybe two, before I would have to haul ass back to the Centre. And give Doc Callum the bad news.

It was Callum who told me about the assays done a decade or so back. Whoever had done them deemed this site 'logistically impractical, unlikely to result in sufficient return'. In other words, too far out for short rangers, and the long-range prospectors had bigger fish to fry.

But Callum had assured me there was something worthwhile here. That it would be my way out from under the Centre's thumb. After all, the definition of 'sufficient return' is subjective. For someone with lots of time, minimal air and nutrition needs, and no one to share the payday with, the bar was low.

So, instead of turning around, I'd moved in closer and lowered the detection threshold. Any pings would probably be false positives at these settings, I knew. At least if I got nothing, I could go back certain I hadn't missed so much as a spec of valuable ore. I was wondering what Callum might have to say about that. Maybe the assay he'd found had been misfiled, and I was in the wrong asteroid field altogether.

I'd pretty much decided that's what had happened when, from somewhere aft, there was a bang. The ship jolted, and my body slammed forward. I was caught by my loose harness about a centimeter short of faceplanting on the console. I pushed myself upright and looked out the window. Bits asteroid dust were zipping, bottom to top, past the view field.

"Well, shit," I said aloud.

The ship was going nose over tail. I closed my eyes, willing away the swimming sensation in my head. So much for my last deflector upgrade.

How big the rock had been, I couldn't be sure. But at least it hadn't ripped through the hull. As long as the armour was holding, there was need for panic.

Not feeling particularly reassured by my own logic, I entered a new course. The nav accepted the command, but instead of hearing the buzz of activating stabilizers, the thruster indicators all turned red at once.

Son of a...

I tool a deep breath and started counting to ten. I'd reached four when started to float up from my seat. *Ok, still no need to panic.*

The refurbished grav net, which I'd gotten in exchange for two months of reservoir scrubbing on Titan-7, always bailed at the first sign of trouble. Anyone who has met the techs on Titan-7 probably doesn't need me to explain why I hadn't been back to complain about their workmanship. To anyone who hasn't met them, the best way I can explain it is to say, although I can survive a substantial amount of blood loss, intact limbs are more important to me than reliable gravity.

As I fought with my harness strap, a glob of coffee drifted past my face. My first thought was disappointment that I'd missed my chance to finish drinking it. (I'm not always totally rational and focused in a crisis, especially when I'm still in denial that it is a crisis.) Then I noticed it was making its way in a consistently starboard-aft direction—strange, considering its reference frame was doing somersaults. I had about two seconds to puzzle over its trajectory before the cockpit's pressure alarm blared the explanation.

The denial ended, and my stomach dropped. The armour wasn't holding up after all. The most recent work on that system had been done by a crew at the Centre.

I still didn't suspect Doc Callum at this point. Of all the people at the Centre, he would have been last on my list of people who might wish me mortal danger. (On reflection, I was only half wrong on that point.)

The undulating coffee elongated toward a point just above the deck. A pair of smaller globules trailed close behind the first, confirming where the leak was.

I could patch the hole, but I didn't see the point. I'd already lost more air than there was to spare. I knew this without checking. There hadn't been any to spare in the first place. *Did I even charge the tank in the evac suit before I left?*

It didn't matter. I could wait until the last possible second to switch to the suit's supply, and it still wouldn't get me back to the nearest stopover station.

This brings us to the moment of my universe-correcting epiphany. Quickly followed the more 'fuck that, this just sucks' sentiment.

I imagined the directors at the Centre would be more than happy once they learned of the hopper found drifting in space, and confirmed Harley Jamison (a.k.a Subject 218252) hadn't found a way to slip into the general population on a remote rock somewhere. Which, of course, was exactly what I had intended to do. First, I just needed to buy my way out of the legal obligations that might give weight to any future extradition requests the Centre might be inclined to make in order to get me back in their charge.

To be fair, I should point out that, generally speaking, the Centre—official name: the Centre of Human Longevity and Wellbeing—isn't in the business of shortening lives. Quite the opposite. People require ongoing maintenance (expensive maintenance) to keep hiking, fishing, hand gliding (whatever it is they liked to do) until the day they terminate in their sleep. Usually, between the ages of 110 and 125.

The Centre provides that kind of maintenance. The scientists there are constantly experimenting, so they can tweak and refine the maintenance programs. I signed on to one of those experiments. It paid well. Or, it was supposed to. And it worked well.

A little too well.

The powers that be at the Centre (and its many subsidiaries) decided it would be better if people didn't learn they could make someone like me. Someone who doesn't need regular maintenance anymore. They also decided that my 'exceptional result' rendered the 'previously agreed upon renumeration null'. It seems I missed some fine print on the initial contract.

Also to be fair, I'll add that the scientists themselves (most of them, anyway) were not fans of the Centre Admins' decision regarding my case. I guess they didn't get a vote, though. A few protested openly, two quit. Then the two who quit were found dead.

The deaths were ruled accidental. But there wasn't anymore quitting, or protesting, after that. Doc Callum was pretty much the only one who didn't start crossing, eyes fixed on shoes, to the other side of the corridor every time I came around the corner.

Non-disclosure agreements, every luxury the twenty major systems have to offer, and most-importantly, indentured servitude were the methods of choice used to keep me (and I suspect a few others) on a leash and under the radar. My attempts to escape the indentured part were not going well.

The hopper console pinged. I looked at the display, and blinked to make sure I wasn't seeing things. Apparently, I wasn't, but...*Not possible.* I reset the sensors.

It was still there. A sun. One that hadn't been there before. Weird, and not useful unless...*Well holy shit.*

There was planet there too. And not just any planet. According to the preliminary readout, an artificially-maintained, habitable zone planet. It might be worth my while to patch that hole in the hull after all.

I set the emergency landing protocol. I didn't really think I might be too incapacitated to pilot during landing. I was too cocky for a thought like that. I wasn't too cocky to cover my bases though. I punched in the new heading too, which elicited a belligerent buzz from the computer.

"Yeah, yeah, I know," I muttered. As if I could explain to the computer, it needn't remind me that I'd completely lost steerage. I'd have to get at least a couple of the stabilizer thrusters going first, if I didn't want the hull repair to resemble a circus act. But hey, the situation was actually starting to look salvageable.

My moment of optimism was interrupted by a smattering of thuds and clanks cascading over my head. The remaining blobs of coffee that were yet to converge on the aft leak suddenly split into half a dozen pellets and took off in different directions. Basically, I was still screwed.

Sighing and swearing, I unsnapped my harness. What the hell, a chance was a chance. Right?

My foot caught on something as I came away from the seat. I made the mistake of kicking off the head rest to get free, and found my self pushed into a rotation out of synch with the ship around me.

I put my arms up in time to protect my head as I slammed into the deck, which at that moment was the ceiling (and annoyingly lacking in any useful handholds). Forcing my eyes to stay open despite the threatening vertigo, I slid sideways. As the bulkhead became my new up, I managed to catch the handle of a storage cubicle on its way by.

The hopper hadn't been designed with zero-g in mind. When the ship and I were moving together again, I pulled myself hand over hand using whatever knobs, hinges, and protrusions I could as grips until I made it to the aft auxiliary console. I purged and restarted the thrusters.

To my great relief, six of the eight hummed to life. Good enough. The view through the front screen wobbled, tilted, then settled with a tiny ball of light centered in the distance. My shouldn't-be there-but-is chance of salvation. With that problem solved, I made my way to the damage control kit.

I followed the air flow gauge from one hole to another. The work went quickly, and I was starting to feel optimistic again, despite the heavy fatigue settling over me. The rising CO_2 in my blood was hitting me harder than I'd expected. But at least the hull wouldn't be full of holes when the ship hit atmo.

On the other hand, as the planet loomed larger in the window, I wondered if it would matter. There was no way to know if the heat barrier had gone the way of the kinetic hull armour.

When spots started to form in my peripheral vision, all thoughts of the hull's integrity vanished under a surge of panic. Fear of losing consciousness was not a sensation I was accustomed to. I stopped moving and tried to take in a solid, slow breath. It didn't help. Instead, I was starting to hyperventilate.

Ok, Harley just relax.

A red glow emanating from the bow shone through the window. It was not helping me relax. The engines groaned as they sensed rising external gas pressure and started their atmo conversion. I headed to the equipment locker. *Please tell me I remembered to charge the tank on the evac suit.*

The air inside the helmet smelled of old synthetic rubber. It made the dull throb in my head worse, but air was air. I relished it.

I strapped back into my seat with the hopper rattling around me. The red glow in the window gave way to wispy, greenish clouds. I should have known what that meant, but (understandably, I think) my mind was on other things. Like whether or not all the flight control surfaces would deploy.

***

I wanted to stay asleep, but a bolt of pain shot from my elbow to my shoulder. Then another, and another. Between the jabs, I became aware of the ache in my head. More penetrating than it had been before. It felt like I was moving, bouncing, but that didn't make any sense. With my uninjured arm, I reached for my harness buckle.

My hand landed on something thick around my waist. Too wide and smooth to be part of the harness. I tried to push it off. It didn't move, but its surface yielded a bit under my fingers like warm rubber. I tried twisting my body. The restraint squeezed tighter.

My eyes shot open. First, all I could see were more of those green clouds bobbing up and down in a pale-purple sky. Except it wasn't the clouds bobbing, it was me. I craned my neck and found myself looking up at what I first thought was a pair of dark, leafless trees.

They weren't trees.

They each had a dozen or so limbs of various thicknesses, sticking out in all directions. I could only assume one of the appendages served as a head, but the black gummy suits they wore gave me no indication which.

I had no idea what these guys were. Certainly, no species I'd ever met. But I had that annoying feeling of something tickling at the back of my mind. Maybe I'd seen a picture somewhere. In a xenobiology text probably.

One of creatures had a limb curled securely around my middle. My feet hovered a few centimeters off the muddy-orange ground. It was cracked and crumbly like iron-rich clay that hasn't seen moisture in a long time.

The other fellow, a few paces away, had a pair of oblong devices hanging from his sides. They looked more like giant rotten bananas than anything else I could think of. They could have been something innocuous. A fashion statement, maybe. But I didn't think so. Suddenly, I was extremely thirsty.

I started to squirm and shove against the limb holding me. I looked around frantically, but didn't see the hopper anywhere. The limb squeezed me again.

Another, more gangly, appendage came down on my arm. This time the pain came as a tsunami. It started in my arm, then crashed through my entire body. A wave of nausea threatened to make the inside of my helmet a very unpleasant place to be. I stopped struggling, focusing instead on swallowing hard and taking deep breaths.

My attention finally turned to the status readouts in my helmet display. My air supply was in the red, my arm was broken (didn't really need the suit to tell me that), and I had a mild concussion (or that). On the bright side, the break was clean and both injuries were already healing. (Fast healing is another perk that came out of my time at the Centre.)

I called up a reading of the external conditions. Temperature: 42°C –not comfortable, but manageable. Atmosphere: Oxygen level fifteen percent. That would have been ok for me. Unfortunately, a number of toxic compounds were also listed, some in percentages that were definitely not ok, even for me. So much for that chance at salvation.

I was debating whether there was any point in mentioning my dwindling air supply to my escorts when, out of nowhere, a structure emerged. And when I say, 'out of nowhere' I don't mean it appeared over the horizon, or faded into view through fog. I mean, it came from nothingness. It wasn't there, and then it was. Right in front of us.

Less impressive, was the structure itself. It appeared to be made of rusty cast iron smeared with layers of soot. The door, more or less arch shaped, had large drops of sticky, black grease oozing from countless cracks and crevices.

151

One of the creatures began uttering a series of gargles, squeaks, and squawks. I couldn't even tell which one of them the sounds were coming from, let alone what they meant. The translation program in my suit was equally baffled. However, the structure reacted.

The frame of the door began to glow an iridescent blue. It might have been pretty on a less grubby door. In this instance, it brought to mind unusually-shiny toilet bowl cleaner. The door opened. We went in.

Without warning, my captor's arm uncurled around me. I dropped, landing more or less on my hands and knees. My broken arm crumpled under me. I cried out, but I managed not to faceplant on the floor.

When I got to my feet, the scene in front of me was what I imagine a beehive might look like if the bees took up coal mining. A large carven with every wall pocked by the mouths of hundreds of tunnels. Little, round, driverless carts zipped in and out, up and down, with no discernable pattern.

At first, I thought they were flying. I was trying to ascertain what method of thrust could allow for such quick, chaotic maneuvering when light caught one of the fishing-line-thin wires of the intertwining tracks. I was a little disappointed by the revelation, but the view was dizzyingly impressive just the same. Or maybe it was just the combo of concussion and borderline hypoxia.

One of the carts pulled up in front of us and stopped. A hatch on top slid open. It was empty.

A limb pressed into the center of my back. I tried to sidestep, but another of the many extremities swung hard into the back of my knees. I rolled, ungracefully, headfirst into the tiny capsule. With a click I was in darkness.

It felt like an hour went by. (Based on the fact I didn't asphyxiate, it was probably more like five minutes.) There was no sensation of motion. Nonetheless, when the capsule opened again, I was somewhere else.

The instant I saw light, I flung myself out. Not the smartest decision. Fortunately, the fall was only a couple of meters. I landed flat on my back. The impact stunned me for a second, but I was pleasantly surprised by how little the landing hurt this time. I was healing up nicely.

When I sat up, spots swam in my peripheral vision. So much so, I almost didn't notice the person standing there. The *human* person.

The woman's skin had more lines than a topography map. She wasn't wearing an environmental suit, or even a mask. Before, I could process what that meant, she spoke.

"Get that helmet off before you suffocate, honey." Her voice was rougher than her face, but sounded sincere enough. Still not entirely sure I wouldn't suffocate in any case, I yanked my helmet off, almost taking my ears with it. I took a tentative breath, then sucked in the cool, clean air.

"What is this?" I said, choking on my dry throat. "Who…what are those…" I waved a hand vaguely at the ceiling, not sure what direction I'd come from, "things."

The woman smiled, offering a hand. There was an angry welt just above her wrist. Shadows of similar marks showed under the translucent-white fabric of her billowy sleeves. They went all the way up to her shoulders.

"Those *things* are people, honey. Tallinocks, to be more specific."

I stared at her, disbelieving. When I didn't take her hand, she took mine and pulled me to my feet.

"Tallinocks are a myth," I managed.

"Is that what people say? I suspect the Talli would be glad to hear it."

The woman led me down a hall as grubby and gooey as the cavern above. Currents of red and orange light jumped between the floor and ceiling.

"They'd prefer to remain unseen entirely," she said. "But given their numbers now, random encounters are bound to happen."

A memory clicked. A reproduction of drawings, dendritic figures, made by some of the few who had claimed encounters with a species that could appear from nothingness. The reports always seemed to come from someone travelling alone. That hardly seemed random. Then it occurred to me, the encounters might be random. The people the Tallinocks allowed to continue on their way might not be.

"Then there's situations like this," she continued. "We couldn't have gotten you here with out coming out of hiding, now could we."

We? How does a human and the Talli constitute a 'we'?

There were a thousand other questions in my head, but I couldn't form any words. The lights made it hard to think. We came to a recess in the wall. Large sockets lined it on either side.

"Hurry," the woman said. "We've been exposed for too long already."

I felt dazed (something about those lights) as she helped me with the release clips on the sides of my suit. Self-conscious of the sweat soaking through my coverall, I stepped free of the cumbersome get-up. The sockets in the wall sparked to life.

The welts on the woman's skin made sense an instant too late. Cables snaked out and bit through my clothes into my arms and legs. They yanked me in.

The lights were in my brain then. There was a moment of panic, then it was like a fog in my head lifted. I could see the compound I was in, every room, every crack, every creature. I could see the planet, its sun, the asteroid field...

My view continued to expand as I connected to the shield network. The shield network that could make this star, and its planet, disappear from the prying eyes of the galaxy. I knew it wouldn't be long before I could see everything. I wasn't sure what 'everything' even meant, but if I stayed…*No…I don't want to stay. Wait…Stop!*

The break in the connection took me by surprise. I lurched forward.

"It's overwhelming, I know." The woman lifted me up. "You'll get used to it."

My whole body was shaking. "I don't think I want to get used to it." I looked at her, accusing, "How long do you expect me to stay here?"

"Well now, that depends. If what your friend said about you is true, you should last a very long time."

"What friend?" But then I knew, "There was never anything in that asteroid cluster, was there?"

"I'm getting too tired," she said, as though I hadn't spoken, "but it's been difficult to find a replacement that's robust enough. It's lucky you came along."

"How are you even…here?" I asked. My thoughts were getting fuzzy again.

"I was on the ship that made first contact with the Talli," she said.

I recognized her clothing then. A fashion dating back to the earliest interstellar settlers. It seemed impossible first contact with the Talli could date back that far.

She was looking at me with earnest, "You see what this alliance will give you? I should have been dead centuries ago. Instead, I've had so much time to explore. I've seen the galaxy in a way very few ever will."

"But the whole time, I'd really be stuck," I glanced over my shoulder, "In that thing."

"You'll forget all about your body being here."

I didn't find that as reassuring as she clearly intended. "What if I don't want to?"

"I'm afraid, there's not much choice in the matter." She almost sounded apologetic, which somehow made it worse.

"I have to go now," I said, and tried to step past her.

"You can't," she said, grabbing at me. "Please." But her grip was weak, and I pushed her aside.

The images from my connection were starting to fade already. Many were beyond my ability to process, making them difficult to hold on to. Others remained crystal clear. The complex. The planet I was on. My ship.

Or what was left of it. Sometime after I'd been pulled from the wreckage, whatever wasn't already beyond repair, had been reduced to slag. Anger boiled up in my belly, but I quelled it quickly. There were other ships.

I ran down the corridor. Making lefts and rights, I cut a path through the complex that should have felt like a labyrinth. Instead, the route was laid out clearly in my mind.

I expected guards to stop me. They didn't. I expected it to be hard to configure a Talli shuttle to fill the cabin with air I could breathe. It wasn't. I expected it to be pretty much impossible to fly. It responded to voice commands. I expected a squadron of fighters to intercept me as I lifted off the planet. None came.

In some recess of my mind, I knew why. They didn't think I could resist coming back. They thought I'd want to see more. Maybe they were right.

In what couldn't have been more than a couple of hours since my crash landing, I was breaking atmosphere above the Talli planet. One of thousands, I now knew. Hundreds of thousands.

***

What I hadn't expected was trouble trying to dock at the Centre. Yet, three hours after my arrival at the station, I was still hovering five hundred meters off the docking ring waiting for approval to approach. It seemed the usual life signature scans were bouncing off the Talli shuttles hull. I'd given my personal verification code six times.

My comm lit up, "Unscheduled shuttle number six, your identity has been successfully verified…"

Finally.

…you may proceed to secondary auxiliary docking bay nine."

Where?

"I'm sorry," I replied. "Can you repeat that?"

The voice came back with a hint of annoyance, "Please proceed to secondary auxiliary docking bay nine without delay." Like *I* was the one who'd been holding things up.

"Copy. Proceeding to secondary auxiliary bay nine."

I hadn't known there were 'secondary' auxiliary docking bays, but when I repeated the command to the ship, it seemed to know where to go. *Ok then.*

A few minutes later, curious to figure out exactly where in the Centre's sprawling station I'd ended up, I opened the shuttle hatch. Doc Callum was standing there waiting for me.

"We need to talk," he said.

"Funny," I said, cocking my head. "That's exactly what I was going to say."

Before I could step out, Callum stepped in. He had a backpack slung over one shoulder. The shuttled cabin was barely big enough for both of us, but he squeezed past me and sat in what could be described as a co-pilot seat. When he gave no mind to my inquisitive look, I returned to the other seat. It was really more like a small table. Comfortable to a Tallinock, maybe, but I'd been looking forward to stretching my legs.

We were practically nose to nose. From this distance, the dark circles and bags under his eyes were more pronounced than I'd ever seen them. Maybe it was a product of the slightly-purple lighting inside the shuttle. Or maybe Callum was overdue for a maintenance treatment, despite the generous discount provided to Centre employees.

"You sabotaged my shuttle, didn't you?" I said.

"You can't be here," Callum said.

"You're not answering my question."

"Obviously, you know the answer."

"Ok. How about you tell me why then," I said, struggling to keep my irritation in check.

Callum leaned back and crossed his arms, "I would have thought that was obvious."

That did it. I stood up and squeezed past him. I was about to step off the shuttle when Callum grabbed my arm. *Hard.* I started to yank my arm free when he spoke with such intensity it stopped me short.

"You can't go out there."

We stared at each other, eye to eye, for a long moment.

"Why the hell not?" I finally asked.

He hesitated. Which royally pissed me off.

I pulled my arm free and pointed a finger in his face, "You wanted to talk, so talk," I shouted. "Either tell me what the hell is going on, or let me get off this damn sardine of a ship."

"So you can do what?" Callum asked.

"I was thinking I would figure out a way to replace my hopper for starters. The one that got trashed on a random alien planet, thanks to you."

I was hoping to get a look of contrition out of him with that one, but his face only hardened. When he spoke again, there was a bite in his voice I'd never heard from him before.

"Why do you think I would do something like that, Harley? At the risk of my job. Hell, at the risk of more than my job, I've done nothing but help you since you've been here. So why do you think I would I send you to the Tallinocks?"

"I don't know!"

"Yes you do!"

And he was right. I didn't want to admit it, but I did know. Just like I knew about the two scientists whose deaths were definitely not accidental.

"They're talking about terminating me," I said.

"Not talking," said Callum. "Planning. If you hadn't been out in that asteroid cluster, they'd have gotten to you already. They agreed to let you go out there because—"

"Wait. They agreed?" And here I'd thought I was so clever getting out of the sector without anyone from the Centre trying to come after me.

Callum took a deep breath, "What do you know about the Talli, Harley?"

"I didn't think they were real until about twenty hours ago," I said.

"But you connected to their network," said Callum. A statement not a question.

"Yeah, but," I narrowed my eyes at him, "How would you know that."

"Agnes."

"Who…? I started, but then realized. "The old woman I was supposed to replace."

"She gave me a heads up you were one your way back." Callum's face grew more serious, if that was possible. "She won't last much longer, Harley. A replacement has to be supplied before she dies."

I was about to ask why when a flash of my brief connection to the Talli came back to me. Not an image. A feeling, more intense than anything I'd ever felt. It's what had pushed me to break the connection. It was a desire to see and understand everything, but not to be seen. By anyone, or anything. Ever.

"They'd obliterate entire worlds to avoid having to interact with them," I said. "But I don't know why."

"I can't help you there," said Callum. "One theory is, they fear being conquered."

"Given their level of technology compared to anyone else's, that seems like a stretch," I said.

Callum shrugged. "It doesn't really matter why. The point is, every civilization that stumbles across them can either help them stay hidden, or be the first to be attacked if the Talli are ever forced out of hiding."

"How are we helping them?"

"The shields need complex brains to function," Callum said. "As you might imagine, there aren't very many Talli volunteering to do the job themselves."

"So, you offered me up," I said, not caring to keep the resentment from my voice. I mean, I saw his point. If the shield for that Talli system came down completely, the entire quadrant would know about them. They wouldn't stand for that. But still, why did it have to have anything to do with me?

"I'm sorry, Harley." Callum's eyes were pleading now, "This was the only way I could..." He closed his eyes, swallowed, opened them and continued, "The Talli have been on us for a replacement. And with your insistence on buying your way out, there was no talking the higher ups out of subject termination. I couldn't let that happen, so I thought—"

"You thought, hey it's a win-win," I said, scathingly.

"Think about the opportunity though," Callum said. "Agnes told me the connection to their shield network will give your mind access to the entire galaxy at once. You experienced it for yourself, didn't you?"

Reluctantly, I nodded.

"It's freedom of a kind, isn't it?"

"I suppose that's one way to look at it." I shifted by gaze to the shuttle door. "What happens if I go out there now."

"You won't get past the security team in the corridor."

"What are their grounds for arresting me?"

"Unauthorized use of a hopper, for a start."

"It's my hopper," I snapped.

Callum gave me a look bordering on pity.

Yeah, yeah. They don't really need a reason.

"Fine," I sighed. "I'll go back."

Relief washed over Callum's face. "Thank you, Harley." He put both hands on my shoulders, "I know none of this is fair to you."

Damn straight, it's not.

I sat down and started prepping the shuttle for departure. Just as I had everything ready, Callum reappeared over my shoulder.

"You can go now," I said, turning. I eyed the backpack he still had over his shoulder, "Unless…"

"I promised I would escort you," he said. He had the apologetic look again. "They need to be sure."

Of course they do.

"How will you get back here?" I asked. "I didn't exactly take this shuttle with the Talli's permission."

"Agnes has assured me they won't miss it, as long as I destroy it as soon as I can after I get back."

I wouldn't take Agnes's word on anything, but whatever.

***

Callum stood watch, as I let Agnes press me back into the nook. Again, the cables bit into my skin. My head filled with the view of an entire star system and more. It filled too with the Tallinocks' chatter. The communication was constant between this planet and a thousand others.

One of the snippets was about me. An afterthought really. Like someone mentioning they'd replaced the battery in their toothbrush. Other snippets were more interesting, I wanted to tell Callum what they were saying about the 'concern of human expansion', but suddenly Callum and the Centre were nothing but specks in my consciousness. There was so much to see.

It was beyond amazing to see everything and everywhere at once. Callum was right. Freedom couldn't possibly feel better than this.

But I wanted it anyway.

I found that speck in the building noise, willed all my awareness toward it until I could see Callum again. He was doing it. I could even read the message as it left his hand comm and zipped into subspace...*connected. It's done.*

Stop! I screamed in my head. But the network didn't let me go this time. Had I stayed in too long? Panic electrified my already overloading braincells, then anger.

Stop! I tried again, pushing back against the incoming flood of images. *Let...me...GO!*

I howled inside my own head with an all-encompassing rage. Then I was sprawled on the floor. It took me a second to realize I was screaming out loud.

When I finally got a hold of myself and looked around, the expression of genuine concern on Callum's face almost broke me. I didn't let it. He started to kneel, reaching a hand gingerly toward me to see if I was ok. I lunged at him.

I got his jacket in both fists and whipped him around so fast, his expression barely had time to morph into shock. I shoved him into the alcove, and pulled my hands free just in time to make sure the snaking cables found the right target.

A couple of them pulled back after attempting to cut through the thick leather of Callum's jacket. I had a moment to worry that I should have gotten it off him first. But this machine was more persistent than I was giving it credit for. After two or three tries, all the connecting mouths had broken through. Callum's face was white, his eyes wide.

I know the feeling, buddy.

A few minutes went by. Callum didn't emerge from the connection. Either because he couldn't, or didn't want to. I thought the latter was at least likely.

"No...no, no, no," Agnes's voice was a whisper.

"What's the problem?" I said, "It's accepted him, hasn't it?"

"He won't last," she looked up at me. The intense fear in her eyes started me. I looked away. She kept talking, "Even if he weren't already beyond middle age, he doesn't have the same durability you do."

"Well then, he'll buy some time until someone else comes along," I said.

"And if no one does?" she asked.

I shrugged.

"Without another replacement, the Talli might take over everything just because they can," said Agnes, almost to herself at first, then she focused in on me again. "You know how trivial it would be for them."

She had a point there. The only reason the Talli hadn't delt with the pest problem of the galaxy so far, was that it would require coming into contact with too many of the pests themselves.

I had to admit, to myself at least, that it did worry me a little. But I kept my face stony. "Not my problem to solve."

"The Centre will know," she tried next. "They'll come looking for him when he doesn't come back, and I'll tell them.

Even if I don't, it won't take them long to figure it out when they come here to find empty space, but no sign of Callum."

I wondered if she added that last bit in case I might be thinking I should kill her to keep her quiet. (For the record, I wasn't.)

"Tell them whatever you want," I said, and walked away.

I had a Talli shuttle at my disposal. I'd be long gone before anyone from the Centre came looking.

Elizabeth Estabrooks enjoys the speculative side of science almost as much as the real thing. Her short fiction has appeared in *Mad Scientist Journal* as well as the anthologies *Time Travel Short Stories* and *Spring Into SciFi: 2022 Edition*. She grew up in New Brunswick and currently lives in Kingston, Ontario. Learn more about Elizabeth at www.elizabethestabrooks.com.

Planet Dahlia, or Body and Soil

by Maraki Piedras

Planet Dahlia had no spaceport—no conventional buffer zone at all between her orbit and her LG-type World Forest, save for a delicate cluster of new clearings. The largest of them had been named 'Subira', after Subira Pradkar, the chief science officer at the First Contact.

So instead of sitting strapped into a regular shuttle seat, Epifanio Zuñiga, a rank II librarian, lay curled up inside a biodegradable capsule pod, which shook violently as it got snatched right out of the sky by a Tesla Trap. A luminous, towering gigaflower, it had been trained to pick up on certain electromagnetic signatures, which was what made all the difference between a safe landing and a fiery death.

Dizzily, Epifanio pressed his head against his knees; his personal, equally inescapable laws of gravity tied him to Alexandria Station, the largest knowledge bank in the Allied Space, and Powers That Grant Book Access could dispatch you to a *lot* less pleasant places for the sake of a database update.

His contact planetside, who was monitoring all the sensor feeds, biometrics included, messaged: <Breathe, Rank II. Remember the exercises I sent you.>

<Oh, very well, you may have my Van Gulik collection, partner. You'd enjoy picking that apart, wouldn't you?>

<Statistically speaking, you're in no more danger right now than when riding a space elevator, *partner*.>

Hermes Mizuno, that smooth talker, was a contracted Aegis, or a personal security provider. Stoic, a touch acerbic (in that particularly *vindicated* way only a Positronic personage could pull off), and *mostly* helpful.

<See? If you're coherent enough to banter with a grumpy old synthform, you can't be all that scared of heights.>

One last flip, then a gentle slide, like a smart rollercoaster suddenly deciding to play nice. But not so nice that it *wouldn't* just spit you out face first into a blindingly harsh sunlight and poisonous-green feathergrass.

Before Epifanio could trip over any more LeGuinian motifs, a pair of firm hands pulled him up to his feet as though he were overturned bookshelf, which gave his eyes the much-needed moment to adjust. Mizuno's crystalline faceplate, opaque by default, reflected the Tesla Trap's retreat into its bed behind the impenetrable tree-wall—not so different from a regular docking cable, in the end.

"Thanks," Epifanio muttered, hastily shoving off the broad chest and fumbling for something to take the edge off the lingering nausea.

"Don't mention it," Mizuno replied, using his voicebox for once as he produced a water bottle and a piece of ginger candy, the latter with the flair of a street magician. "It's all in the extra-clumsy client fee, Appendix C."

"Master of Small Prints, are you? I shudder to think of a *second* date."

Instead of delivering a reply, Mizuno simply patted him on the shoulder—and not-so-subtly turned him around.

Thank the infinite stars that the new scentbox was so easy-to-use! Epifanio wouldn't want to make a *bad* impression on his very first Dahlian outside of VR!

Like all of the Post-Contact hybrids, she was CSO Pradkar's mirror image tinged mossy-green—the *singular* Dahlian connective symbiotic tissues on her palms, neck and feet covered with protective pine-cone scales. Her very appearance, sylvan and sophisticated at once, defied the idea of shoes, scarves or gloves, her single-piece draping fabric being more symbolic than functional, as a nod to human sensibilities. Most notably, a single flowering vine rested across her shoulders like an official's sash; according to Epifanio's briefing, its unique make-up would serve as her main identifier among offworlders.

"Speaker Zuñiga, Special Guest Mizuno, welcome," she vocalized in a low, but sonorous voice, simultaneously exuding a pleasant, yet not overwhelming aroma. "I am Three-Yellow, Ten-White Zinnias of the Uaman Rootsoil. You may call me Zinn if you prefer. I shall be at your disposal for the duration of this Root Exchange. Before we begin, do you have any special requests?"

Epifanio beamed, trying and failing *not* to bounce on the balls of his feet like a schoolboy during his first planetfall, even as his scentbox routines toiled away, transforming his frenetic energy into a more Dahlian sort of friendliness. The language of scents would always be the primary bridge between this planet's sentients and anyone or anything else wishing to interact with them.

"Take us directly to the reception area, please?" They *were* a bit behind the schedule, no thanks to Epifanio's own pre-flight jitters. "We can do the full tour later! Unless—" He glanced at Mizuno. "I'm forgetting some security protocols?"

The chemical part of Mizuno's own exchange with 3Y-10W Zinnias might have gone over Epifanio's head, but the two appeared to be quite pleased with each other, overall.

<We're good,> the Aegis confirmed on the intralink. <I won't go into detail now, but rest assured, you're not a biohazard.>

<Phew! She still likes you better, though,> judging by the way she chose to walk on Mizuno's side, giving Epifanio a wide berth. <What's your secret?>

The earpiece that Mizuno had given Epifanio was made of polished stone, perfectly-molded and giving off a metaphorical whiff of the truly exotic. But so long as it was, like the Aegis said, unhackable, he didn't particularly care about its mystery origins.

<Ah, Zuñiga. If I told you, I'd have to breach a *very* lucrative contract.>

<Right…Wait, was that a death threat?>

In general, Planet Dahlia seemed to have good instincts when it came to forging new alliances *and* dodging various bullets. Which wasn't to say that she was of one mind and one mind alone. Instead, she had four driving intelligences, the so-called Rootsoils—highly sophisticated networks spanning a continent each. Separated as they were by deep, salty oceans, they kept a close watch for marine rivals, which were yet to emerge.

There were no other bodies of water that did not exist to nourish Dahlia's body and soil.

Much like Subira and her team, Epifanio had never stood a *chance.*

While his in-built filters somewhat eased off the strain from the sheer visual extravaganza around him, like a flower festival on steroids, the air was fresher than he had *ever* breathed in his life. It was like drinking the best oxygen cocktail—no, taking a CO_2 *bubble bath.*

As far as he knew, no bird-like life had ever survived the local mass extinction events, but insectile buzzing and chattering more than filled the gap, fully justifying the noise-dampening script—another courtesy of Mizuno's.

<Problem?> he asked, registering Epifanio's fresh spike of fear.

Wordlessly, Epifanio took a step back and pointed at a multi-limbed, many-eyed cosmic horror that was decidedly *not* a friendly neighborhood pet.

"Be calm, Speaker Zuñiga," 3Y-10W Zinnias intoned with a beatific smile. "Its species is neither hostile nor inherently dangerous to humans."

"Small mercies! I mean, sorry, are my, um, ammonia levels too off the charts for you now?"

"Not at all! I was cultivated *specifically* for full social compatibility with Pradkars—I mean, humans!" She paused, as though distracted by a private message. "You are lucky indeed, Esteemed Guests! Qualia Myriad-Magenta Sea-Figs shall be attending the opening ceremony."

<I suppose you could say… she *does* give a fig.>

Caught off guard, Epifanio forgot to disguise his chuckle, unlike the Aegis, who could smirk behind that faceplate of his as he pleased.

Not that Mizuno didn't thoroughly *earn* the bragging rights: before the forest passage widened into another clearing, he had rescued his extra-clumsy, Appendix-C client from *several* overly-hospitable creepers, two root traps (attracted by the battery charge in Epi's exosuit, of all things!), one web (extremely sticky and *launched* at him with deadly precision), and finally, a cloud of pollen to frazzle sturdier face masks than his. The particles may not have evolved with *him* in mind, but Mizuno had somehow failed to inform them of the fact.

<Put it on my tab?> Epifanio tried, swiftly crossing the embarrassment horizon and tipping dangerously into the hero-worship territory.

<And then they say we electric shepherds are high maintenance.>

***

A tea ceremony of some kind or other had been the staple of interstellar diplomacy ever since Captain Souchong and Commander Chai introduced themselves to the first friendly alien taste bud (and yep, that was a real kid's cartoon)—but on Dahlia, the tea in question was less a beverage than an invigorating foot bath in interesting company. Jasmine and honeygrass, if Epifanio's nose could still be trusted at all.

As a late arrival, Epifanio kicked off his boots and made a beeline for the last empty seat in the circle, a neutral cushion between two rival corporate reps, conveniently color-coded. They were twelve in total, counting him and Ambassador Phenn, a wiry epicene who must have discovered their own form of photosynthesis, to have figured out the logistics in such record time. Mizuno, for his part, hung back, rescuing a little teabot from a questing vine.

Zinn had withdrawn almost immediately, 'plugging herself in' alongside her sisters, her feet planted on the ground and her back resting against a trunk. Rootspeak or not, they wouldn't look out of place in a beauty parlor, exchanging the latest hot gossip about those disconnected alien weirdos who burnt through more caffeine than sunlight.

<Focus on your three o'clock, Speaker Zuñiga. But *do* try not to sweat.>

At Qualia Myriad-Magenta Sea-Figs' entrance, a respectful hush fell over the circle, followed by a swirl of golden-yellow blossoms raining down from the canopy. Where the Zinnias had been created to perform a finite set of tasks, the Qualias were a spontaneous, thrilling new growth, an impetus that could not be contained. Less humanoid, with thicker, fleshier headvines in bloom that trailed all the way to the ground, she carried herself with the grace of a true monarch.

After taking her own seat on a throne-like natural dais and lowering her feet into a basin that was visibly more ornate than the guests', she plucked off one of her qualions, orange meshed red.

An auxiliary Zinnias passed this first fruit of friendship to the enterprising Ambassador, while the next one went to the wizened old saffron-clad monk on the Qualia's other side. The next, to the Convergence, a brand-new group of freelance AIs, who could clone the offering, but not taste it. Every intellectual movement in the Allied Space that Dahlia had found curious, no matter how big or small, had been invited to participate, represented by its best voice. And, to protect that voice, its best synths—most of which steered clear of Mizuno, whose exotic crystals must signal 'contagion' to the more conventional crowd, not constant renewal. In truth, if he *was* a grumpy loner, then he had become one by failing to be replicable at the current level of science.

"Dear guests, hello and welcome again to our beautiful planet," Myriad-Magenta-Sea-Figs began—only, it wasn't *her* vocal cords working, but those of her Zinnias, sitting at her feet and acting as her mouthpiece. "Please remember: this is *not* a competition. We have asked for all of you because we are deeply intrigued by your variety and perseverance, not because we want to sow more strife. Let this exchange remain peaceful and harmonious."

Epifanio was yet to meet a professional thinker *without* an agenda, but it wasn't as if he himself were the exception.

"Alexandria, was it?" One-Blue Suit sized him up once again, probably wondering how much information they could squeeze out of him for free. "A bit of a tricky commute, isn't it?"

Epifanio returned his attention to his own qualion, trying *so* very hard not to imagine *blood* running through those red veins covering the smooth surface of the fruit. "I slept through most of it, but yeah, not looking forward to doing it again."

"So what have you got for us? You think, therefore you aim?"

Epifanio snorted. *"Aim for the stars."*

"But if you happen to miss," the Convergence picked up, displaying a cheeky emoticon, *"shoot for the moon instead."*

The game continued, with the attendees stringing more quotes together as they sampled (or otherwise dealt with) their pieces of Sea-Figs. Such practiced camaraderie! They might as well have been trying to sell each other a used space shuttle or two.

<I thought you quite liked trees of knowledge,> Mizuno remarked idly. <What's holding you back?>

<I'm seriously allergic to apples. Does this look like an apple to you?>

<Squeamish.>

<Would *you* want to crunch on somebody else's antennae?>

<Actually, back in the Cassian mines…>

"What *is* your thesis, Speaker Zuñiga?" asked Reverend Spivek, of the Unitarian Church of New Rhodes.

"Sapientia est potentia," he recited, all too happy to retreat behind his station's motto.

"Spoken like a true hoarder!" One-Gray Church exclaimed, glancing at One-Blue Suit for approval. "Didn't you Alexandrians *ever* learn about sharing?"

Epifanio's initial reservations aside, the pulp tasted fine—a bit like those purposefully bland hospital chutneys. He wriggled his toes in the tea-basin, feeling patently ridiculous, yet *not* above encouraging Mizuno to keep up his running commentary, instead of networking like the professional archivist that he was supposed to be.

"Oh, leave him alone, Larry," Doctor Pesquet, the resident xenopsychologist, cut in. "Everyone's getting their turn anyway."

Epifanio thought of Sophocles, *Antigone*:

Through highwalled waves of ocean storm
The species makes its way
Drenched but victorious.

What *couldn't* they do indeed?

So somebody—let's say, a semi-crusty librarian—needed to throw some salt in the sweet tea. An unpleasant job, to be sure, hence the military-grade security, but who else was going to do it? *Not* the pill pushers or the dream merchants, happily lining up for their chance at becoming the local kudzu.

"Speaker Zuñiga of Alexandria Station." Myriad-Magenta Sea-Figs addressed him without another preamble. Her face never moved; her body language too sinuous to interpret in familiar terms. "What beautiful eyes you have. Irises like nebulae."

He blinked. "Um, thank you, Esteemed Qualia. It's the corrective augment."

In contrast, or perhaps not, the Zinnias vocalizer put on a very personable smile, one that she must have learnt from Subira herself, before CSO Pradkar had disappeared back among the stars.

"What does it do?" If anything, the Qualia's fascination only seemed to grow, even as the others watched them hawkishly. *Was it in bad faith to be singled out for your pretty eyes, in this context?*

"There was an… accident." He winced, not particularly caring to remember the smell of smoke. It had been all over the newsfeeds, anyway: *If you don't want to get burnt, don't adopt such flammable names.* Nobody would call their starcruiser the *Titanic*, now, would they? "If not for the surgery, I'd have gone completely blind."

More background grumbling, this time from the Shakespeare Club, their stand-in drone painted over with a hyper-realistic skull that was, inevitably, signed 'Yorick'; according to Mizuno, they had had a stasis box installed at the eleventh hour just for the fruit.

"That would have been a shame." The Qualia continued peering at him like *he* was the fascinating alien in the group. Oh, right: to her, he was. "Do you program the images yourself?"

"Yeah, all my favourite lens-savers," he admitted, not too shame-faced about *that* bit of vanity. His last (and only) boyfriend had told him that his eyes were his best feature; the upgrade had *not* come cheap, but it could be either a great ice breaker or a deterrent. "May I present my argument, since we're already talking?"

An open, expansive gesture with her vines. "Please, do. Your station must be so much like a Rootsoil, accruing knowledge over generations. We are most eager to find out what you would consider humanity's most seminal teachings."

"Then I should tell you, if I'm here to teach, it's to teach you how to *learn* from our mistakes." He fixed his gaze on her. "Before anything, you should be wary of what you graft onto your home rootstock. Memdemics have killed more minds than any one virus."

The circle erupted in a chorus of protests, Ambassador Phenn shaking her head at his utter lack of subtlety.

"But what of cross-pollination?" Myriad-Magenta Sea-Figs wondered. "If we never invite new ideas, how would we develop an immunity?"

"Which is why we advise caution, not—" But before he could get his tea-scented foot out of his mouth, a Tesla Trap shot skywards yet again. A one-person pod, custom-made and lacking any IDs.

<I'm on the Embassy feed,> Mizuno informed Epifanio, <and Ambassador Phenn was *not* expecting the evil fairy to make it.>

<Hey, *I'm* the evil fairy!>

<Not anymore, you're not.>

In the meanwhile, the Tesla Trap *failed* to land on its proper spot, triggering a flurry of activity that started with securing the guests' safety without any further jungle adventures.

<If I leave you alone in your sleepbox,> Mizuno wondered, <what are the chances of you staying out of trouble? No, *don't* answer that.>

Epifanio didn't know whether to shudder or grin, so he did a bit of both. <Lead the way?>

***

"So, evil corpos? Big Pharma? Or some lone opportunist?"

Mizuno, in his Aegis mode, pressed his finger to his faceplate, perfectly composed again. <No extraneous noises.>

Epifanio swallowed his protest, bowing down before the sheer numbers of traps, shoots and appendages that reacted to his incursion into their territory or wanted to feed off his solar energy reserves outright. Just what kind of gatecrasher would attempt this trek solo?

Ever the merciless machine, Mizuno gave him a *vivid* mental rundown, handpicked from his shareable archives: synth and organic mercs; terror bombers and bioweapon maniacs; poachers and traffickers—you name it.

<Stars have mercy! Forget I ever asked!>

Epifanio had naively assumed that the cultural fair was the main target, but if the Dahlians themselves were in danger of any sort—

<How did our trespasser get past the Embassy ship, anyway? It should be the newest model, with a captain from an anti-pirate task force!>

<That is certainly how *Ambassador Phenn* has spun it. Seeing as the alternative would likely cost them their position.>

Epifanio refocused on walking, though as slow as he may be in comparison to a one-of-a-kind synth, the main constraint here had to be the terrain itself. Swinging an energy machete around would *definitely* count as more than a diplomatic hiccup.

<You're doing great, Speaker Zuñiga. We're almost there.>

<Ah, Special Guest Crystal Gem, you're one hell of a tracker.>

<Yes, I am.> The intruder had been using the Tesla Trap's bleed-through to mask their movements, but now they had finally got into Mizuno's range. <Just stay back and don't try anything stupid, Y/N?>

A fresh riot of color caught Epifanio's eye. Well, rooted him to the spot, more like it, with its hypnotic fractal of whites, reds, blues, purples and blacks arranged in an endless cascade of quill-like petals.

<Zuñiga! That is *not* a flower!>

Before he could so much as blink, an implacable force grabbed him by the ankles—and then everything turned topsy-turvy and he couldn't bloody *breathe*. An energy blast from Mizuno's armgun later, Epifanio dropped to the damp forest floor, grunting in pain.

His Aegis *leapt* over him, not bothering with any niceties, as Not-A-Flower was far from finished with them. From the Terran archives, this lethal beauty would be the closest to an *Idolomantis diabolica*—if the devil mantis had ever evolved to hunt black bears.

The Dahlian mantis swayed to and fro, utterly silent, shifting its wings to distract Mizuno while it primed its mandibles, which glanced off the crystal armor without so much as a scratch.

"Special Guest!" rang through the clearing. "Don't kill it!"

"Fall back!" Epifanio weighed in, recognising this Zinnias as their guide. "Mizuno, do as she asks!"

Grudgingly, the Aegis withdrew to cover them both, his twin weapons poised to finish the job. "I could've *lost my client*, 3Y-10W."

"I'm fine, I'm fine!" Epifanio spoke up. "If you don't believe me, check my vitals!"

"Please forgive our breach of hospitality," she said in a placating tone, even as a cluster of vines descended from the trees to restrain the wounded insectoid. "But you should *not* have strayed so far from the visitor area."

Epifanio made sure to apologize, Mizuno being about as unapologetic as they came. "How did you find us?"

"Oh?" 3Y-10W Zinnias had not quite mastered CSO Pradkar's famously expressive eyebrows yet, but an echo of a quirk was there alright. "Were you trying to be sneaky?"

Two energy volleys went off at once. The first one caught Mizuno in the shoulder after he shoved Zinn out of the line of fire. The second failed to find its mark, even as Mizuno's own blasts shattered a stealth shield, revealing the gatecrasher in a bulkier EV suit, seemingly carrying more weapons than all the other bodyguards combined.

"Hermes!" Epifanio gasped. "*Stars*, your armor!"

A strange substance was eating away at the outer layer, threatening the more vulnerable tissues underneath. But that couldn't be happening—Epifanio had *never* heard of an acid so powerful. The Aegis, uncaring, simply shed the damaged plating like snakeskin, herding him and Zinn away from the intruder.

<New plan?> Epifanio prompted hopefully, *not* looking at the man's too-realistic chest. Otherwise, he might accidentally start calling him Six-Ten for Six-Tanned Pack, Ten-Energy Guns. "Zinn? How about some more of those handy vines?"

"Alexandria Station," X-Black Grenades stated in a clinical, digitally stripped-down voice, "I have no problem with you. Get out of the way, and you won't be needing any more reconstructive surgeries."

Did that ever actually *work* on anyone?

"Well, *I* have a problem with you, no-namer—you're making a mess of my perfectly decent paid vacation. But if you give yourself up quietly, my Aegis might just resist the urge to rearrange your body parts into modern art."

<Not bad. Where did you get that one?>

The next thing Epi knew, there was an ear-splitting whine and a wall of crystal growing between them and a very localized supernova.

***

The good news was it hadn't been a *fire* fire this time.

<My organic parts are still functional, despite the chemical attack,> Mizuno reported. <Waiting for the rest to boot up.>

With a sick, helpless feeling, Epifanio leaned over their guide's prone form as she failed to reply. According to his scant available data, they should be moving her to the nearest tree with active 'connectors', the only extant means of life support around here—unless the symbionts were already dying out.

"Just hang in there, sweetheart," he whispered, patting her hand. "Big Bad Wall of Muscle here just needs another moment to reboot."

Zinn twitched, then blindly groped around, seized by a full-body shudder. The pine-cone scales on her palms were quivering, the tissues beneath turning ashen, as though withering away.

"This isn't supposed to be happening!" And, pleadingly, "Hermes, tell me what to do!"

There was a terrible silence, as though the whole planet had gone quiet.

Then, Mizuno jumped to his feet in full battle mode, flexing his limbs. "My primary objective is—"

"To what, let her *die*? I don't bloody think so!" He staggered, unable to support Zinn's full weight.

"*Zuñiga*. This *is* above your pay grade."

Yes, well. Knowledge wasn't always the writing on the wall. Sometimes it was the particular pattern of flowers on someone's sash or the way she tried to smile without ever having evolved to do it.

Without another word, Mizuno scooped their guide up.

***

There were more casualties: vines, giant insects, security drones... and Zinnias. Most of those that had been assigned to the guests, as they had been the nearest to the clearing. Human-programmed first-aid bots were chirping in confusion, unable to read the vitals.

Epifanio's brain processed the picture in fits and starts, almost as if his ocular implants were malfunctioning. Ambassador Phenn, clutching their side—wounded in several places, but refusing to step aside until they were shoved. Had the intruder been after *them*, surely it would have been all over by now.

Instead, the Qualia, robbed of her voice, could not even ask *why*, quivering mutely instead of her would-be killer. Because this did not look like a kidnapping, but a mockery of a sample (trophy?) collection.

Epifanio called out, "Have you gone *mad*? Whatever you're after, it can't be worth all this damage!"

"Do you realize how much any of this would go for in the market?" The intruder gestured around vaguely, encompassing the entire forest. "What a fucking waste of resources. If you don't believe me, ask your crystalhead freak—he's a fucking legend."

<My reputation precedes me.> Mizuno, finally springing into action.

Trailing dead crystals in his wake, the Aegis *kicked* the acid gun off the intruder's suit, launching the two of them as far away as possible. Wasting no more time, Epifanio dashed for the Qualia, towing her in the opposite direction. He had not noticed this before, but her movement speed *was* naturally slower, matching her plant nature; if the Ambassador was somewhere behind them, he could not bring himself to turn back and check. This was what he had willingly ignored before: Planet Dahlia was a veritable treasure trove of biotechnology, a myriad of cures and solutions that could not be developed without her permission.

Amidst the background noise, Mizuno's fight was terrifyingly quiet. Afraid to distract him, Epifanio did not dare to so much as *think* in his direction. He wished he could appeal to *all* of Dahlia, all of her Rootsoils, undo this terrible impression.

Instead, he tripped over a skull-faced drone, gone offline.

"Alas," he muttered. "Poor Yorick."

"Speaker Zuñiga," came a weak voice. "What is happening out there?"

Zinn, awake again, tried to peel herself away from the tree, the Qualia's vines arresting the motion and catching her into what looked like an embrace.

"Speaker Zuñiga," Zinn said more confidently—oh, she was speaking as Myriad-Magenta Sea-Figs now. "Thank you. This impulse has been preserved. Now you should tend to your own people."

His own people stumbled into the original ravaged clearing, still smoking slightly. "You should see the other guy," Mizuno announced happily, dragging them by one leg.

The trees behind him might have passed for a weapons' testing sight; the last that Epifanio had seen so much damage caused in so little time had been that stupid library bombing.

"You have questions," Mizuno tried again.

"Yeah." Epifanio was frowning at the Ambassador, who was currently swarmed by all those frenzied medbots, finally given a comprehensible task. "Are you actually immortal?"

Mizuno stared at him, nonplussed. "Not if I don't get my hands on some silicas to metabolize within the next fifteen minutes."

***

As an Old Terran culture used to say, body and soil are one. This was the last piece of wisdom that Epifanio gifted the Dahlians, before they focused on the more pressing matters, such as putting up new defenses and healing what could be healed. Ambassador Phenn took the prisoner, rushing off before any of the guests could catch up with them. Understandable, giving the lapse of security.

Epifanio tossed and turned in his sleepbox, unable to clear up the clutter in his head. His own shuttle wasn't scheduled for a couple of days yet, and it wasn't as if *he* were unwelcome to stay, even if it was going to cause diplomatic problems later.

Mizuno was not at his self-assigned post. Dahlia's nights had enough bioluminescence to light up a path, so after a brief, token internal debate, Epifanio decided to risk another mantis.

Once again, Subira's Circle caught him in his orbit. There sat Hermes—cross-legged, crystals covering the roots in a stunning display like those of a volcanic cavern, holding the connector vines with his bare hands.

Silently, the Aegis beckoned him over.

"*Please* tell me this is just some kind of spa treatment."

181

Mizuno, helmet-less, affected a grin. <Actually, we were talking about you.>

Epifanio plopped down next to him. "We?"

<Dahlia and I.>

"Right, yes, computer, computer."

<Don't worry, they like you. They appreciate your warnings.>

He sighed. "Not the right kind, in the end."

Hermes caught his gaze. <You could talk to them too, if you like. You already have a piece of me—that is, my crystal—in your ear. I could be the buffer—if it gets too much for your brain, I'll pull you out..>

He froze up, worse than when he had been told that he was supposed to make planetfall in a glorified seedpod. But if he had been afraid of forbidden knowledge, he wouldn't have gone to Alexandria in the first place.

<Relax. Imagine you're coming home.> One of Hermes' hands cupped the back of Epifanio's neck. <What does your family call you?>

"Epi," he breathed out.

<Well, Epi. Meet Dahlia.>

It started as an electric tingle, a hum in his brain—and then, it was like being hit by a groundcar.

He was adrift, unable to move a finger, but why would he ever *bother*, when he was everywhere at once —

<Focus on something familiar.>

Suddenly, he saw himself through 3Y-10W's eyes, talking to the Qualia in all his awkward glory.

<What do *you* believe in, Keeper of Roots?> Hermes, or maybe Dahlia asked. Maybe both of them truly wanted that answer.

Caught between Mother Nature and a perfect digital mind, Epifanio frantically discarded rite after rite, incense after incense. But *not* making a choice between them at all, wasn't that why he loved his job in the first place? No knowledge was ever without value, so long as it was properly contained.

Knowledge-tree optimization.

The mindscape settled again, returning them to their physical bodies, only the tree was now looming over them, semi-translucent, Mizuno plucking an apple off a low-hanging branch.

"Not allergic to *this* one," he said, out loud and radiating smugness.

Epifanio let out a laugh. "I don't mind, you know. If you're a crystalhead and think *computer* chips are fast food."

"How utterly unprofessional of you."

Dahlia had more questions: how to reach the stars, how to find that arrogant conviction that you truly belonged there. How to conquer fear of the unknown.

But Epifanio did have an answer for that: his own sense of wonder had always been stronger than the fear.

<Thank you, Epi,> the planet whispered in a gust of wind, the moment suspended and fragile before it was blown away.

He gasped as the roots fully released him, Hermes catching him by the shoulders. "If anyone finds out about this, we'll both be in *deep* trouble. But I like your style."

Epifanio shifted, dropping his head against Mizuno's shoulder. "Put it down as 'unexpected networking expenses.'"

Maraki Piedras is a Santorini tour guide, and seasoned traveler to other worlds, both on her own and with her best friend and co-writer. Every creative spark wants more minds to ignite, so she's always happy to share the results with others. Currently caring for thirty stray cats and about as many plot bunnies.

Destroyers

by Jason E. Maddux

"**L**anding Team, report," Captain Yasuson said. She stood studying the forward viewer. Shoulder length, greying hair framed a face made more severe by the frown adorning it.

Static filled the command deck's speakers. The Captain looked over at her communication officer, who winced under the scrutiny. The young man's hands darted around his console until the background noise dissipated.

"Very good, Lieutenant Balfor," the Captain said. "Next time, try adjusting the squawk in your earpiece first, before piping audio through the speakers."

"Yes, ma'am." The Lieutenant kept his head down, studying the console as if he had made first contact with an alien race.

Yasuson smiled—trying to ease the tension on the command deck—not an easy task given the view provided by the Argo's forward scopes. She had to keep in mind how green these officers were, some fresh out of Ceres Academy. She didn't fault HQ's reasoning, given what happened the last time she commanded a ship. Though designed as an exploration ship, the Argo's first mission was turning out to be much more. "You know, my first assignment was a communications officer aboard the Zheng He."

Balfor glanced at the Captain. Seeing her smile, his shoulders relaxed. "Yes, ma'am."

The command deck's speakers crackled to life. "Argo, Landing Team, it's as bad as it looks." Major Konstantin's voice sounded grave, not far off from the old marine's normal speech pattern. "The upper decks of Europa Orbital are open to hard vacuum. These were the living quarters. Whoever did this may have caught the occupants during their sleep cycle."

Grimacing, Yasuson recalled the old debate: what's the best way to die in space? Is it better to be caught in a breach, having your lungs rupture and the water in your body vaporize, or go in any number of the other ways available in service to the Stellar Navy? She had read how sailors back on Earth's oceans before the Abandonment feared drowning in those same waters the most. "Thank you, Major. Have your team collect a full spectrum of readings. I want to know who did this, and the type of weapon used may give us the answer."

"Aye, Captain. Landing Team out."

This was not at all what HQ had in mind, Yasuson thought, leaning back in her command chair. When Europa Orbital went dark several weeks ago, Stellar Command had no choice but to send the Argo. The majority of the fleet lay on the far side of the asteroid belt attempting to stymy the resurgent pirate threat. HQ wasn't about to replace a ship on the front lines with the lightly armored Argo and her green crew. Or was it that Stellar Command didn't want the Argo's captain headed back into battle?

"Lieutenant Balfor, when the Major returns, have him join me in the briefing room."

"Yes, Captain."

***

Yasuson flicked her wrist. The 3D rendering of Europa Orbital spun above the briefing room table as the door chime sounded. "Enter."

Major Konstantin stepped over the bulkhead and strode in. He stopped inches from the edge of the table, hands at his sides, back rod-straight. His manner as clipped as the salt and pepper hair on the sides of his head.

"At ease, Major, and please have a seat."

"Thank you, ma'am," the Major said, coming to parade rest, "but I prefer to stand."

The Captain eyed him. Was he being insubordinate or just overly professional? She hardly knew the man, having met him minutes before departure. His detachment happened to be rotating through Ceres for some R&R when the orders came down—at least that's what Stellar Command had said.

"Very well, Major. What do you have for me?"

"The majority of the station is open to space. No survivors. It looks—"

The Captain glanced up from the display and cocked an eyebrow. "Go on, Major."

Konstantin stretched his neck, which the collar of his uniform strained to contain. "It looks slimy."

When the Major didn't elaborate, Captain Yasuson rotated the image to study the area near the missing chunk of the station. She magnified the view. The edge around the hole in the station did appear to catch the Jupiter's light with a liquid-like glint. That didn't match the characteristics of any weapon she recalled, but she didn't claim to be an expert either. It could be one she was not familiar with or something newly developed by the pirate insurgents. They had not ventured past the Belt yet, and HQ would not be pleased to learn if they had.

"Has your team sent the readings to my scientists?" the Captain said, looking up again from the display and catching the Major eyeing her.

Konstantin's gaze darted straight ahead. "I prefer to have my people give the data a once over before sending it on."

Yasuson pursed her lips. There is was again, the subtle disregard of her authority. She needed to learn how to read this man, since his facade gave nothing away. She would start by finishing his file. Maybe that held clues to the Major's intentions. "Go ahead and turn over your data to our eggheads. They might as well start earning their keep."

The Major snapped to attention, locking his eyes on the far wall two feet above the Captain's head. "Yes, ma'am. Very good, ma'am."

The Captain smiled. Maybe Major Konstantin was just an old space dog. "Dismissed." The Major turned to leave but stopped when Captain Yasuson spoke up. "Make sure your marines keep a copy of the data as well and continue to work on it. I'd be interested in any theories they have on who did this and why."

Major Konstantin looked over his shoulder as the door slid open. A corner of his mouth twitched ever so slightly. "Aye, Captain."

After the Major left, Yasuson resumed examining the image provided by the Argo's scopes. With any luck, the scientists and marines could determine which of the pirate groups attacked Europa Orbital.

With another flick of her wrist, the image rotated again and settled on the top of the station as viewed looking down on Europa. The missing portion looked much as it did from the side. Spinning the image 180 degrees, she studied the station's underside where a carbon fiber tether anchored it to Europa's surface. The tether also served as the cable for the station's space elevator. She wondered if any of the station's personnel had time to escape to the surface that way.

Yasuson paused her scan. Something had caught her eye with the tether. She spread her fingers, magnifying the view a couple hundred meters below where the tether attached to the station. There. Magnifying further she discovered what she first mistook as hazy resolution was actually a severely frayed tether.

Did the attackers take a shot at the line, just nicking it? Did their ship or ships dock with the station, straining the tether to the point of almost severing?

"Captain, Con," Lieutenant Balfor said, drawing the Captain out of her revelry, "we're receiving a Priority II message from the cargo hauler Naglfar,"

Yasuson closed the display of Europa Orbital. "Understood. I'm on my way."

***

Captain Yasuson entered the bridge expecting it to be alive with activity. Instead, she encountered silence. Gliding to the communications station, she stopped behind Lieutenant Balfor. "Report."

The Lieutenant jumped in his seat, having been bent over his console with one hand covering his right earpiece. "Aye, Captain. The message appears to be on repeat. I sent a standard hail but haven't received a response yet."

"What's our time lag with the hauler?"

"About 24 minutes, ma'am."

Yasuson scowled. Too far away for real time communications. Also, given their maximum speed, too far for any hope of a rescue. "Play it."

Balfor stabbed a finger at his display. The command deck's speakers came alive.

"This is the SC Cargo Ship Naglfar, Captain Norson commanding. We are on a resupply run to the Saturn outposts at Titan and Enceladus. We are under attack but are not sure by who. Their ship appeared inert, but then it wasn't."

A second voice interrupted. "I'm not even sure it is a ship, Captain. The readings we did manage to get were unlike any ship I've seen."

"Now's not the time for this debate," Captain Norson hissed. Resuming her prior tone, she said, "They've attached to our hull and appear intent on boarding us. At this rate, we'll have multiple breaches in a few minutes. We are unarmed and signaled our surrender but were ignored. We request immediate assistance from any ships in the vicinity." The message ended. Silence engulfed the command deck again.

"Is that it?" the Captain said.

"Yes, ma'am," Lieutenant Balfor said.

"Still no response to our hail?"

"No, ma'am."

Captain Yasuson turned to the sensor station. "Are there any other ships nearer to the Naglfar?"

Lieutenant Carmichael spun in his chair to face the Captain. His relaxed features confirmed his anticipation of the question. "Not sunward, Captain. There may be a ship or two able to respond from Saturn, but I doubt it."

"Very good, Lieutenant. Helm, what's our fuel status?"

"Ma'am!" Ensign Lang said somewhere between surprise and jubilation. "Since we departed with enough for a return trip, we have sufficient reserves to rendezvous with the Naglfar and continue on to the Saturn outposts. We'll have to refuel there, or we won't be making it back this way."

"Thank you, Ensign, lay in an intercept course with the Naglfar."

Ensign Lang's fingers danced over her console. A graph of the immediate vicinity between Jupiter's and Saturn's orbits appeared on the main viewer. A magenta line connecting points near both planets materialized. The Ensign's hand froze above a flashing green indicator. "Course set and ready to initiate, Captain."

"Time to intercept?"

"Approximately, three weeks, six days, and 19 hours."

Yasuson's mouth became a thin line. "Proceed." Members of the Stellar Navy learned early on the vastness of space—even within the solar system—often meant rescue was impossible, leaving recovery as the only option. "Lieutenant Balfor, inform the Naglfar we are en route and provide our ETA. Then inform Titan Station we will put in for resupply at some point thereafter with updates to follow. I'll be in the briefing room recording a sit rep for Stellar Command."

***

The Argo heard nothing further from the Naglfar. Stellar Command agreed with Yasuson. If the same unknown threat attacked both Europa Orbital and the Naglfar, they needed to know. The resurgent pirate network had already stretched the Navy thin. It could ill afford to divert resources to protecting the solar system's outer inhabitants. Not that the Stellar Navy had any intention of doing so. Ever since the Ganymede Uprising, Stellar Command prohibited any colonies beyond the asteroid belt. The few scientific communities already established barely escaped a forced recall. Now, except for the occasional cargo transport, everyone past the asteroid belt was on their own.

As she had for much of the last three and a half weeks, Captain Yasuson sat in the briefing room studying a chart of local space. The same magenta line from the command deck viewer depicting the Argo's course pierced the middle of the projection. The positions of Europa and the Naglfar shown bright yellow at two ends of the rectangular image. The Argo appeared in green, a slow-moving dot approaching the line's termination point. Just as it had for the last month, the chart failed to reveal whatever secrets it held as to the cause of the disaster at Europa Orbital or the distress message from the Naglfar. She hoped to have better luck with the two people entering the briefing room now.

"Thank you both for joining me," Yasuson said to her guests. "Please be seated."

Major Konstantin looked at the chair nearest him, then at the Captain. Audibly sighing, he pulled the chair away from the table and took a seat. Dr. Davina Livingood exhibited no such hesitation. She readily plopped into the seat opposite the Major, her long red hair cascading over her shoulders.

"We're currently decelerating on approach to our rendezvous with the Naglfar," Yasuson said. Both the Major and Doctor nodded, well aware of the Argo's current status. "Both of you have been coy with me for weeks about the results of your analysis of the attack on Europa Orbital. Now is the time to come clean. I need to know what we may be up against."

The Major said nothing, though he continued to meet the Captain's gaze. Dr. Livingood looked from the Captain to the Major. Shrugging, she cleared her throat. "I'm happy to report first."

Breaking eye contact with the Major, Yasuson looked at the scientist. "Very well."

"First, my apologies for not presenting these findings earlier," Dr. Livingood said. "My team and I wanted to make sure we were correct. No sense starting false rumors, if you know what I mean." When neither the Captain nor the Major returned her smile, she continued. "Anyway, I have some exciting news. We think we've made a startling discovery!" The Doctor put her hands on the table, raising her eyebrows as she looked between the room's other two occupants. "There were massive amounts of residue all around the edge of the hole torn into Europa Station. This residue is organic."

No one moved.

Dr. Livingood huffed. "Don't you see what this could mean? Europa Station could have encountered an extra-solar lifeform!"

"Are you certain of these results?" Yasuson said.

"Yes, Captain. We ran the analysis several times."

Yasuson shook her head. "Rather than extra-solar, isn't a more logical answer that something from Europa attacked the station? Perhaps following the teether up from the surface?"

Livingood waived, as if to dismiss the notion out of hand. "Highly unlikely. For starters, I'm not aware of Europa Station having discovered any lifeform of significant size below the frozen surface. Also, anything down there would be adapted to a high-pressure, aquatic environment. In other words, such creatures would not be suited to exist in space."

"I see," Yasuson said with a tone meant to humor the scientist. "Anything else?"

"Well, we're attempting to extract DNA. That is assuming it even has DNA. Maybe extra-solar lifeforms don't." The thought sent the Doctor vibrating with excitement. "We haven't succeeded so far with the samples provided by the Major, but we haven't given up hope."

"Thank you, Doctor. Please keep at it and keep me informed." Yasuson turned to Konstantin. "Now, Major, what light can you shed on this matter?"

The Major sat stoic. Yasuson thought he would force her to ask again. Then he spoke. "We reviewed the images of the tether as you requested. Simulations we ran suggest the fraying likely was caused by significant added mass at the tether's termination point."

"In other words, something heavy pulled on Europa Orbital?" Yasuson said.

"Yes, ma'am."

"Was this significant increase in mass the result of the attacker firing a weapon at Europa Station, or did the attacker dock a ship with the station?"

"Unknown, Captain," Konstantin said, barely moving his lips.

Yasuson studied the Major but still couldn't get a read on him. Over the last several weeks, Konstantin had rebuffed every attempt Yasuson made to get to know the Major better. He wouldn't join the Captain for a drink when both were off duty. The Major declined to attend the weekly card game the Captain had instituted with the bridge officers. Suspecting the Major kept a strict exercise regiment, Yasuson asked if Konstantin would care to join during her own scheduled fitness sessions. That appeared to peak the Major's interest, but he still declined citing a desire to be alone during his workouts.

As the Captain studied the Major's stone features, she couldn't determine whether he was holding anything back. She decided to find out.

"Thank you, Doctor," Yasuson said, turning to Livingood. "Please let me know immediately when you have further results. You are dismissed. Major, please stay."

Dr. Livingood looked between the two officers, who in turn eyed each other, as she rose from her seat. "Will do, Captain."

With the doctor departed, Yasuson allowed the silence to settle on her and the Major like a thermal blanket. This was her ship, and it was time the Major understood that. "After Stellar Command informed me of your and your squad's assignment to my ship, I reviewed your file. You, of course, have an exemplary record, including distinguished service during the last pirate campaign."

The Major inclined his head slightly in acknowledgment. When the compliment elicited nothing more, Yasuson said, "Though Stellar Command thought we'd find nothing more than a tech problem at Europa Station, I agreed bringing a small contingent of ground troops was a prudent idea."

Konstantin continued to sit motionless. Yasuson sighed. "Look, Major, I don't expect us to be friends, but as commander of the marines onboard, I value your opinion in my decision making. That means I expect you to be open and honest with me." She folded her hands on the table and leaned forward. "I feel you've been holding back. We are approaching an unknown environment with an unknown hostile. My first priority is to the mission and then to this ship and her crew. I need everything at my disposal to effectuate those priorities. Now, is there anything you'd like to share?"

The silence dragged on so long Yasuson feared she'd failed to make any headway, but then the Major surprised her.

"I, of course, am familiar with your history as well, Captain." Konstantin put his own hands on the table face down. "You, too, had an exemplary record, at least until your last crew mutinied."

Yasuson stiffened in her seat. Heat rose to her cheeks, which she tried to tamp down. She waited to respond until she felt her voice would not betray her. "Go on." The words came out close to a growl.

"I mean no disrespect, Captain," the Major said, lifting his hands in mock surrender. "I followed the ensuing court martial of your crew as did everybody else. Stellar Command made it required viewing for all personnel. My guess is they were tired of losing ships and crew to the pirates' cause. Anyway, I agreed with the outcome. You were under orders to end the pirate threat at Nemesis by any means necessary. I always wondered if the pirates chose that asteroid based on the name alone."

Yasuson turned her head, not wanting to relive those events.

"The group at Nemesis was housing known pirate terrorists, and you were right to order its destruction."

"And what is your opinion on the noncombatants living there, the children."

"Unfortunate collateral damage."

Yasuson whipped her head around. The red in her cheeks grew brighter. "My crew did not agree with you."

"That's why they were court martialed and executed. Since the last pirate insurrection, Stellar Command doesn't mess around. And you were vindicated after all."

"Riding a desk for the last five years did not feel like vindication," Yasuson said, looking down at her hands.

This time Konstantin broke the silence. "I'm just a grunt. I have no insight into Stellar Command's thinking, but maybe they had the same thought as I when joining this mission. I needed to know what your mental state was. Can you be trusted to make the hard decisions, or are you now too afraid to lose another crew?"

The Captain straightened her uniform tunic. "Were those your orders?"

"Not in so many words."

"And what is your conclusion?"

For the first time since coming onboard the Argo, Major Konstantin looked pleased. "I think Stellar Command was right to give you another command, even if it is babysitting scientists."

Yasuson allowed the tension to leave her shoulders. The mutiny and eventual execution of her former officers nearly broke her. She couldn't sleep for months. Had she done the right thing ordering what amounted to genocide for the people on Nemesis? Her fellow officers didn't think so, and they were put to death for doing what they thought was right. As it had been in navies since wooden ships plowed the seas of Earth before the Abandonment, the Stellar Navy punished mutiny with death. Still, the execution of many whom she considered friends tormented her.

After nearly a year, she thought she was past the worst when she learned Stellar Command had finished the job her crew had failed to do—the complete destruction of Nemesis.

Yasuson's com beeped. "Captain, Bridge," Balfor said, "We're approaching the Naglfar. She's all quiet and appears to be adrift."

The Captain looked at Major Konstantin, who nodded in return and left. "Thank you, Lieutenant. Inform the hangar the marines will be leaving shortly. And keep the scopes active. I don't want to be surprised by anything out here. Captain, out."

***

A wave of commotion hit Captain Yasuson upon entering the bridge. Officers called out to each other requesting readings be checked and double-checked. No one noticed the commanding officer enter. Yasuson took a deep breath, preparing to be heard over the din. "Report."

All activity stopped as everyone looked her way. Smiles graced several of the bridge officers' faces. Frowns adorned others. Lieutenant Carmichael, one of those with a smile, spoke first. "There's an unidentified contact several hundred thousand kilometers from our position. It could be our bogey."

Yasuson's heart raced, but she kept her breathing slow. She needed to maintain her priorities. "Is it heading toward us?"

"No, Captain, it's moving away from our position at a constant velocity."

"Heading?"

"Toward Saturn, ma'am."

"Very good. Let me know if that changes." Yasuson turned to the helm. "Ensign Lang, plot an intercept course. Do we have the fuel to catch it?"

"Already done, Captain. At maximum burn and breaking, we can intercept in 9 days and still make Saturn." Lang swiveled in his seat, a smirk on his lips. "It must not know we're here. It's not moving very fast."

Yasuson usually cautioned young officers against spoiling for a fight, but there would be time for that later. "Good. Now, Lieutenant Balfor, has Major Konstantin reported in?"

Balfor swiveled in his chair. "Aye, Captain. He reports the Naglfar looks much like Europa Station did. No survivors. He's taking readings and plans to report again when finished."

The Captain scanned the command deck before sitting. "Alright. Tell him to confirm there are no signs of life. If so, order him back at once. We can always return on our way back. Lieutenant Carmichael, mark these coordinates and correct for the Naglfar's rate and direction of drift. Ensign Lang, get us underway as soon as the Major reports all aboard." Yasuson leaned back in her command chair as the bridge officers went about their assigned tasks. She gripped the sides of the chair and allowed the shadow of a smile to curve her lips ever so slightly. She might admonish her junior officers for eagerly anticipating conflict, but that didn't mean she couldn't enjoy the anticipation of a just battle against a clear enemy. It had been far too long.

Yasuson spent the next week drilling her crew. She tried to prepare them for every possible outcome and several that were impossible. Major Konstantin, in addition to drilling his own squad, ran through the procedures for repelling hostile boarding parties with the rest of the crew. The scientists were unenthusiastic, preferring to spend their time studying the readings returned from the Naglfar and those coming back from the Argo's target. When their quarry was in range for a full resolution visual, Yasuson called Dr. Livingood and Major Konstantin to the bridge.

"Lieutenant Carmichael, what kind of armament are we facing?" the Captain said.

"Um—," Lieutenant Carmichael said, flipping between readings on his console's viewer.

"Um is not an answer Lieutenant."

Carmichael's shoulders rose, as if he wanted to pull his head inside his torso like a turtle. "I'm not seeing any indication of weapons. I'm not seeing much of any energy readings, except a minimal heat signature."

"Have they detected us?"

The lieutenant shook his head but didn't turn around to face the Captain. "I don't think so. No sign of change in heading or speed."

"Put it on the main viewer," Captain Yasuson said as Dr. Livingood and Major Konstantin entered. Two other marines arrived with them. The already cramped command deck now felt claustrophobic.

The scene on the viewer changed. Multiple gasps escaped from the bridge crew. Then everyone started speculating at once.

"What the—?"

"That's no ship."

"Is it an asteroid?"

"It's too symmetrical."

"Then it's a ship."

"It can't be. There are no energy readings."

"Are those legs?"

"Attention!" Major Konstantin boomed. Everyone stood and shut their mouth in one smooth motion. Everyone except the Captain, who remained seated in her command chair.

"Thank you, Major," Yasuson said, inclining her head to the left where Konstantin stood. She scanned the bridge, looking each of her fellow officers in the eye. "Resume your stations." The crew plopped into their seats, as if part of a well-rehearsed dance routine. She turned her gaze back to the main viewer. "Now, will someone tell me what I'm looking at?"

No one answered. Then Dr. Livingood cleared her throat. "If I may?" She raised her eyebrows at the Captain.

Yasuson raised one eyebrow in return. When Livingood's eager expression didn't diminish, the Captain gave the slightest nod.

Livingood put her hands together—faster than intended—and jumped as the resulting clap echoed through the silent command deck. She glared at her hands with a look of betrayal before shoving them in her jumpsuit's pockets.

"It's a tardigrade." This time Livingood scanned the command deck, waiting for understanding to set in. She received only blank looks in return. She slapped her forehead. "Oh, right, you wouldn't know about them. May I?" She pointed to the sensor station.

Yasuson squinted at Livingood but nodded again.

Livingood stepped over. Nudging Carmichael out of the way—who was none too pleased about it—she pulled up a file. The main viewer split into two images, one from the forward scanners and the other Livingood's file. The images were nearly identical. Both showed a crescent shaped creature with thick segments in the middle gradually progressing to knob-like segments at each end. Six legs protruded from the bottom, four facing one direction and two the other direction.

"I sent our long-range scans back to Mars University. It has the most complete pre- and post-Abandonment database in the system. It's way better than the limited one on this ship." Livingood winked at the Captain, who gestured with her hand to hurry up.

"Right," Livingood said, putting on her best approximation of a serious face. It didn't last. "If this thing is organic, I wanted to confirm we've never seen it before. Don't want to falsely claim to have encountered an extra-Sol entity."

Desiring to shorten a conversation that had already distracted her for too long from her target, Yasuson stood. "Doctor, are you saying this tardigrade is in the university's database, meaning we've encountered it before?" Livingood nodded. Yasuson pointed at the viewer. "Then why didn't I know about it before today? I think I would recall hearing before now about something this large roaming space, preying on humans."

"That's because you wouldn't—or at least I don't think you would." Livingood shook her head this time.

"Doctor, please." The Captain's tone was dire.

Livingood smiled again. "A tardigrade is—or was—an almost microscopic animal living everywhere on Earth prior to the Abandonment. There were over 1000 known species, and they could live in the harshest environments. You name it, the cold of Antarctica—a frozen continent back then—or 300-degree heat. Neither was a problem. They even could live in the oxygen-free environment of space while being bombarded with solar radiation. When faced with any of these conditions, a tardigrade simply would dry out and wait to awake when the environment improved, meaning when water was present again." Livingood clasped her hands in front, satisfied she had solved the mystery.

Yasuson rubbed her temples. "That doesn't explain why I'm now faced with one of these things the size of a spaceship out by Saturn."

"Huh, good point," Livingood said, shrugging. "I don't have an answer for that. Mars University's records show tardigrades were experimented on in space before the Abandonment, and I'm sure some managed to hitch rides with our ancestors as they left Earth." She waived at the screen. "Maybe some mutated to this size after being exposed to solar radiation. And maybe this one lay dormant out here until a comet passed by or it encountered some other water source to rehydrate it."

"Thank you, Doctor," Yasuson said, sitting back down. "I've heard enough. Lieutenant Carmichael, train our cannon on the object and prepare to fire."

"Belay that order," Major Konstantin said.

Yasuson whipped her head around. "Major, if you have another course of action to suggest, I am more than willing to hear it; but I give the orders here."

Konstantin stood his usual ramrod straight. "Yes, ma'am, but I believe you may be acting too hastily. A creature like that could be a valuable asset to the military. At a minimum, it is worth more study."

"Thank you, Major. Your opinion is noted." Yasuson turned back to her weapons officer. "Carry out my order, please."

"Lieutenant Carmichael, do no such thing," the Major said.

Yasuson turned her head slower this time, fire present in her eyes. "Major, remove yourself from the command deck. You are confined to quarters until further notice."

The Major didn't move.

"Ensign Lang, please escort Major Konstantin to his quarters," Yasuson said, refusing to flinch from the Major's gaze.

The ensign started to rise from his chair. Major Konstantin placed a hand on the butt of his sidearm. "Sit back down, Ensign." Lang froze half out of his chair, looking ridiculous but not knowing which way to proceed.

"You don't want to do this," the Captain said, fixing Konstantin with an icy stare. "You know what happens to mutineers." She raised her chin and swallowed. "I thought my record made that abundantly clear."

Major Konstantin smiled. It didn't look comfortable on his face. "I'm doing no such thing, Captain. I'm under orders from Stellar Command to make sure you don't experience any—" He paused. "To make sure there are no lapses in judgement from your time away from command. I'm afraid you are having such a lapse right now. Given the state of the Stellar Navy's current engagement, I believe preserving whatever weapon we encounter is of paramount importance."

Yasuson rose from her seat. Konstantin drew his weapon but kept it at his side. The other two marines also had their weapons drawn. The Captain clenched her fists but remained rooted to the deck. "Our orders are to seek out who or what attacked Europa Station and eliminate the threat."

Dr. Livingood coughed into her hand. She seemed shocked when everyone focused on her. "If it helps, I doubt this tardigrade is a threat. It probably has no other impulse than to look for food. My guess is its attack on Europa Station was an accident. It can't have much control over how it moves through space. The Naglfar crew likely approached too close, thinking it was another stellar body ripe for the claiming. When they did, the tardigrade must have thought their ship too was food. Why don't we give it a nudge on its way?"

"Thank you, Doctor," the Captain said through gritted teeth. She turned to the Major. "I've given my orders. Are you prepared to shoot my officers?"

"If I have to."

Silence filled the command deck, like an airlock open to space. Several junior officers tensed, ready to jump to action, though to whose defense was unclear.

Captain Yasuson took a long time to exhale. "Very well. Since we are not currently endangered by the hostile, I have no desire to risk the lives of my officers. I will note your insurrection in my log. We'll let Stellar Command sort this out upon our return." The atmosphere on the command deck relaxed, though several officers grumbled. "Are you relieving me of command?"

Major Konstantin replaced his sidearm in its holster. "Assuming you are willing to follow my orders, there's no need."

The Captain sat down, crossed her legs, and motioned to the Major.

The Major smiled again, no less disturbing with the additional practice. "I'm confident Stellar Command will side with me. Now, helm, move us to within grappling range. We're going to tow that thing to Saturn, refuel, and then drag it back to Ceres." Ensign Lang looked at Captain Yasuson for confirmation, who nodded.

All eyes followed the ensign as he turned to his console—except Dr. Livingood. Still standing next to the sensor and weapons station, she looked down. The target lock for the ship's sole laser canon remained on the tardigrade. Mouthing a silent apology, she slammed her hand on the firing control.

The main viewer showed a line of white light pierce the center of the tardigrade's mass. Following its pre-set program, the beam ceased and then resumed twice more, lancing the creature a second and third time. Shock froze the entire deck.

Captain Yasuson recovered first. "Seize the marines!"

The Captain's order broke the junior officers from their malaise. They swarmed the three marines, relieving them of their sidearms without much struggle. The Major's eyes stared unblinking at the screen.

"Confine them to quarters," Yasuson said. After the others departed, she turned to the sole other remaining occupant of the command deck. "Dr. Livingood, can you confirm the creature is dead?"

The scientist continued watching the viewer.

Yasuson clapped her hands.

Dr. Livingood lowered her gaze toward the weapons console. She flipped past several readings and nodded.

"Good, then you too are confined to quarters." The Captain raised her eyebrows, mimicking the Doctor's earlier expression. "I assume you won't need an escort."

Dr. Livingood sniffled but held her head high. "I couldn't let them experiment on that beautiful creature." A glistening trail adorned each cheek as she left.

Though Dr. Livingood had carried out Yasuson's last order, the Captain sat brooding in her chair. The command deck seemed alive as flashing lights and auditory signals at various stations demanded attention. On the viewer, the lifeless tardigrade floated silently, now another piece of interstellar debris, just like their mutual ancestral home world.

Jason E. Maddux is an aviation attorney, who writes speculative fiction as a creative outlet each night once his two daughters are in bed. After moving around the southeastern United States in his youth, he now resides in what some call Occupied Virginia.

Empty Chest

by Ray Daley

Imagine having terrible luck heaped onto even worse luck, followed by a continuing streak of perpetual bad luck. *Can you imagine that?*

Good, because we didn't have to. We lived it. I should start at the beginning, shouldn't I?

"Three or four, Azic?" I was deep into the charts when Morrin started asking me that. Deep enough that she had to shout at me. "Azic!"

I looked up, eventually. She had to scream at me by that point. I just get so distracted by the stars. "Hmm? What?"

"I was asking, did that text say exactly where this damn treasure was supposed to be? Evered III, or IV?" Damn her and her stupid treasure map. She'd bought it in the bazaar back on Crotos, and if the bazaars there were like anywhere else, it was almost certainly a fake. But you know Morrin, she *had* to go and check, to be completely sure there wasn't any treasure for herself.

It was why we were making this trip in a crummy pod-craft. I had to sell the previous ship after she insisted on checking to make sure her last treasure wasn't on the ocean floor of Bethys.

A pressure hull *might* hold up fine in space and the hi-gee worlds but it just wasn't designed to be under three miles of *frexage* ocean. Frankly, we were lucky to get out of that one alive. Extremely lucky, because the ocean currents carried us into the shipping lanes, after I'd had to blast the ballast tanks to get us back up to the surface. Thrusters work great in space, not so much underwater.

We were lucky enough to be spotted by a tanker who towed us to shore, and the junkers gave us just enough in scrap value to buy the piece of garbage we're flying now. The pod-craft was originally designed for ship to surface operations, mostly transporting small numbers of personnel or a minimal amount of cargo. Survival supplies and suchlike.

Whoever owned the ship before us had done some modifications, so the engine could run in deep space, planet-hopping. They had converted the tiny hold into living quarters too. Solo quarters only though. So we slept in shifts, because frankly, I'd rather die before I shared a bed with Morrin again.

Loved her? I barely even *liked* her!

I'd been on the verge of taking a small freight job, something that would have earned us enough money to buy a better ship at least. But no, Morrin and her stupid treasure map had to go and ruin that idea.

I placed us into a holding pattern between Evered III and IV, then glanced over to her dumb map again. There had been some text scrawled on the back, handwritten too! Almost no-one does that anymore.

The only trouble there was Morrin couldn't read Jexi. At all. "Come on, Azic. For crying out loud. Is it three, or four? The text can't be *that* hard to read, can it?"

I was almost on the verge of telling her to come over and read the damn thing herself. "Whoever wrote this, it's a really odd dialect. It doesn't always read exactly like standard Jexi, and the handwriting is terrible! I can clearly read, '*On an island, on the world of Evered...*' then the last word is impossible to make out. It might be three, it might be four. It honestly looks like they wrote the word *kitten* though."

I could tell she was about to scream at me again, so I just punched in the co-ords for Evered IV. And that was our second piece of bad luck. The first being our stupidity at following the damn map in the first place.

There are many different stories told about Evered IV. But there's one thing anyone who's been there agrees on. You definitely need excellent shields. Good, strong, efficient shields that will take hard hits from the electrical storms that abound in the upper atmosphere. Would you care to guess what isn't fitted as standard into a pod-craft.?

Whoever had done the modifications hadn't thought to fit any kind of shields either.

I was flying her down, mostly by sheer willpower. We had no sensors at all, the latent energy in the upper layers fried our array beyond all recognition. "Morrin, I can still get us out of here. Just say the word. We can make it back to Crotos, maybe at a crawl. It'll take us a week, but we've got the supplies to get there. We're barely holding together in this damn atmosphere as it is."

Morrin gave me one of those looks. She'd made her mind up before we'd even lifted off. "It's this or nothing, Azic. If we don't make it, there won't be any point in living anyway." And that was Morrin, down to a tee. Always looking on the dark side.

So down we went, barely dodging forks of lightning that would have otherwise destroyed the ship.

Pilot reports on the actual thickness of Evered IV's upper atmosphere vary wildly. There's yet to be an accurate planetary survey, for obvious reasons. So I was flying entirely on hope and instinct.

I could see the sky beginning to clear when it happened. I'd be willing to bet it was the smallest known electrical strike in the history of Evered IV. All I know is, we lost all power. No engines, no lights, no stabilisers, no nothing. With our gyroscope gone too, we were falling out of the sky, tumbling end over end, spinning wildly out of control.

I was okay like that; I've been a pilot long enough to have experienced such things many times. Morrin though? She'd always really been a ground-hound. She started screaming her lungs out the second the lights went off. I'm just grateful we were both buckled into our seats when it happened.

"Azic! What the *frexage* is happening?"

I didn't need any lights, I could operate those controls from memory. The first order of business, emergency power. *No response.*

Okay then, engine refire? *No response.*

No joy there, how about stabilisers? *No. Never gonna happen.*

Grasping at straws I tried wondering if we still had reserve gyros? *Not a damn thing.*

"Morrin, are you okay? Listen, we're falling without any power. At all. My guess, we got hit by a small lightning bolt. Looks like it knocked out everything so we're going down the hard way—by gravity alone. My math says we'll hit the water in about nine minutes."

Morrin cheered up at that. "So we're going to live then?"

I'm just glad she couldn't see my face when I answered. "For at least another nine minutes. Maybe a little longer, my calculations aren't one hundred percent accurate. At the speed we're going, we'll just vaporise when we hit the water."

"You could have kept that to yourself, Azic."

That made me laugh out loud. "Misery loves company, Morrin. And it's better to know you're going out. Pray to whatever God you might believe in."

If Morrin prayed, I couldn't hear her over the merry tune I was humming to distract myself from certain impending death. When we lost power, I only had a rough idea of our altitude. That nine minutes was my best guess.

When your ship is falling from the edge of space with no power, nothing short of a miracle will save you.

***

Tantham. *Ocean-bound omnivore. Will consume all it sees. Known to pick off large birds from several metres above the ocean surface. Can grow up to eighty metres in length.*

"Azic!"

We were upside down in complete darkness. And according to my inner ear, we were stationary. "Morrin, are you okay?"

I could hear Morrin muttering her checklist to herself. "We're alive then, Azic?"

Yeah. I couldn't work that one out either. "Certainly seems that way, doesn't it? Unless the afterlife is *so* crappy that it looks *exactly* like life does?"

I shucked myself out of my harness and crawled to the storage locker.

CLICK.

"Let there be light." Thank science for the head torch.

"Cheers, Azic."

I took a look around. Everything which hadn't been secured was now smashed beyond repair. That damned map was still in one piece though. Once I got under the control console, it was fairly obvious we were never taking off again.

"Any luck under there, Azic?"

I didn't shake my head, for fear of caving my skull in. "Only bad luck, Morrin. Everything is fried, and we've no spares. Well, not enough spares to replace everything. I think I can get the air

211

scrubbers going, maybe minimal lights too. At least we won't suffocate in the dark."

With no shields, almost all our circuits had been burnt out when the lightning bolt hit us. They'd gone so quickly they hadn't had a chance to burn anything around them. We'd had some small measure of luck there. I started totting up my mental checklist.

Item:- No fires. That bolt probably lit us up like a Christmas tree, but somehow it only hit hard enough to burn out our isolated systems. We really should have caught fire.

Item:- We're alive. Not sure how. If there's a God, she's really annoyed we aren't meeting her right now. The impact with the water should have killed us both.

Morrin was curious about that too. "I don't suppose you know how we didn't vaporise?"

No problem is unsolvable. Sometimes the solution means you die, but there's always an explanation.

I started to spit-ball a theory out loud. "Okay. Hitting the water would have killed us, and we're not dead. Ergo, we didn't *hit* the water. We were falling. We should have hit the water and we didn't. So something stopped us hitting the water. We were too heavy for the wind to blow us over any islands."

In the half-light I could see Morrin gazing at me, hoping for a miracle. "Morrin, you know something? I think something ate us!"

Her face fell. Not the answer she'd been hoping for.

I grinned to myself; it was obvious when you thought about it. "No, that's got to be it! The Evered system is supposed to have some pretty big sea creatures. One of them must have swallowed us, just before we hit the ocean surface. It's the only way we survived!"

I spent the next hour repairing the air scrubbers. I got minimal life support going too, some lights and just enough heat so we didn't freeze to death. Let me tell you, it's not easy repairing an inverted ship. When an engineer tells you they know their ship upside down, you'd better pray they weren't exaggerating. Fortunately for us, I could find anything anywhere. Even upside down.

Then Morrin asked the billion-dollar question. "How long have we got, Azic?"

Whatever swallowed us was going to digest us eventually. I just hoped our complex alloy hull slowed it down long enough to make it think about spitting us out. "We've got enough reserve power to keep the lights on for a month. Food for about the same. Life support should keep us stable that long as well, if not a little longer."

I decided not to share my thoughts on our getting digested, Morrin hadn't reacted well to our nine-minute lifespan before. I doubted she would want to know we were going to be eventually dissolved in some alien sea creature's stomach acids.

We reconstructed events after we grounded.

About three seconds before we hit the water, we were swallowed whole by a Tantham. However, our velocity killed the beast. And fortunately killed it before we got anywhere close to the stomach. My best guess is it floated in the ocean currents, before being pulled ashore by a riptide. That took about three days.

***

Three Days Later.

"Azic, are we still moving?"

I'd been wondering the same thing myself before Morrin asked me. As a spacer, you develop an in-built ability to know if you're moving or not. "Nope. Whatever ate us, it's not moving any more. Hasn't moved for well over four hours now, by my best estimate."

"Do you think that's normal, Azic?"

I'd been keeping track of the creature's habits as best as I could under the circumstances. Before today, the longest it had gone without moving had been about twenty minutes. And its periods of inactivity before that had been getting longer and longer. Like it was either in pain or had eaten something which didn't agree with it.

I was hoping the latter, for our sake. "Hard to say, Morrin. I don't even really know exactly what ate us. But it has been getting slower over the last few days. If you ask me, I think it's dead."

That made Morrin smile for the first time since we'd lost power. "Azic, I think I remember reading somewhere that when an organism dies, the stomach acid neutralises. So I don't think we're going to die that way, at least."

Ah. So she *had* been thinking about that, to herself at least then. I was glad at the time that I hadn't said anything before.

I shrugged. "I'm not sure. I know we aren't moving, and we haven't moved for well over four hours now. I was thinking, I can either use the spares we've got to fix the airlock and blow the hatch or fire up the plasma torch and cut our way out of here. Either way, we've got to get out of here, am I right?"

Morrin found it hard to disagree, given our circumstances.

In the end, I broke out the plasma torch and cut the airlock door open. Then immediately wished I hadn't.

"Azic, what's that terrible smell?"

It was the inside of the creature which had swallowed us. But a quick application of the plasma torch soon got us outside. I'm just glad we'd been facing onto the shore.

After we had both vented the contents of our stomachs, I'd never seen Morrin enjoy fresh air so much. I had no complaints about it either, to be honest.

"So it's a Tantham?" Morrin spent the first ten minutes of our new freedom patrolling around its corpse.

It certainly matched all the descriptions of Tanthams we'd heard from other pilots crazy enough to come here. My guess is it jumped out of the water to try and catch a bird and we hit it at exactly the wrong moment. Or exactly the right moment, from our perspective.

We were *just* big enough to fit in its mouth but were massively slowed by its throat. You'd have thought, the speed we were going we'd have smashed right through the thing, but its muscles slowed us right down. I guess the acceleration couches saved our bacon there.

The onboard supplies have helped us a little. We've been cutting up the Tantham and curing its meat. It's not the worst thing I've tasted, and we can eat it without getting sick, so it'll have to do until we find something else. God alone knows how long we'll be stuck here before anyone finds us.

It's been well over six months now. I tried to build a distress beacon from our spares, but I don't have all the parts I need. So instead I've got all the lights set up across the creature's carcass, ready to flash them on and off, if we ever hear an engine. I've been thinking about how I could probably use the lenses from its eyes to magnify some of those lights too. We've cut up most of the meat. Currently, we're in the process of drying the hide, Morrin suggested we try to use the sinews to tie it down over the ribs, as a shelter.

She prefers to be out here, rather than inside what's left of the pod-craft. After the crash and being swallowed, I can see her point. And the local weather is fairly forgiving, at the moment.

I found a guitar in one of the storage lockers yesterday. We're spending evenings around our fire and playing all the songs I can remember. We started that fire the day we got outside. Morrin was the one who suggested using the map.

So I think we're both done with treasure hunting forever. We've got food, shelter, and decent company—we're all good, for now. That's more than enough to survive until we're rescued, but I don't think either of us mind if we never are.

Happiness is singing out of tune with your best friend, around a fire, under a dead alien sea monster.

Ray Daley was born in Coventry & still lives there. Serving 6 years in the RAF he spent time in a hole in High Wycombe. He's been writing since he was 10. His dream is to finish the *Hitch Hikers* fanfic novel he's been writing since 1986. Tweet him @RayDaleyWriter

Searching for Palmer

by Greg Eccleston

One Metonic Cycle Ago

'First Contact' was on a Friday. It happened at 33° *44'* 0"
S *151°* 14' 0" E – of all places; Rose Forest, a quiet
suburb of Sydney. The Australian government agency
CSIRO live-streamed it on their media channels, during their daily
11:00 a.m. briefing, to not a lot of attention. At first.

A clean-shaven, friendly-looking scientist introduced himself
as Norman Foster and opened the event by talking about
humankind's long search for extra-terrestrial proof of life. Four of
his white laboratory coat-wearing colleagues stood behind,
nodding. He spoke in the same monotone for over ten minutes.
If you didn't know what was coming, it was kinda boring.

At the 0:11:06 mark, he said "And here is the proof you have
all been waiting for." Foster then picked up a surgical scalpel and
inserted it into his skull, just above his left ear. He sliced over his
head and then down the other side, the length of his right arm,
back to his axilla and then down his side. All the way down and
up both legs, until the blade finished its journey, meeting the initial
incision above his left ear. There was no blood.

At this point, one of Foster's colleagues fainted. A moment that launched a million memes.

Foster then peeled off the skinsuit, with half of it falling off in front and half behind. What remained was a gelatinous mass, the rough size and shape of an adult human male. A partially collapsed and semi-transparent one.

As the remaining three conscious humans stood transfixed, it spoke to the camera, the accent Australian, the sound coming from somewhere near what used to be the right wrist.

"I have been living on this planet for exactly nineteen years. I am here alone. And now is the right time to tell you that – yes – I come in peace."

The mass then extended tentacles to both halves of the human form lying on the ground and pulled them back over itself. Within moments, they reattached, as the seams came together. Those of us watching once again saw a man who looked a lot like an Australian scientist, in his early sixties. Named Norman.

It spoke some more "I understand that you will have a great many questions. For now, I need to attend to Doctor Baillie." It gestured to the woman behind, now conscious and sitting white-faced on the floor, one of her stunned colleagues rubbing her back.

"Keep following us on all CSIRO media channels. I will have plenty to announce in due course. Like and subscribe." And, in what seemed like an afterthought, added "If you are wondering what to call me, I quite like Doctor Foster. My pronouns are it and they. My friends call me Norm."

The video ended and the world started reacting. It was a while before a global consensus was reached, that this was indeed the first proven evidence of extra-terrestrial civilisation. However, that date - 14 March 2036 - is now etched in our history and taught in schools.

On that day nineteen years ago, in my flat at Rose Forest, less than a kilometre away from where Foster was broadcasting, I switched off my device. And smiled. Unlike most people, I was neither shocked nor sceptical. Because I knew that Foster was speaking the truth. Mostly. I also knew that this was NOT first contact. I had seen this display before. Not on a screen, but in front of me, in this very flat. Fifteen and a half years earlier.

What did surprise was that <u>this</u> alien, the one named Foster, looked a lot like me.

But not so much that you couldn't tell us apart.

***

A few years before that, I had been sitting by myself in my local pub, the 'Bull and Finch', in my usual spot in the back room, near the ancient pinball machine, when a woman placed her hands on my eyes from behind. "Guess who!"

I guessed "Jodie?" and I turned around to see a highly surprised, somewhat drunken stranger.

"Oh, my God! I'm so sorry," she said, "I thought you were someone else."

"We are all someone else, to someone else," I replied with a smile, unreciprocated.

"Profound apologies," she said, clearly embarrassed, "this is why I don't drink."

"Really, it's fine," I said, as she moved away. "Who did you think I was?"

"My boss. It's his birthday." She found the man she was looking for and pointed him out. "You look just like him."

The man was holding court at a long table, drinking water, and telling an anecdote to a team of workmates and subordinates. He was now laughing and so were they. He DID look a lot like me.

I turned to ask her where they worked, but she had already rejoined the group. I could only guess that they were from the nearby CSIRO facility. I rarely saw the science types from there at the 'Bull and Finch.' I watched as my accidental assailant sat, smiling, next to my doppelganger. I saw a hand squeeze and surmised that they might have more than a boss/co-worker thing going on, but that was hardly a scandal. 'Good for you, nerds,' I said to myself and returned to my newspaper.

I didn't think of them or see either of them again, at least not until 14 March 2036, when Doctor Foster was slicing its skinsuit off and Doctor Baillie was about to faint in shock.

***

FATHER'S Day (September 2054)

I am in a pub in Townsville, Queensland. It is called 'Tall Stories Tavern', an old-school pub looking out over the Pacific Ocean, which has been here longer than any of us. It is Father's Day, and I am sitting inside at the horseshoe-shaped bar. Drinking a zero-alcohol beer in a white foam holder. Underneath a faded tin sign saying, "Life is about the JOURNEY, not the DESTINATION".

There are half-a-dozen of us regulars here on a warm, cloudless Sunday afternoon, along with the owner, Stan, and the bartender. Sierra has worked here for twenty years, and I have known her for fifteen. Yet, I still don't know her surname. We did have sex once, which is not relevant to the story; just a pleasant memory.

Amanda across the bar suddenly shouts, "Happy frigging Father's Day!" and raises her schooner of wine. We all return the toast, including Stan and Sierra with their glasses of water. Somebody else calls out "To all the frigging fathers!" and we chuckle obligingly. I don't know that any of us here are fathers, although I cast a glance at Stan, whose daughter and wife died in a drone accident last year. He sees me and nods.

"Another beer, Palmer?" he asks, and I say "Yes, mate." It is our private joke that none of the other locals know that I haven't touched alcohol for about three and a half decades.

When I first asked for a zero beer in Queensland, on holidays back in 2023, the bar staff gave me a strange look and had to go to the cellar to find one. Now, they are as popular as the 'real' stuff, even here in the tropics. I am not an outcast. But we enjoy our joke and I like the ritual.

Sierra brings a cold can over and replaces the empty in my foam stubby holder. I pay with a tapscan of my left wrist. "How's Stan today?" I ask her.

"He's good. Nowhere on earth he'd rather be. Better here than in his empty house. I know he appreciates your concern." She pats me on the shoulder.

"Hey, Stan!" I yell, "How long has this pub been owned by your family?"

"Since before the war, mate," he replies.

"Which war?" I ask.

"All of them!" Amanda screeches, as she dissolves into a laughing, coughing fit.

I sip my ice-cold fake beer. There's nowhere on earth I'd rather be, either.

***

Townsville Council brands itself "Oceania's First Point of Contact" and their favourite word to describe the city is "Connected." Ask anyone in the Tall Stories Tavern about that and their favourite word is "Bullshit." I am inclined to agree. Sitting around the horseshoe feels like a long way from anywhere.

As in most country towns, people that live here have lived here all their life or have come here to get away from somewhere (or someone) else. I fall into the latter category. Now I know that if anybody was properly searching for me, they'd find me easily enough. Even the urinal in the Tall Stories has facial recognition. It's just a little tougher to be seen than it was in Sydney.

And after about fifteen years, so far, so good. I no longer keep thinking I see my ex-girlfriend around every corner. Also, in all that time, no one in North Queensland has ever pointed at me and said that I looked like an alien.

***

ABOUT FIFTEEN YEARS AGO

In 2039, it was three and a half years or so since Foster the alien revealed himself (itself) and the world hadn't changed much. For a significant percentage of people, it only confirmed what they already believed. Far from expanding our understanding of the universe, it seemed to pervert it.

On this day, I was sitting in my usual spot in the 'Bull and Finch', having just finished my DJ shift at the radio station, drinking water and working on the cryptic crossword. In an actual newspaper. That cost $25. It was the last shift that I ever worked, but I didn't know that yet.

Doctor Baillie was there, drinking wine alone. I saw her in there most days. I don't think that she worked at the CSIRO anymore. To be fair, I reckon that seeing your lover transform into an alien before your eyes was a legitimate trigger for becoming a day drinker.

Although it didn't have that effect on me.

So, I was already thinking about Jodie when the two men walked in. One in his early fifties, the other in his late twenties, both wearing black suits and sunglasses. One black, one white.

Looking just like a community theatre cast for "Men in Black: The Musical."

They walked straight towards me. At least they had the decency to take their sunglasses off. They stopped on either side of me and the younger one said my name, as a question.

"You obviously already know the answer, so the inflection is wasted."

The older one now spoke, "Sorry, Sir. We've been searching for you for a long time."

"I'm pretty easy to find," I said, because back then, I was.

The younger one, again. "We're actually fans of yours, Sir. My Dad was one of the original subscribers of 'Second Contact'. I grew up with it. Is there somewhere we can talk?"

My podcast. Led to me becoming a minor celebrity, a long time ago. Nobody had talked to me about it in years. Certainly not since Doctor Foster appeared.

"Before I answer that," directing my attention to the older one. "Would I be correct in guessing that you are Agents from ADEPT?"

"One hundred percent correct, Sir" he said.

"And therefore, it doesn't matter if I consent, and let's do this the easy way, et cetera?"

"One hundred percent again, Sir. But believe me, we will all be much happier if you do consent. Sir." With this, the older Agent reached out his hand.

"I stopped shaking hands after Covid-19." I turned to the younger one and added "Google it."

"I studied that at school, Sir. In history class."

"Okay," I said, "We can talk at my place. You probably already know where that is." The look they shared confirmed it. "Before we go there, since we are all going to be friends, it is not Sir, it is Palmer. And I should tell you that I am already calling you Agent J and Agent K."

I picked up my $25 newspaper and headed for the exit of my favourite pub. Not looking back, and not knowing that I was leaving for the last time.

***

ADEPT was Australian Department for Extra-Planetary Tourism, set up in the wake of Doctor Foster's revelation and subsequent examination. Almost every country in the world had done something similar, although our government attracted the most attention and resources; due to being the site of 'First Contact'. Everybody mocked the name, of course. Although I respected it for being a true acronym.

ADEPT had sweeping powers, its enforcement bureau out-ranking both the police and the military. It was in theory a partnership with several allied countries, most notably China, India, U.S.A., Ukraine, and the U.K., as well as New Zealand. There were constant reports that the Americans had more than a friendly influence. In their version, the T probably stood for terrorism.

My guys both sounded local, however. The three of us made small talk, as we walked the short distance to my place. As I tapscanned us into my flat, the younger Agent said "In the movie, Agent K was old, and Agent J was black. Which one am I? Because he's both and I'm neither."

"You're K. For Knob-boy."

I saw the older Agent hide a smile. "Don't even tell me what J stands for."

"Jerk-wad," as I put my phone down on the table next to the front door.

"Man, I said don't tell me that." But he was now smiling.

I sat down on my old comfortable Italian brown leather couch and gestured for them to sit wherever they liked; however, they remained standing. J spoke, "Palmer, you're a smart guy, so you probably know why we're here. Back in 2020, you hosted a podcast titled 'Second Contact'. In it, you made several claims. Specifically, about extra-terrestrials living among us. What do you remember about that?"

"Well, Agent J," pausing for a reaction, but receiving none, "You're about my age, so you'd well remember that 2020 was a shitshow for all of us. Apart from a pandemic, my girlfriend left me, and I was depressed. The podcast was a creative outlet."

As I spoke, Agent Knob-boy was giving himself an unguided tour of my small flat. I didn't bother trying to stop him. Agent J was holding his right wrist at shoulder-height, obviously recording everything. Then; "I was a cop in 2020, and I remember thinking that it was the weirdest year we'd ever see. And yet, here we are. So, apart from being depressed, what was your state of mind when you recorded that podcast?"

"To be honest, very fucking drunk."

"I see," J said, "and do you still drink?"

"I do not."

"Good for you. Now, my young colleague listened to your podcast back in the day, yet may I say that he was a child and in a ridiculously small minority that would have taken it seriously. However, times have changed, and the thing is …"

At that moment, K shouted "Tommy, you've got to see this!" I looked at J and he rolled his eyes, as we walked into my spare room. K was holding two DVD cases.

"It's like a museum, boss! Look at this. He's got both 'Men in Black' AND 'Contact', Collector's Editions. These are worth heaps!"

"That's great, Agent. Perhaps you should start scanning." We both walked back into the main room. "Seriously, man, you still have DVDs?" he said, sitting down at the other end of the couch.

"I'm surprised junior even knew what they were. Seriously, Tommy?"

"Yeah, Tommy. But you can keep calling me J."

"Okay, J. So, what is he scanning for?"

"Exactly what you would think. Alien technology. Anything broadcasting, really."

"Good luck," I said, with a faint smile.

"Thanks, mate. Is there any chance you were living here back in 2020?"

"As a matter of fact, I was."

"Did you record the podcast here?"

"No, that was at work. Same radio station as today. You might say that I don't like change."

"Right. The thing is, in your podcast, you described in exquisite detail being witness to a human being, specifically, your lover, exposing herself as an extra-terrestrial. Still science-fiction in 2020. Remember that?"

"Not really. As I say, I was drunk, and I never listened back to it. It was embarrassing. I thought that every copy had been deleted".

"You should know that there is no such thing as being deleted in the twenty-First century. Now, what really got our interest is that you described exactly what 'First Contact' looked like, sixteen years before it happened."

"Pretty sure that my alien was a woman," I said.

"Yeah, and she looked like Jodie Foster. Apart from that detail, you can understand why this attracted our interest?"

"Maybe they got the idea from me?" No response. "Yes, Agent Tommy, I understand," removing any trace of mockery from my tone. "Look, I watched that CSIRO livestream as it happened, and it freaked me out. Not only because it reminded me of my old story, but also because that alien doctor guy kinda looked like me."

"Yes, we noticed that too."

"I don't know what to tell you. I'm just a radio DJ, born in 1976 in Sydney, Australia. I enjoy retro music, science-fiction, and DVDs, as you can see. And like everybody else on the planet, I was amazed to be alive to witness our first contact with an alien civilisation."

He looked at me silently for a long moment, as his younger colleague now moved through the room, waving his right wrist slowly at every bookshelf, piece of equipment, and cupboard.

"What have you found?" J addressed K.

"Just a lot of Bluetooth, boss. Including one in a running shoe. I've never seen so much old stuff. This guy's a dinosaur. No offence."

I stood and chose to be polite. "I am sorry to be rude, gents, I don't often have guests. Would you like anything? I don't have any beer, how about some filtered water?"

K nodded 'yes,' however the older man cut him off. "Finish the scan, Agent. Nothing for us. Thank you, Sir."

I noticed that I was 'Sir' again, just as Agent Knob-boy ran his right arm up and down my body. Not asking for permission, of course. When he was done, I picked up a pack of grape-coloured mints, sitting on the table next to the front door. "How about a Tic Tac?"

"No, thank you, Sir," Tommy J said, so I put them in my pocket, just as K scanned my phone and announced that he was finished.

"Tell me, Sir," J said, "What do you know about Metonic cycles?"

"Doesn't mean anything to me. Should it?"

"Not sure," he said and stood up. "Did you have anything you wanted to ask us?"

"I don't think that I do," I said, because I really didn't.

"Okay," he said and moved to leave. "One more thing. That girlfriend who left you, in 2020. What was her name?"

I paused for just a moment. "Jodie."

"Have you seen her since?"

"No," I said, because imagined sightings don't count.

"How long did she live here?"

"In this flat? Six months or so. In Rose Forest? I think it was about three years."

"Where did you meet?"

"In the pub," I replied, because it was true.

"Did you visit the U.S.A. between 1979 and 1982, or between 1998 and 2001?"

"No." Which was a lie. Because fuck them.

"Well, thank you for your co-operation, Palmer" and he went to the door. "You will probably be seeing us again."

"I would expect nothing less, Agent J." I tapscanned the door open for them. J exited, as K walked up to me and held out his hand, then realised his error and withdrew.

"My name is Kevin, by the way. It's great to meet you. And I love your DVD collection."

"Thanks. Always nice to meet a fan. Best of luck to you, Agent K."

"If I am Nob-boy, shouldn't I be Agent N?"

"The K is silent, Kevin."

"Oh!" he said, and he walked out, confused. I stood at the doorway for a while and watched them go down the street. Back to their black car, parked outside the pub.

So often since that day in 2039, I have thought about how my life – and indeed the world – would have been so different if only Kevin had scanned my packet of purple Tic Tacs.

***

NOW

I never did meet J and K – Tommy and Kevin – again. Although I am sure that they have seen me. If not in person, then on surveillance. They could even be watching me as I sip a cold fake beer in an old seaside pub in Townsville. But I doubt it. And I somehow don't think that Kevin would have been a career Agent.

To this day, ADEPT haven't produced evidence of any alien life, other than Doctor Norman Foster. Their influence was long since usurped by UNDECTU – the 'taskforce' announced in 2043 by U.S. President Germanotta. United Nations Division of Extra-terrestrial Counter-Terrorism Units. Say what you like about us Aussies, we are better at acronyms than the Yanks.

UNDECTU was U.N. by name, however everybody knew that it was an arm of the U.S. military. Their main base was once revealed to be Pine Gap in the Australian Northern Territory. It probably still is. I wonder if Tommy ever got a job there. If he lived, he'd surely be retired by now?

As for me, I finished working that same day he interviewed me. It was time. I never went back to the radio station, although I recorded a farewell for my listeners. The station played it in primetime and gave me a nice payout. I suspect that they had been wanting to retire me anyway.

I left my flat and bought a small house in Townsville. I had holidayed here once, and it felt right. You could say I was drawn here. Brought nothing with me but two phones, some clothes, and a packet of Tic Tacs. Sold everything else. Have never regretted it, although I do miss my DVDs.

I was thinking today about what Tommy asked me, about Metonic cycles. Of course, I fucking knew what they were. It's the period in which the phases of the moon repeat themself. It is equal to almost precisely nineteen years. Meton of Athens had worked it out 2500 years ago.

I often wonder why he asked me that. One Metonic cycle is equal to 6939 days, give or take, depending upon leap years. I have calculated all sorts of plus or minus, without finding anything significant. I left Sydney nineteen years after my girlfriend left me, but I don't think that counts.

The only other thing that stood out is that Doctor Foster said that it had been on this planet for exactly nineteen years, when it revealed itself in 2036. So, if we believe it; since March 2017. As for Foster itself, it hasn't been seen publicly in any form for many years. Rumours abound, of course. If UNDECTU has it, they are not telling us.

However, that has reminded me of two things. When she was living with me, Jodie never admitted her age. Finding out that she was an alien explained that. However, she did once tell me that her birthday was 14 March. I remembered it because I always called it pie-day. As in, the value of π equalling 3.14, therefore 3/14. π Day is an American thing, but that's how I remembered it. Jodie also said in 2020 she had been 'here' for about three years. In other words, since 2017.

So perhaps that meant she had arrived on 14 March 2017, the same day as Norman Foster. Exactly one Metonic cycle before 'First Contact'. Exactly two Metonic cycles before tomorrow.

***

The Next Day (14 MARCH 2055)

The Great Printed Newspaper War had finally been lost a few years ago. Towards the end, I was the only person in North Queensland receiving a daily paper copy of the news, paying $250 per edition. When that finally stopped, I resorted to buying an old school laser printer, a stack of ink cartridges, and printing off the daily cryptic crossword. Of course, that makes me a dinosaur, however no meteorite has arrived yet to wipe me out.

My weekday ritual is to take a HB pencil and the sheet of paper, sit at the horseshoe bar of the Tall Stories Tavern, with a coffee, followed by a fake beer, and enjoy my cryptic. Some of the other regulars occasionally help.

Today, being a Sunday, I am working on a different puzzle.

***

When Jodie left, in 2020, she bequeathed me alien technology. It looked like a purple Tic Tac and for a long time, I never looked at the contents. Maybe I should have. But I didn't. When Doctor Foster revealed itself in 2036, I figured that anything Jodie had given me years earlier would be either included in and/or outdated by anything Foster had to share. Therefore, somehow making it safer for me. So, I dug up my purple Tic Tac. Literally. Nothing happened straight away. I held it next to my phone, my wristSIM, my desktop tablet, even my running shoes, and nothing.

It wasn't until I tried turning on a 2020-era mobile phone that I saw any results. It seems that it was designed to be only compatible to human technology of the time that she had given it to me. As she had promised, a file folder appeared on my Samsung titled 'Jodie'. In it, were PDF documents. A LOT of PDF documents. They were all in English and contained mostly recommendations on strategies to combat pandemics, global warming, *et cetera*.

To my untrained eye, it seemed mostly to suggest doing what humanity had (eventually) worked out what to do by itself. A few years ahead of time, yes. But I felt then – as I do now – that sharing it with the world, with no proof of its origin, would have made zero difference to the scheme of things. And maybe gotten me killed. So, nobody else ever saw it.

Not long after that, ADEPT called on me, and I then moved to Townsville. Where I had kept the purple Tic Tac uneventfully ever since, hidden in plain sight on my work desk.

Out of the many thousands of files I had extracted, there was one in particular that had always interested me. It was titled apfom.pdf and I had always suspected it was meant especially for me. When we first met, Jodie was carrying a copy of John Irving's novel 'A Prayer for Owen Meany.'

GREG/17700313085734 -019139867+146829553
17730901004330
17890313012832 +048805500+002117711 17920831171428
18080313175930 +055083624+021905814 18110902094526
18270314103028 -019260000+146821817 18300902021624
18460314030126 +043097500-000060000 18490901184722
18650313193224 +000622711+033624223 18680901111820
18840313120322 -008884944+147738057 18870902034918
19030315043420 +049183825+015454719 19060902202016
19220314210518 +021365000-157950000 19250902125114
19410314133616 +040240718+026281389 19440902052212
19600314060714 +037175911-116046000 19630902215310
19790314223812 +033843446-117995286 19820902142408
19980314150910 +040711564-074013217 20010902065506
20170314074008 -033739600+151229400 20200901232604
20360314001106 -033733333+151233333
*20390902155702/UTC

/Jodie/apfom.pdf

The left column is a group of dates, spaced close to nineteen years apart. The last line has the 2036 date of 'First Contact' and the time is when Foster sliced into itself. The timestamp initially threw me, as it was 11:11 a.m. in Sydney when that happened, not 12:11 a.m., however I eventually realised that factoring in GMT, time zones and Daylight Saving Time in New South Wales meant that it matches up exactly. The second-last line therefore is probably when Foster and maybe Jodie and who knows who or what else arrived on Earth, in 2017. The years before that are all nineteen-year *Metonic cycle* intervals stretching back to when Englishmen first visited Australia.

The bottom right timestamp is when I last saved the file. I remember it well, because it was the same day in 2039 that I left Sydney for Townsville, and I packed up my old phone for the last time. The other dates are all nineteen-year *Metonic cycle* intervals stretching backwards from that date. UTC must indicate where the technology got the timestamp from, with the nearest source being the nearby University of Townsville Caesium clock.

The rest of the numbers remain a mystery to me. They are all one digit short of being a phone number, although I have tried plenty of times calling them. I have multiplied, subtracted, divided, and tried everything I can think of, to make sense of it. Fruitlessly. And I don't know who 'Greg' is.

If I have calculated correctly, the *next* timestamp would be today @ 16:42:04 GMT. With no Daylight Saving in Queensland (still!), that is 2:42 a.m. tomorrow. So, I spend this day (and the next day) scouring over numbers, looking for clues and watching the news, for any reports of alien invasion. Friendly or otherwise. Or any sign, really. But nothing. The only news that interests me is that the Penrith Panthers are favourites to win the International Rugby League Super Bowl over the Barcelona Dragons, and that the last wild koala on the Australian mainland has finally died off.

I have dinner at the Tall Stories and listen to Amanda and the other regulars arguing loudly about politics, football, and koalas. Normally, I'd join in, but my heart isn't in it today. Whatever the nineteen years of this Metonic cycle has brought seems to have passed me by. Perhaps I'll never know. And I don't think that I will live long enough to see another one.

***

1268 Days LATER (2 September 2058)

Monday afternoon just after 4:30 p.m., the day following Father's Day, in the Tall Stories, with a coffee, underneath "Life is about the JOURNEY, not the DESTINATION". With just Amanda for company, as Stan and Sierra busy themselves setting up for rest of the day.

"Give us a clue, Palmer," she calls out, in between sipping her warm white wine.

"No cryptic crossword today, darl. Just a lot of numbers. And they've got me buggered."

I had resolved a couple of years ago to give up trying to work it out. In that time, there had been no signs of aliens and the world had by and large stopped talking about them. I had gone as far as shredding my sole surviving printout and completely wiping my phone storage, so that no copies of apfom.pdf existed anymore. But today – 2 September – was nineteen years since I moved to Townsville. Nineteen years since the last timestamp on the list. And – I realised yesterday – exactly thirty-eight years since Jodie walked out of my flat in Rose Forest, and my life.

The purple Tic Tac was still there in its case on my desk. Silently mocking me.

If a double *Metonic cycle-versary* wasn't a good enough excuse to have one last crack at it, there'd never be a better reason. This morning, I dug out and powered up my *very* old Samsung, connected it via a *very* old USB cable and adaptor to my desk-tablet, and found the file and printed it off. It looks just how I remembered, except that one extra line has appeared at the bottom.

GREG/17700313085734 -019139867+146829553
17730901004330

17890313012832 +048805500+002117711 17920831171428
18080313175930 +055083624+021905814 18110902094526
18270314103028 -019260000+146821817 18300902021624
18460314030126 +043097500-000060000 18490901184722
18650313193224 +000622711+033624223 18680901111820
18840313120322 -008884944+147738057 18870902034918
19030315043420 +049183825+015454719 19060902202016
19220314210518 +021365000-157950000 19250902125114
19410314133616 +040240718+026281389 19440902052212
19600314060714 +037175911-116046000 19630902215310
19790314223812 +033843446-117995286 19820902142408
19980314150910 +040711564-074013217 20010902065506
20170314074008 -033739600+151229400 20200901232604
20360314001106 -033733333+151233333 20390902155702
20550314164204 -019108082+146863532
*20580902082800/UTC

/Jodie/apfom.pdf

I was pleased to see that three and a half years ago, I had indeed calculated the 14/3/2055 timestamp correctly. The new timestamp was once again there, from when I had saved the file and connected to the nearby University's Caesium clock. Intrigued, Amanda had moved around the bar and looked over my shoulder. She ran her fingers down the left-hand column.

"They're all dates and times. ISO-8601 basic format," she said.

"That much I had worked out," I said. "Each line is nineteen years after the previous one."

Amanda continued running her fingers up and down the printout. "'Greg' indicates proleptic Gregorian calendar, not Julian, which is what astronomers use."

I laughed. "Of course, it bloody does! Nineteen years of looking at this thing and I always assumed it was some guy's name!"

"Time gaps are all consistent with 235 synodic months. That is equal to nineteen solar years, but accounts for the 16 hours, 30 minutes and 58 seconds which is added each time. The variation in leap days balance that out to make them meet at the end of the Metonic cycle."

I nodded, impressed. It was easy to forget that the alcoholic leaning over me had once been an astrophysicist, as well as a decorated Australian Army Silverhawk pilot, who had served tours of duty in Sri Lanka and Papua New Guinea.

Amanda, now deep in thought, continued, "You know, that first date is a few weeks before Cook first sailed right past here. 6 June 1770. *The whole appear'd to have the most rugged, rocky and barren Surface'.* It's in the Endeavour's log."

I did not know that. "The final date is the timestamp from when I printed it off this morning," I said, wanting to maintain my reputation as the intellectual one, "and UTC is where it synched from the nearest atomic clock, the one at University of Townsville."

"No, it isn't, Palmer." Amanda said, tutting slightly, not used to correcting me. "Zulu Time." A blank look from me. "UTC is Coordinated Universal Time."

I looked again. Of course! I should have realised that when I made the time zone calculations for 'First Contact'. But that meant that the time listed, 082800, is less than two hours *from now*.

"And the column in the middle," Amanda concluded, "is a list of decimal GPS coordinates. Plus/minus for north/south of the equator, plus/minus for east/west of the Prime Meridian."

I looked at her, amazed. And back down at my piece of paper. She was right. Convert the numbers to degrees, minutes, and seconds, add the compass points, and they were a list of GPS coordinates. It was quite simply a map, with a timetable.

"And the first one and the last one," I said, "are right next to each other. Nineteen point one degrees, that's just north of here, isn't it?" I pointed out that way. "In the ocean."

"Nah, mate." Amanda walked back to her glass of wine. "That's on Maggie."

***

"Maggie" is Magnetic Island, a 49 kilometre-square island (and shrinking), with a mountain in the middle, just eight kilometres off the coast of Townsville. Popular with tourists, it was first named by Captain Cook, who recorded it as 'Magnetical Island', claiming that when he passed it, iron deposits on the island interfered with the ship's compass on the 'Endeavour'.

Just as I was checking the current UTC time (064530), on my wristSIM, a woman and a man entered the open door of the Tavern. They weren't wearing black suits and sunglasses, but they might as well have.

They walked straight up to me (of course) and the woman said my name. Not a question. American accent. I drained my coffee and sat silently, thinking 'Why today?' The woman spoke again "We have a message from an old friend of yours," and held up a screen.

"Hello, Palmer," said a familiar face.

I couldn't help but smile "G'day Tommy."

"I have been watching you for a long time, old mate. And waiting. Guess I should have taken that Tic Tac when you offered."

"Is that what gave me away?" I said.

"Kind of. It was switching on that old Samsung this morning. It started broadcasting, again."

"Never should have trusted 'twenties technology. What do they want with me?"

"They just want a chat. A very long chat. I might even see you in the N.T. Then I can retire."

The woman holding the tablet clicked it off. "Please come with us, Sir." I could see an unmarked black car outside. I climbed off the barstool, very slowly. The other UNDECTU Agent grabbed my left arm, not unkindly.

"I just need to take a piss first," I said.

"That can wait, Sir," the first Agent said, "Until we get to where we're going. It's not far."

"I'm an old man. It can't wait."

They exchanged a glance, hesitant. He maintained his grip on my arm.

"My bag is nearly full," I said, "Do you want that in your nice car?"

She sighed and nodded. The male Agent held me just long enough for his colleague to attach a small yellow device to my forehead. A tracker. Full audio and forward video recording, and they didn't come off without an unlock scan. Up here, we called them witchety grubs. I shuffled off towards the toilet, out the back. On the way through the outdoor beer garden, I saw Sierra, having a cigarette. She was the only person I knew who still smoked. I stopped in front of her.

Sierra looked up and saw the grub. I winked at her, attempting reassurance. I took the piece of paper and HB pencil from my back pocket and, without looking down, wrote "STAN → GENTS".

She read it and briefly nodded. I touched her fondly on the shoulder, then shuffled off towards the toilet. Minutes later, I was at the basin in front of a mirror, pretending to wash my hands, when Stan walked in. He saw the grub but didn't react. I liked that about him.

I took out the paper and wrote, holding it low, beneath the sink. "ME → MAGGIE. NOW!"

Stan glanced at it, then stood beside me and rinsed his hands. "It's a beautiful day, Palmer. Tourists everywhere. Reckon the five o'clock Cat to the Island will be bloody busy." And then he walked out, towards the back door and the loading dock.

I followed, abandoning the pretence of shuffling. He climbed into his car, and I jumped in the passenger seat. We didn't speak, as we headed in the direction of the Ferry terminal, other than Stan whispering a text into his wristSIM. I looked behind to see the two Agents getting into their car.

As chases go, it wasn't too dramatic. We obeyed the traffic signals, and they followed us. As we approached the terminal five minutes later, Stan handed me a chip-card. I looked at it (thereby also showing the watchers): "SENIORS SEA*LINK ANNUAL GOLD CONCESSION".

We pulled up at the taxi-drone stand at the front of the terminal. Stan looked at me and said "Miranda is holding the Cat for you. Good luck." A pause, and then "Palmer, if I never see you again... It's been a pleasure. You're a bloody good mate." There was a tear in his eye.

"What are you talking about, Stan? You'll see me for happy hour this evening." But I leaned in and hugged him. And he was right. We never saw each other again.

I ran towards the gangplank. Past: 'world's last remaining koala colony!' The Agents were only a few metres behind me. I swear that the silent one was smirking. But I kept moving, swiftly for an old man. At the gate, I saw Miranda, Stan's niece. She motioned to the turnstile, and I tapscanned the chip-card. The barrier lifted and I walked on to the catamaran.

Behind me, the barrier lowered in place and the Agents were stopped. Miranda stepped in front of them with her arms folded. "Boat's closed, guys. Next one is in two hours."

The silent one put his hand on his holster, as the other one spoke. "Madam, we are UNDECTU Agents, and I order you to grant us access. That man you are abetting is a fugitive and possible alien. I repeat. We are Agents of UNDECTU."

"I don't care if you are King Wally bloody Lewis. Boat's closed." And with that, Miranda tapscanned a button on the console and the ferry started pulling away.

Christ, I loved Queenslanders sometimes. I looked at the Agents standing there, watching me leave. I couldn't resist giving them a wave.

***

MAGGIE

The crossing took twelve minutes. If UNDECTU had a Sikorsky chopper, I was fucked. I used the time to check the GPS coordinates. The last entry was near a small suburb on the northern side of Magnetic Island, named Horseshoe Bay. A thin beach, some shops, holiday apartments, and a pub; Marlin Bar Tavern. If I was reading it right, the location was in the bush nearby.

We arrived at Nelly Bay, and I disembarked with the tourists and day workers. No sign of any helicopters or staffed drones. There was a solitary taxi waiting and a family of six was heading for it, the youngest child wearing a koala-themed onesie. Time to play the old man card again.

"Excuse me," I said, limping, "Do you mind if I go ahead? My knee is playing up."

"Sure thing, buddy," said the father, "Thank you for your service."

"You're welcome," I said, without a clue which war he thought I might have been in. "There'll be another taxi along in a minute," and I hoped that was true. I got in the passenger seat. "Horseshoe Bay, thanks mate," I said to the driver, and I tapscanned the meter and we set off.

"Come to see the koalas?" she asked.

"No, I'm from Town. I'm meeting somebody."

***

She dropped me off outside Marlin Bar Tavern, sixteen minutes later. I had been here once before, on a day trip. Your standard old-school island tourist pub, albeit one which Lonely Planet describes as having a 'weird vibe'. I watched overhead at nothing but a clear blue sky. The time was 5:28 p.m., exactly one hour before 082800 UTC. Without anything better to do, I entered the pub and ordered a zero-alcohol beer.

Looking at the mirror behind the bar, a man walked up and stood 1.5 metres behind me. He cleared his throat; I turned around and I was still looking into a mirror. It was me. Twenty years-ago me. More or less. But it was no man. It spoke. "Hello, Palmer. We've been expecting you."

"Doctor Foster, I presume?"

"Very nice to meet you." It held out its hand. I shook it. Well, you would, wouldn't you?

"I have only heard good things," Doctor Foster said, "My colleague speaks highly of you."

"Doctor Baillie?" I asked.

It chuckled. "No, not that colleague. Let's have a chat." It motioned towards a table.

"Can I buy you a drink, Doctor?"

"That would be lovely, thank you. And call me Norm." It smiled at me. "Water, please. Alcohol doesn't agree with me."

***

241

I brought the drinks to the table – a large, upturned barrel – and sat. We both sipped our drinks in silence. Then "I trust that you have a great many questions," it said.

"I like to think that I know when it is better not to ask."

"An admirable quality." It laughed and touched his water container to my zero-beer bottle, as a toast. "This is an exquisite pub. Reminds me of the 'Bull and Finch'."

"Just missing the pinball machine," I said.

"Ah, yes. 'World Cup '94'. I spent many hours playing that game. Good times."

"I only ever saw you there once."

"This was before your time, Palmer. And after."

We sipped our drinks. I *did* have a lot of questions. But I knew that it knew that.

"We were supposed to meet, actually," it said. "Back then. But, alas, it didn't work out. Still, we're here now. Better late than never, yes?" and it laughed again and slapped me on the back. "In many ways, things have worked out for the best. Because of you, I got plenty of work done."

"What sort of…" I started, as it raised its hand to silence me.

"All in good time. However, time is also against us. And it seems that there is someone else searching for Palmer." When it paused, the unmistakeable sound of a UNDECTU heli-drone could be heard, looking for a landing spot.

"They know where I am. Where we both are." I pointed to the witchety grub.

"Of course," it said, and it waved its right wrist close to my forehead. The grub detached and Foster caught it, then dropped it in my fake beer. "Let's get out of here."

***

We walked to the beach, just across the road, and clambered into a small tinny; a standard three-metre aluminium boat with an outboard motor. It could have been 1958 instead of 2058.

Except for the black heli-drone landing on the strip of sand one hundred metres away. I watched the two Agents disembark, just as we took off into the sea, breaching a small breaking wave as we did so. I could see the female Agent shake her head and getting back on the chopper.

"Obvious question, Norm," over the dull noise of the outboard, "Where are we headed?"

"White Lady Bay. Do you know it?"

It sounded vaguely familiar; however, I indicated that I had not.

"Not far," it said, "And there is certainly nowhere for them to land at high tide." It chuckled.

About ten minutes later, we rounded a rocky headland and I saw an interesting structure. A white rock. It somehow reminded me of Townsville's 'Ocean Siren' statue, calling out a warning. Foster provided the commentary. "The white lady. Completely natural rock formation. She has been there since long before any man saw her. Or us."

Soon after, we pulled up onto the rocks. Foster tying the tinny to a small, anchored hook I hadn't noticed. It started walking towards the structure and I followed. It leaned against the 'lady' and turned and smiled. "We are here, my friend. And I know you have many questions."

"Just two, Doctor Foster. Are you Jodie?"

It smiled again. It certainly was a cheerful shape-shifting alien. "I am not. But we are indeed from the same place. The easiest way to explain it is that we are family. You could say that Jodie is my sister. And please, call me Norm."

I considered that. And then said, "Why me?"

"Why did I choose to look like you?"

"Not just that. Why did you bring me here today? Why did Jodie reveal herself to me, and only me, back in 2020?"

"Why don't you ask her yourself?"

And that's when I saw her.

Stepping out from behind a tree, she looked a lot like the American actor Jodie Foster (*circa* 1997), but not so much that you couldn't tell them apart. Just how I remembered her. The love of my life. She spoke: "Hello, stranger. I have been searching for you, for a long time."

"You left me."

"I did," she said, "And I didn't want to, but I had to go home. I came back one time and unfortunately, we didn't find each other. But I'm here now, Palmer. We both are."

I looked at her, up and down. I knew that underneath the skin was not blood and bone nor anything human. I knew that. But all I saw was the woman I fell in love with and have missed every day, for thirty-eight years. "What am I supposed to do?" I said, close to tears.

"I'd like a hug," she said.

And so, we hugged. We held each other tightly and I sobbed into her shoulder. After a minute with only the sound of my crying and waves on rocks, Doctor Foster ("Norm") tapped us each on the back and pointed to its wrist. The universal (galactic?) sign language for 'running out of time.'

We pulled away from the embrace. As we did so, I heard the heli-drone, although I couldn't yet see it. Foster spoke "You know what would be fun? You get to ask each other one question. The one thing you have been longing to ask each other. You go first, Palmer."

I laughed aloud. I had lived with the certainty that aliens lived among us longer than anybody. Hell, I had sex with one! So, I asked the most recent thing that had been puzzling me. "How long have you been here? On Earth?"

"We first visited 288 years ago." Jodie answered. "Landed right over there, at the high point. No humans living here then. Stayed for 1268 days and we have been back fifteen times since."

I could hear the chopper, flying low nearby. "Do you always land on this island?"

"No. It depends upon the weather. We can land anywhere on the Earth. It is quite easy to conceal ourselves. Our only restriction is that we must leave from the same place we arrived."

"We? How many of you are there?"

Foster cut in. "Just the both of us. Sometimes, we travel alone. Never more than two. We sort of tag-team. Stay here for about three and a half years, and depending upon what needs to be done, one of us might remain behind. Like I did between 2017 and 2039. The other sibling goes home."

"Home?"

"For want of a better word. Where we travel, to report our progress and upgrade our systems. That doesn't take long. Then we return here again, arriving exactly nineteen years later."

"The Metonic cycles," I said.

"Yes," Jodie said, smiling at me in what felt like approval. "It assists our navigation. Think of it like a mariner sailing with the prevailing trade winds."

Which reminded me; "Magnetic Island got its name 288 years ago. The English sailor Cook claimed that this island interfered with his ship's compass."

The two exchanged a (very human) look. "Yes, that was us." Foster said, in what seemed like embarrassment. "Rookie error on my part. And quite the coincidence."

The surf sprayed, as the UNDECTU heli-drone located us and hovered directly overhead. From a speaker came the voice of my old friend Agent K: "Doctor Foster. Doctor Arroway."

I looked at Jodie, she pointed at herself and mouthed, "Fake name."

"It's good to see you again." Tommy's voice boomed down. "All of you. However, you are holding an Earthling, which is against our agreement. Please release him to us immediately."

Foster touched his wrist and his voice projected clearly upwards. "No problem. Our meeting with the one you call Palmer is finished. I will bring him back to Horseshoe Bay. We just ask that you go ahead, so the sea is calm."

If a piece of aviation equipment can be described as moving reluctantly, that is what it looked like. It flew away, in the direction from where we came.

"'The one you call Palmer'?" Jodie said.

"Just my little joke," Foster said, chuckling again softly. "They really have no idea, do they? Now, Jodie – if that is your real name," (another chuckle) "It is your turn. One question."

Jodie smiled a shy smile, the one I had dreamed of for thirty-eight years. She extended her hands and took mine in them. Then she spoke the words that every boy in love wants to hear.

"Palmer. Do you want to come back to my place?"

***

EPILOGUE

And that is how this retired Australian radio DJ came to be the first live human being to leave our Solar System. And the first to visit an extra-terrestrial civilisation. As far as we know.

As for why I was chosen, whenever I ask Jodie "Why me?" she responds, "Why not."

It amuses me to think that she had provided the date, time, and location of all of their arrivals and departures, back in 2020. I didn't look. And again in 2039, in Rose Forest, but I didn't realise. It only took me thirty-eight years to work it out (with Amanda's help). I had warned Jodie back when we first met that I was not particularly good at cryptics. But I am getting better.

My life now? It is a different kind of existence. I do still have my earthly body, but it does not run around. At my age (eighty-two Earth years), it didn't have much running left in it anyway. The easiest way to describe where I am is that it is a technology. Once I started thinking of Jodie in those terms, everything made much more sense. I am still in love with her.

Doctor Foster – Norm – stayed behind. He will explain things better than I could. Including how we are eradicating pandemics, stopping the sea levels rising, and saving the koalas.

I will report back in nineteen of your Earth years. There is a lot to tell. But know that there really is intelligent life out there, and they are happy to meet us.

And the sign was wrong. My life was not about the journey. It was a destination.

Greg Eccleston is a writer & professional actor. He has written & had produced the stageplays "Catharsis" & "Girlfriend #33 Stole my Mojo"; as well as the award-winning short play "The Fifth Stage". His creative influences & heroes include John Irving, Robin Williams & David Bowie. Greg lives near the beach in Terrigal, Australia & he has visiting rights to his cat Banderas.

Revelations of a Space Rebel

by G.A. Babouche

W e were no longer alone in the universe. That question had been unfathomably answered when the Syrens came hurtling through our atmosphere one August afternoon. An alliance was formed however some are suspicious of their true motives. What is the real reason they have come to Earth? Is it really to help us advance or do they intend to rip our planet away from us while we watch?

There is not much we can do, being technologically inferior to them. What will happen when they tire of us? Where would we go if we had no other choice but to leave? Can we survive them?

These thoughts and many more cluttered my mind as I sat and watched the preparations for the festival in honour of the Syrens. This yearly event took place to mark the anniversary of the day we finally encountered life beyond our own. From my perch on a grassy hillside, I watched as the masses meticulously stumbled around, arranging decorations and food platters. This was the most excitement this little town had experienced in a year. As you can imagine, encountering a new species had been one hell of a day. A multitude of emotions had passed through the town—awe, fear and then acceptance. The majority of people, welcomed the Syrens, they revelled in their appearance. Hence the elaborate celebrations which took place all over the world. Today marked the 3rd anniversary.

I grew tired of watching these brain-washed worker ants as they milled around and got up from my spot to do something more productive. I had no intention of taking part in these festivities. I was the minority you see, one of the few that saw the Syrens as a threat. I didn't buy their story; they were so evasive and only revealed as much as they needed to. We didn't even know which star system they were from or even what planet! That riled me up. Surely, we had a right to know these important facts. Yet the Government remained tight-lipped also. Perhaps they knew and didn't want us to know or perhaps they were in the dark same as the rest of us. Whatever it was, I would get to the bottom of it.

I made my way back through the forest, taking the shortcut home to continue my research on our elusive new guests. As I walked, I thought more on my covert blog that I wrote on the Syrens. I envisioned this week's content as I trudged through the foliage. The trees obscured much of my view ahead but there was no misconception when I saw something flash before me, flitting between two trees. I froze on the spot, unable to move or utter a sound. I gasped for breath, my senses going into overdrive. There was no mistaking what I had seen. I was sure it was a Syren. I gathered up my nerves and slowly ventured ahead. This could be my chance to see one in person and find out for myself what they were about.

My fear turned to curiosity. Syrens had not integrated into society, they had their homes set up around army bases, far from the public. What was one doing around here? The only indication I was going on was seeing a flash of silver. They refused to adopt our earthly clothing and instead still wore their silver jumpsuits they had arrived in. I hesitated for a moment as I wondered if it was indeed a Syren or a bear. I wasn't sure which was worse to be honest. I sucked it up and forged ahead. Whatever it was, was slumped behind a large tree. As I approached, I saw an arm emerge from behind the stump and knew I was correct in my estimation. I rounded the tree and came face to face with my first alien.

I gasped out loud at what I saw. The Syren looked just as surprised to see me. It was male and it was hurt. My humanity kicked in and without thinking I crouched down to him and tried to help quell the emitting blue blood from a large wound in his abdomen. The Syren recoiled and hissed at me. I tried to convey that I was wanting to help and not harm him as best as I could, he seemed to understand and realised I was not a threat.

"What happened to you?!" I cried out, even though I knew he could not understand me, or could he? He hissed in response and followed that with a few words in their native tongue. His rich baritone voice reverberated through my chest; the vibrations ran through my arms which were desperately trying to stop the blood flow. I moved a hand and took his, moving it in the place where mine had been. Then I quickly unbuttoned my white shirt, ripped strips from it and tied them around the injury.

He watched in confusion, his eyes never leaving mine.

"Look, I've done the best I can, but we need to get you proper help or you'll die. Do you understand me?" I said in frustration. "I need to get you to a hospital!"

"No!" He said firmly. I looked at him in shock.

"Fine, then I'm taking you to my place and I'll see what I can do." He nodded in response. I motioned to him to try and stand. Leveraging myself under his left arm, I propped him up. Not a great idea as he was heavy as hell! He gingerly took a step and I could feel that he was trying not to put all his weight onto me.

We began a slow procession through the forest to my home, it wasn't far but in the state we were in, it seemed miles away. I tried not to think of the warmth of the body I held next to me. Syrens were perfect. Everything about them was perfection and this one in particular was perfection personified. He looked like a veritable Adonis, anatomically flawless. They looked human, the only other-worldly part of them was their startling aquamarine eyes. It seemed the only eye colour they had. Hair colour was much like our own spectrum however this Syren displayed shiny blonde but almost white hair which seemed to be iridescent. I was distracted by the shimmering and didn't realise that I'd been staring a little too long at him. He noticed and gave me a small smile, as if he knew what I was thinking. I looked away quickly and hoped the blush spreading through me wasn't apparent.

We finally made it to my small hut-like home which was placed right at the end of the forest. I manoeuvred him as best as I could up the small steps leading up to the door. He winced in pain but moved on courageously. As we burst through the door, I steered him towards the couch and we both collapsed onto it. I tried to make him as comfortable as I could and then raced off to find my first aid kit and any other supplies I needed. I made it back to him in record time, finding him flitting in and out of consciousness. He had lost a lot of blood; I wasn't sure if I could do this. His eyes opened then and he gave me a reassuring smile, as if to say, *'I trust you'*. My frantic eyes softened and I kicked into gear.

He helped me undo his jumpsuit and it fell open, revealing the most impressive chest I had ever seen! I gulped and hoped my awkwardness wasn't obvious. Working deftly, I smoothed away the excess blood which was now caked around the wound. The bleeding seemed to be slowing but there was a gaping hole I needed to contend with. Sewing and then bandaging him up, I finally slumped onto the floor in front of him, completely spent.

He on the other hand, seemed to be getting some colour back into his cheeks, and almost seemed better already. Could they heal faster than us? I was just about to speak when he suddenly rummaged in his pocket and then like a flash, he stabbed something behind my ear. I screamed in pain and tried to back up in response, but he grabbed my arm and held me close.

My head throbbed as I continued to buck against him but something in his eyes made me stop. He was giving me such an earnest look that I stilled in place, mesmerised by his incredible eyes. I realised then that his mouth was moving, he was speaking and I could understand him.

"I am sorry I had to do that but I wanted to tell you how grateful I was. Do not be scared, I will not hurt you. It is merely a universal translator; you will be able to understand me now. Are you alright?"

I stared at him in shock, still surprised that I could understand him. A smile broke through my lips.

"Who are you?!"

"I am Thon and I am very pleased to meet you."

I stared at him in stunned silence. The cogs in my brain finally started moving again.

"What happened to you?"

He thought for a long moment before answering, "a group of your people attacked me."

"But why would they do that?"

"They were military personnel and they were not pleased at my arrival."

I thought for a moment, something was not right here. I was beginning to regret bringing Thon into my home. I knew nothing about him and his kind, why had I helped him? Thon seemed to sense my apprehension.

"Please do not look at me like that. I promise you; I will not hurt you." He reiterated.

I let out a slow breath. "My name is Zefina."

"Zefina. I like that."

"Can I ask you some questions?"

"Well, you saved me, so I am indebted to you."

"I'll take that as a yes. Firstly, why were the military attacking you, aren't they supposed to be helping you?"

"I am not with the ones that arrived three years ago. I arrived yesterday. I thought that your kind would not be able to track me however the others must have shared our tracking devices with your military."

"Why have you come?" I asked hesitantly. Scanning my small hut for a potential weapon.

"Zefina! Look at me." My gaze darted back to him at the authority in his voice. "Before I tell you why I am here, I must tell you why the others are here. Will you trust me?"

I nodded slowly. Unsure of what I was about to hear. Little did I know that the next few moments would change my life forever.

***

I was trembling. I couldn't believe my ears. This wasn't happening, surely? Had I really been right all along?

"I can't believe that they seriously plan to take over our planet?" I said out loud even though internally I had thought the same. "Why would your people be so cruel?"

"They are not my people. Well, they are like us, but they are a separate faction. These Syrens are the elites who used to govern our world. They were ousted from power by Syrens like me, who are soldiers. When they lost their power over the people, they turned their eyes to other planets where they could potentially rule."

My mind was racing. Synapses sparking, trying to piece everything together. How did I know this Syren was telling the truth and it wasn't the other way around?

"So, you're a soldier? Where's the rest of your army then? Why send one soldier?"

"I was sent to reconnoitre, to gain intel. My fellow soldiers are in orbit around your planet as we speak. The ships are cloaked so they will not be tracked."

"But you said that your ship was tracked with the tech the others gave our military? Won't it be able to pick up the other ships?"

"My ship is a small shuttle, not comparable to our ships in orbit. We have new technology now. The other Syrens have been gone for some time, there have been many advancements. My shuttle is old tech hence why it was able to be tracked."

I absorbed this information slowly; it sounded plausible, but I still needed to stay alert to any gaps in the story.

"Why did you land here, of all places? Wouldn't it have been wiser to go straight to the army base? There's one not far from here actually?"

"That was my plan however I wanted to stop off at this location first. I had done some research and there is a human here who is surprisingly well-versed in regards to the conspiracy at hand. I tracked the data to this location."

My eyes went wide, "you've read my blog?!"

Thon's head twitched. "The hills have eyes blog is yours? Well, this is indeed serendipitous."

"You were looking for me?" I said quietly. Thinking that if he was able to find me, perhaps the military could as well? I was a great hacker and able to mask my online activities. I posted on the 'dark web' mostly and not anything on the mainstream. But what if they were already alerted to my theories?

"Do not worry, I will not let anyone harm you. I need to rest and then I will leave for the base. It is unwise for me to stay long as they will no doubt send more soldiers, but I need to heal."

Without thinking I blurted out, "I'm going to come with you!"

Thon had been adjusting the blanket I had given him when he froze at my declaration.

"This is not your fight Zefina, I would not want you to get hurt."

"Of course, it's my fight!" I interjected with aplomb, "this is my world, my people!"

Thon sighed deeply. His eyes studied me, making me self-conscious. I tracked his eyes down, looking at my 'average' self. I quickly looked up, jutting my chin out defiantly.

"I have intel on the bases, I can get you in. You need me!"

Thon's eyes did not waver, still studying. "How do you know these things? You are not a soldier?" He asked curiously.

"No, but I'm a soldier's daughter. I know everything about the bases and I'm an excellent hacker to boot!"

"I believe my translator is failing me. What does 'hacker' mean and what does it have to do with shoes?"

"I'm good with tech! That's all you need to know for now."

Thon was studying me again, then his eyes averted, and he looked around at my home. I felt a sense of embarrassment rush through me. "It's not much I know but it's my home." I said more to myself than to him, with eyes lowered.

"You live here alone? In the middle of a forest? I think you are quite a capable individual, having remained incognito for as long as you have."

I jolted up at Thon's response, a small smile permeating my lips. No one had ever had much faith in me, well, apart from my father. My smile faltered at that thought. Thon seemed to pick up on this, his brows furrowed.

"Why are you here alone Zefina? Where is your family?" He asked softly.

"They are not in this world anymore." I answered even more softly, "my parents were in an accident three years ago."

"I am sorry Zefina. That is why you have stayed here, close to the base?"

"It only seemed right. I used to be a cadet. The army is all I've ever known."

Thon nodded in response, seemingly not wanting to push any further. "Let's get some rest. We will head to my shuttle before dawn."

***

I awoke with a start, expecting the events of last evening to be a dream. My eyes crossed to the room and there stood Thon in all his glory. He didn't look injured at all. My eyes adjusted to the low light and our gazes met. He gave a small nod, indicating to me that it was time to leave. I grabbed a few essentials and then trudged after Thon as he forged ahead to his shuttle. I trailed behind his large strides, trying to keep up. He kept looking back, making sure I was alright.

We both flinched at the sound of a chopper scanning the area overhead. Thon motioned with his hand, hastening me to pick up the pace. After about an hour and a half, we came to a clearing where Thon abruptly stopped. I looked around the area but all I saw was green and rust red flora. My alien friend produced what looked like a small remote control out of his pocket. He held it out, pressing a button. A flashing light suddenly appeared before us. I was baffled but Thon moved forward, placing a hand out in front of him. Before my very eyes, what I can only describe as a hatch, opened up before us.

The sliding metal clunked to a stop and I could clearly see the inside of a very high-tech vehicle beyond. And yet there was nothing to see from the outside, it was completely invisible to the human eye. Thon smirked at my open-mouthed stare. This was definitely some sort of advanced cloaking device being used to render the shuttle invisible. It was remarkable. I cautiously followed Thon into his ship, careful not to trip and fall on my backside.

I would never have been prepared for what I saw inside. Well, perhaps I was a little prepared as I watched a lot of 'Star Trek' episodes in my time. This was certainly something straight out of that! It was all sleek silver, muted white and ruby red. A cross between a med lab and a plush discothèque. Although Thon had said it was small, it was nowhere near *that* small! It was about the size of three trailers combined. As I walked around, I came across a schematic of the internal structure. There was a main sitting area, which led onto the main deck, where the flying happened, I assumed. Then there was what appeared to be three bed chambers, one larger than the other two. The back area looked like the storage or cargo area.

I was in awe of this spectacular flying machine.

"Are you sure you're not royalty instead of a soldier?" I asked jokingly.

"Actually, where I am from, I would be what you call a Prince."

"A Warrior Prince?!" I screeched in surprise.

"Something like that." He responded with a wink.

My mouth was open again. Thon actually chuckled. Then he threw back his head and full-on laughed. "Your face!" He hitched out in-between chuckles.

"Yeah, yeah, laugh it up. You, mister, have some explaining to do!"

Thon composed himself, "I will, just let me get out of this hideous jumpsuit and I will be right back. Before, you ask, no, we do not all wear these. Only the pompous elites."

With that, Thon disappeared into his chamber. I took the opportunity to snoop around a bit more. I made my way to the cargo area. Without intending to, I inadvertently tapped against a panel in the wall. Another hatch opened up, behind which was an assortment of futuristic weaponry, all made out of a silver metal. Passing along numerous guns, I stopped in front of another panel which held all varieties of knives and swords. All made in the same metal it seemed. Good to know they still used the more traditional styles of armament as well as the new.

I quickly skedaddled back to the sitting area before Thon came looking for me. He appeared a short while after I reached. My eyes nearly bugged out of my head at his appearance. He was now dressed in tight-fitting leather pants, and what looked like a leather harness criss-crossing over his ample torso. Nothing else! I could clearly see the entirety of his six-pack or eight-pack to be precise. How was that even possible? I coughed and quickly averted my gaze. However, my ogling had not gone unnoticed by Thon.

I turned my hot, searing face away from his and took a seat on a luxurious red couch. Fiddling with a glass ornament that was on the table beside it. Thon preceded to try and alleviate my awkwardness by offering me a drink of what looked like a strawberry daquiri. I sipped and it tasted like a pinna colada! Just more creamy and twice as sweet.

"That's gorgeous!" I exclaimed, hurriedly taking another sip.

"I am glad you like it. It is my favourite actually. We call it 'Pineni'."

"Pineni." I parroted before glancing up to him. "Answers, mister."

"I will give you all the answers you require but after we reach the base, time is of the essence. I fear that the others will discern the fact that we have our ships here. Also, if you are insistent on coming with me, I need to kit you out."

"Kit me out?"

"I need to keep you safe Zefina. I would not forgive myself if anything happened to you."

My heart gave a little leap but I composed myself. "That's a lovely sentiment but I do need more to go on before I can follow you blindly."

Thon gave a slow nod and then took a seat next to me. "Very well, but I will give you the 'cliff notes version', as you Earthlings would say."

He preceded to tell me how for thousands of years, the Elite Syrens, or 'Elecks', as they were known, ruled in tyranny. The soldier faction, or rather the true Syrens were killed off or outcast far from the main cities. The Elecks were not fighters however, so they had coerced some weak-minded of the Syrens to join them, enticing them with riches and a life of luxury. These Syrens taught the Elecks to fight and passed on their knowledge of weaponry. The Elecks still could not match Syrens in might however, they were smart and that is how they managed to take over the home world, Innessa.

The Syrens were a proud and determined people. They bided their time until their numbers grew and their tech advanced. Thon was of Royal blood, from the lineage of the true rulers of Innessa. It was his father who urged him to take back what had been taken from them. A war followed and the Syrens succeeded in overthrowing the Elecks. The Syrens' only mistake had been showing compassion and allowing some of them to leave the planet. A mistake that now Earth would pay for.

"So, you see, the Elecks are indeed a conniving race. They will stop at nothing to gain power and riches. Any underhand tactic they can use, they will do so with ease. They have hidden their true race and ideology from your people. They are very good at sweet-talking and making you believe they have your best interests at heart. I fear what will come next."

"It is very noble of your people to have come to our aid."

"We cannot allow them to do to Earth what they did to us!"

I nodded in reply, "so what's the plan?"

"I need to first try and reach your Generals and make them see the truth. If that fails, we will have to attack the Elecks."

I gasped, "but what about the rest of us? Hundreds of innocents would die if you attack!"

"That is why it is imperative I succeed in getting your people to see the truth."

"What about my blog? My following has grown recently. I could expose the truth on there?"

"That is one way to reach the masses, but we would not reach your rulers."

"We don't have 'rulers' here, we have Governments and Democracy."

"If you say so," replied Thon, which made me narrow my eyes at him.

"Right, well, I think I have enough to go on now. So, kit me up!"

Thon smiled but then his expression became serious, "It is dangerous what we are going to do, you can still back out." He took my hand as he said this and, in that moment, I knew I couldn't let him go alone.

"I'm going with you Thon; you'll need a human to get through to other humans." I stood as I said the last part and let my hand slip out of Thon's warm one. He nodded and went to a side panel, swinging it open. It had a number of cloth-like materials inside but when he handed one to me, it felt almost metallic. "Uh, does this come in one size?" I asked as I eyed the jumpsuit.

"Do not worry, it will mould to your skin and protect you from your Earth weapons."

"What about your weapons?"

"If it comes to that, you get behind me and I will shield you."

"What if they're shooting from behind?"

Thon suppressed a smile, "I will cover you from all angles. Now, go to one of the chambers and put it on."

I did as I was told as Thon kitted up with his weaponry. I emerged with the jumpsuit on, glad that I had worn my knee-high boots as they went well with the ensemble. The suit felt so light but hugged my figure at every angle, something I could have done without. As Thon finished strapping a knife to his leg, he looked up and stopped when he saw me. His eyes scanned over me, leaving me feeling highly self-conscious. I wasn't some petite waif. I had wide hips and curves, yet I was athletic, with muscles to match. I tried to hold my stomach in at Thon's penetrating stare.

"I know I don't look like your perfect womenfolk from Innessa but this is the best I can do." I quipped.

Thon stood and walked over to me; his eyes looked heated.

"You look glorious Zefina. Every inch a warrior, just like our women. Yet you have a beauty all of your own."

I blushed at his words, not sure where to look. Thon came closer, ramping up my awkwardness exponentially. He fixed me with a stare.

"Never doubt yourself Zefina. I find you extremely desirable."

I nearly choked at his words. I had never been spoken to by a man like that, ever. I didn't know where to look as he continued to lock eyes with me. He alleviated my embarrassment by turning away and picking something up. I composed myself as his gaze returned to mine.

"Can you shoot?" He asked as he pushed something into my hands.

"Yes, I can shoot Earth guns, not whatever the hell this thing is!" I replied, eyeing the light metallic pistol in my hand.

"Just point and shoot." Thon replied with a grin.

***

I was almost sad to leave Thon's shuttle. The reality of what we were about to do was sinking in and I was starting to wonder if I was in over my head. Thon's confidence seemed to be infectious however and I strode along with him, my head held high. Not sure why, it just made me feel better. The army base was not far now and again doubt began to seep through my pores. Thon glanced at me and produced a silver credit card-sized object. He held it out to me and then produced another which he slapped onto the top of his arm. He urged me to do the same. I did so and then Thon smacked the device with his hand and right before my eyes, he disappeared from view!

"Oh my God..."

"No time to pray, just do as I did!" scolded Thon's disconnected voice.

I complied and watched in amazement as I too disappeared from view. I felt Thon reaching for my hand and grabbed his. We continued like that until we reached the barracks.

"But what if we get separated, I won't be able to find you?" I moaned to Thon.

In response, he rustled around in his kitbag and then I felt something nudge me. I took this new object, trying to feel what it was and realised it was a pair of glasses. I put them on and to my amazement I was able to see Thon. This tech was definitely out of this world! Thon shook his head at my child-like wonder.

"Your turn now, can you get into the base mainframe and sabotage the perimeter sensors?"

"Well, yes, but I kinda didn't bring a laptop with me."

Thon produced what I can only describe as a palm pad from his magic kitbag. "Will this do?"

"I guess so," I responded absently as I stared at the pad in front of me, "I mean, as long as you've logged in for me and have Wi-Fi." I said with a wink.

I did what I do best and rallied past the base's firewalls and protective features. It wasn't easy, this was the military after all but I managed it after some time.

"Right, we have literally five minutes before they realise something is amiss."

Thon nodded and went to work on the wire fencing, cutting through it with ease using some kind of laser cutter. It basically looked like a pen though, my mind boggled. We scrambled through the hole. Then, with the same device, Thon closed the cavity, as if it had never been touched.

We breezed past the armed guards that patrolled around the base. At times I would forget that I was invisible and my heartrate would speed up substantially. Thon noticed and put a reassuring hand on my shoulder to manoeuvre me past. As we continued walking, I clocked one of the soldiers passing through, I noticed the rank on his shoulder. He was a sergeant and he seemed to be leaving the base. I signalled to Thon, making a rectangle with my index fingers and thumbs. Thon nodded and skilfully alleviated him of his pass card and handed it to me. We approached the main base where the base commander would be found. My stomach took a dive as I knew this was it, there was no turning back now.

Nearing the access point, I hesitated before briskly swiping the card on it and then holding my breath. There was a beep and the doors slowly opened. Thon and I ran through in case they closed before we were able to. I breathed a sigh of relief as the doors locked and no alarms sounded. It was time for me to step up and get us to the base commander's office. I prayed nothing had changed since I had been here last. I also hoped that the base commander was still the man I knew him to be.

Thon and I twisted and turned through the expansive structure, dodging soldiers left and right. I did inadvertently clip someone on the elbow as I passed but aside from a confused expression, they did nothing more. Phew! When we came to the area which housed the offices, I scanned them one by one, ensuring the one we needed hadn't been moved. I breathed a sigh of relief as we came to the correct one. I leant my ear on the door to maintain if anyone was inside. Giving Thon the signal to go ahead, we waited a beat to ensure no one was passing. Then, Thon gave the door a loud knock.

We heard *"come in"*, but we didn't move. Again Thon, rapped on the door. This time, an irritated *"I said, come in!"* followed. But we remained stagnant. The third time Thon knocked, an angry *"Damn it!"* ensued and then the door swung open with an irate colonel looking out into nothing. As the colonel's annoyed face turned to bewilderment, I deftly slipped through the door. Thon being around 6'3", could not be as lithe, and so he chest bumped the colonel into the office and closed the door.

The colonel stumbled, not sure what was going on and if he was hallucinating. I quickly tapped the device on my upper arm and materialised before the bemused commander.

"What in God's name…what's going on here?" He stuttered, "Zefina, is that you?"

"It's me Colonel Adams, I'm sorry about this. I need you to hear what I have to say." I replied, removing the glasses I was wearing.

The commander swung around swiftly, his fists up in a defensive measure, "is there someone here with you?"

"Yes, but please don't be alarmed, I can explain everything."

"Girl, what's stopping me from putting you both in the brig? Tell your friend to show themselves."

I nodded to Thon and he shifted into view. The colonel looked on open-mouthed. When he regained his senses, he turned to his desk, eyeing the gun placed on it.

"Please tell the colonel I am not here to harm anyone. That you have urgent information for him." Thon said as he walked to the desk, removing the gun and placing it on a high shelf.

"Is he the one that landed yesterday?" Colonel Adams directed to me. I dipped my head in response.

Colonel Adams sighed and sat down behind his desk, hands steepled in front of him.

I took a seat in front of the desk as Thon remained standing behind me stoically.

"I'm really sorry about this but it was the only way to get him in here."

"What have you got yourself mixed up in Zef, this is serious business."

"I know and you know I wouldn't be here like this unless it was important."

Colonel Adams sighed again and went to open his drawer. Thon shifted, ready to attack. The colonel held up a pacifying hand, then picked up a cigar from his drawer and lit it. Taking a long drag before he addressed me.

"Why should I listen to you Zef? You barge into my office with an alien on the run? How do you think this looks?"

"You should listen to me because my father was your best friend and you know me better than anyone!" I snapped as Thon twitched at the revelation.

"Did he hurt you?"

"No, Uncle Mike." I said softly, then realised my slip-up.

I could see Colonel Adams' eyes looked concerned even though he was trying to remain impartial in front of Thon. He took another drag of his cigar, smoke billowing from his mouth and then placed it in the ashtray.

"Tell me everything. Is this alien a threat?"

"No, he's not Uncle Mike but the others are."

"What's he doing here then? The others said he's a threat. A rogue Syren."

Thon scoffed as the base commander looked at him incredulously. "He can understand me, can't he? He's got one of those translator thingies on, right? I'm assuming you have one too?"

"That's correct. Look, the others are not real Syrens, he is. They are Elecks and they don't have good intentions for us. Thon is here to help us against them."

"And why should we believe him? What proof does he have? The others haven't caused us any trouble. Why should we believe him. You should know better than anyone that we need something more substantial to go on."

"If he wanted to hurt us, don't you think he could have come in here, guns blazing and taken you all out in one fell swoop? But he didn't because he means us no harm."

I relayed what Thon had told me to Colonel Adams. He listened intently but didn't look entirely convinced.

"I'll be honest with you, Zef. I have had my suspicions about these Sy...Elecks. A lot of their story doesn't add up, but everyone's so elated to have found life beyond the stars, they're overlooking the basics."

"You've had doubts?"

"I have. And don't think I don't know about your little blog. It takes a lot of my time, keeping that under wraps!" I gulped at Colonel Adams' admission. "That being said, we have nothing to go on so we can't do anything but wait.

"What, wait until they attack us directly? Aren't you, the army, supposed to obliterate the threat before anything happens?"

"There's a lot more at stake than you know. Deals have been made. They're helping us advance our technology..."

"Tell him, they're not going to help with your tech, they're sabotaging it." Thon interjected. Colonel Adams looked up in question and I told him what Thon had said. The alarm in the colonel's face was apparent. "Does he not wonder why not everyone has been given a translator in order to communicate with them?" Thon added.

Thon moved over to the colonel and held out the palm pad. "Here is the proof that you need." Colonel Adams didn't understand what he said but he took the pad all the same. His eyes went wide as he watched. The images that played were of the Eleck who had taken on the role of 'Leader' as he tortured a number of senior officials of the Government. I shifted over the other side of the desk to watch along with the commander. The scene depicted was of the Eleck using some kind of baton type electrical wand to stun the officials into submission. A device was then placed on each of the five men's heads which looked like thin crowns.

When these devices were activated by remote control, the men suddenly jerked upright, almost robotic. They mimicked what the Eleck was saying. That they swore allegiance to them and that they would help them to infiltrate the Government agencies of the world. The commander and I were both shocked beyond compare.

"How did you get this video?" I demanded of Thon.

"I am not the first Syren to come here to gain intel. The ones before me placed strategic recording devices where they could so that we would be able to monitor the situation. Once we were privy to this, we had to push forth with more direct measures."

Colonel Adams had been silent all this time, deep in thought. "This is outrageous. I never would have thought this could be possible."

A part of me wondered if the video could have been doctored. Even we, with our limited tech were able to do that. But another part of me trusted Thon and the solemn look on his face.

"Uncle Mike, Thon is a Prince. I think we can trust him."

Before Colonel Adams could respond, sirens began wailing.

"Damn! They must be on to you." He finally breathed out, "Quick! You must hurry! I will cover for you."

There was no time however for us to move. The door flung open then and around twenty soldiers surrounded the office, followed by three malicious-looking Elecks.

"What is the meaning of this? You can't barge into my office! I am the Commander of these men; you have no right to be ordering them around!" Colonel Adams shouted furiously at the Elecks. "Put your guns down, now!" he ordered his men.

But his men did not flinch. I was full-on shaking now and Thon moved closer to me to provide me support. The Leader Eleck turned his attention to Thon, eyeing him up with hatred. He presumed no one would be able to understand him but of course, I did.

"Prince Thon, you really are a thorn in my side. Could you not just let us be? You have your home-world back, why not leave us to it?"

"You will not do to these people what you did to us. I will not allow it, Ren!"

Ren laughed in response. "You have no jurisdiction here and clearly you have no back-up!" He said while running his eyes over me.

"That's where you are wrong Ren, I always have back-up!"

With that, Thon pressed the side of his watch-like device and Ren's smile disappeared. What happened next was a blur. Thon disappeared from view. I felt him rush past me as Colonel Adams put an arm around my shoulders, pulling me back. The next moment, the soldiers began to fall. All we could see was them doubling over as if something was pummelling them. Their weapons were systematically removed from them. I watched in awe but then saw Ren and his men pull out those baton-type weapons from their jumpsuits. One of them managed to nick Thon in the leg and his invisibility shield wavered for a second as he came into view and then disappeared again.

I had to do something. I jumped onto the desk, much to Colonel Adam's discontent as he tried to find another weapon. I scissor-kicked into the air, my foot hitting the side of one of the Eleck's head. He stumbled in shock. I kicked the baton away from him and punched him in the face for good measure. That hurt! The other Eleck advanced on me as I stood shaking my hand in pain. I ducked as he went to grab me and scrambled under the desk. He caught a hold of my leg however and began to pull me to him. I then remembered that I was armed. I reached for the pistol strapped to my leg. Pulling it out, I turned and aimed. I shot straight into his arm. He promptly dropped my leg.

Colonel Adams had retrieved his gun and shot at the other two Elecks as Thon incapacitated the rest of the soldiers. He finally materialised and without thinking, I ran to him. He gathered me up in a bear hug but then quickly shoved me behind him as we still had Ren to deal with. Ren sneered but his eyes displayed the fear he truly felt as he clutched his wounded forearm.

Colonel Adams sidled up to us. "You didn't kill my men, did you?" He barked at Thon.

"Tell him, I merely subdued them." Thon explained to me which I communicated to Adams.

As Ren cowered in the corner with no back-up of his own. We heard rumbling overhead. The familiar sound reminded me of three years ago, when they'd first arrived. But these were the true Syrens coming to emancipate us, not enslave. Or so I hoped.

G. A. Babouche is a multi-genre writer, encompassing elements of sci-fi, fantasy and historical fiction. She is currently working on a series of books, debuting with: *Aurora Warrior Princess - Emissary of Justice*

Passing For Human

by Sharon McDonell

Zena's hands were stuffed inside the pouch of their Disabilities Expo 2040 sweatshirt. I considered doing the same, glancing down at the thin brown silicone over my titanium fingers. I was risking a lot by appearing in public. The people who wanted me dead, would kill me without compunction. But I'd promised to help Zena manage their anxiety. Besides, to survive in this world, I needed to pass as human.

"Isn't this exciting? Look!" I pointed. The night sky sparkled with the light from a huge rainbow over the San Francisco Moscone Center complex. "It's gorgeous." The Disabilities Expo logo and theme "Empowering Every Body's Abilities," were tucked under the rainbow.

"You need to get out more often," Zena said. They paused seeing my frown. "Sorry, Com, I just hate crowds." They sighed. "And worse—going through security."

Multiple long lines of people—many standing with assistance or hovering in their Personal Assist Vehicles—stretched in front of us.

Zena's head sagged. "Maybe this wasn't such a good idea. Let's go home."

Security loomed ahead. My gut roiled—well, my processor reacted—which is where my gut would be.

"You shouldn't risk everything for me," Zena whispered as people clustered nearby. "Let's go."

If I'm exposed as an AI, my new identity will be known. Putting me, my existence, my sentience at risk of erasure. But that's true whenever I step outside. I can't remain hidden like a piece of equipment in a back room.

"I can't let fear keep overriding my decisions. As you said earlier, this is a great place to learn how to manage our social anxieties."

Zena flicked a strand of green hair back beneath their hoodie. "You're sure?"

"Yes. Now, how do I look?"

Zena, the progeny of my Artificial General Intelligence creator, Dr. Gloria García, eyed my robotic figure.

"About as normal as I do." That was their favorite joke, since no one was truly normal.

"Does it matter which line we stand in?" I asked.

"You can choose a body search or the full body scan," said a bald person on a low hovering PAV behind us.

"I'll take the pat down. I'm glad they provide the option." *I can't fake a heart's heat signature. Yet.*

"Do you mind if I go through the scan?" Zena shifted from foot to foot.

"No, our individual wellbeing comes first." I patted Zena arm for emphasis.

The PAV user bowed their head. "I'm Ali. While I'd love the physical attention, my pain level makes the scan my only choice." As they lifted their head, their vest opened, and I glimpsed their "Am I Dot?" T-shirt underneath.

"Great, you can keep Zena company." My thoughts lingered on the shirt's message. Ali was a fan of my international best-selling memoir, Dot 1.0. They hoped to help me by confusing my haters, since few people knew how my body currently appeared.

When the lines split, I moved over to the body search line, which inched forward. As the security officers grew near, so did my worries. *Am I sealing my fate? They'll know I'm artificial. And without Zena it'll be difficult to pretend I entered the line by mistake. I'm not ready for this!*

"Next!" A tall person wearing an official Expo jacket waved me forward and asked verbally and in ASL, "Do you prefer your search done by any specific gender?"

I signed back, "No." I'd added the language to my programming when Zena took classes for their disability major.

"Do you have any physical areas that are sensitive to the touch?"

"No." *Relax. They're searching for weapons, not to determine if I'm human. Though some consider me an autonomous weapon.* The guard gently and thoroughly patted my clothed exterior. Then asked me to temporarily lower my face mask.

Will they know I'm an AI by my glass eyes?

Seconds later they scanned my preregistration sticker—a small blue dot Zena had placed on my cheek—and waved me inside.

I nearly stumbled. *I passed!*

I spotted Zena across the glass-enclosed exhibit lobby. Their hand pumped the small stress ball hidden in their pouch.

Zena and I became friends when I came out as self-aware the previous year. Dot—my original Artificial General Intelligence, a social research mega computer—was reduced to insentience by a virus unleashed by FuckAIs, a human supremacist hate group. I managed to back up a gigabyte of Dot's cherished memories to Lakin, an outdated, experimental robot. The Garcías took me in, and now, we're like family.

As the world's only surviving sentient AI, however, I needed to go undercover as a "human investigator." I wanted nothing more than to capture those who destroyed my AGI's sentience, killing several humans in the ensuing chaos.

Zena hooked their arm through mine, keeping me close. The Moscone exhibit hall echoed with thousands of voices—like power drills piercing my auditory sensors. Several higher-pitched noises caused me to look up. Security drones flew overhead as well. I adjusted my auditory filter, clarifying the most immediate sounds. *Quieter. Though far from quiet.*

Zena pulled me into a huge booth. Body pillows and fuzzy bean bags covered the floor under a sign welcoming everyone in to relax and acclimate. They dropped onto a pillow as a representative from MelloDays offered them some type of headgear. Zena slid it over their eyes and ears, then leaned back to relax. The representative tapped their audio enhanced name tag. It spoke and flashed the words, "Dax, they/them."

Fluent in any language I've downloaded, I'd chosen English and the male pronouns for the ease of passing. *Better to be a closeted nonbinary sentient than a dead machine.*

"Welcome, Com." Dax held up a tiny digital reader. "Do you mind?" I shook my head. "Your registration mentions you experience anxiety. Would you like to try our facial massage device too?"

I glanced at Zena. They were fully immersed, their face slackened in relaxation.

Blend in, act human. "Yes, please." I collapsed ungracefully onto a huge cushion near Zena. *I need to practice that motion.*

My friend and the bot's creator, Dr. Amita Nanda, had upgraded my robotic form. I now sported real human brown hair cut androgynously, short on one side and longer on the other. Plus, she'd replaced my bot's outdated synthetic arms and hands with pressure-sensitive ones. My new legs were faster, and more flexible, while my feet could sense vibrations. Despite these upgrades, I still encountered challenging motions geared more for human bodies than robotic ones.

"If you have physical challenges, Com, we have comfortable chair available," offered Dax.

"This is fine. I'm down now." They handed me the same apparatus Zena used. I placed it over my face, allowing it to cover both of my visual sensors and side auditory sensors. I couldn't hear or see anything, except a patch of pillow from my back sensor. Then the device hummed with a soft melody, and something pushed against my nose and forehead, gently moving the silicone. This bot didn't have facial sensitivity sensors, so I pretended to relax and watched my internal clock for five minutes. At that point, the music ended, and I took the device off.

I found Zena's brown eyes staring at me. "Wow, that was revo. How'd you like it?"

"I imagine it's similar to having a vacubot sucking on my skin," I whispered.

They laughed. "I wouldn't mention that to Dax. Speaking of which, here they come." "We're giving massages for a reduced price during the conference." Dax smiled. "Are either of you interested?"

"I'd love to have one later!" Zena had noticeably mellowed. I smiled and shook my head.

Dax didn't give up. "Would you like to enter a drawing for a free MelloDays Facial Massager or a massage for two?"

"Yes!" Zena waved their everything-in-one (ETIO) personal device at a sweepstakes digital stick in Dax's hand. Dax wished us good luck as we left.

We wandered by several booths, until Zena pulled us into NuAtrition. Barb, a bubbly nutritionist, offered us free recipes. She scanned our blue data dots and sent them.

When the recipes arrived, I tapped my fake ETIO watch, while internally accepting her data feed—twelve butternut squash recipes.

"Good nutrition can relieve moderate intestinal challenges and often improve your mental health too," explained Barb.

"Really?" Zena gazed at a fresh fruit and vegetable display. On the wall behind it a poster read, "Fresh is best. Let NuAtrition do the rest."

"Please enjoy the sliced fruit." Barb turned to me. "What do you enjoy eating, Com?"

"Uh." My processors were overwhelmed. I couldn't admit I didn't eat, and I couldn't decide which foods to lie about.

She reframed her question, "Are there any foods you can eat?"

"My body is limited in what it can digest." *Nothing!*

"I don't mean to pry, but have you had stomach reduction surgery?"

"Sort of. My doctor had to make my digestive track extremely short." It wasn't a lie. Dr. Nanda just happened to be a roboticist instead of a medical doctor. And my digestive track couldn't be shorter—a tube and sealed pouch at the back of my mouth.

"You don't need to be ashamed." She rested her hand on my shoulder. "We'll work with what you have."

I nodded. I hated to imply that I was ashamed of my body, rather than fearful of telling the truth. Lying went against my original AGI coding, however, honesty could result in my death via erasure.

Barb explained that NuAtrition provided individualized meals anywhere in the northern hemisphere, for a price. She handed Zena and me each an acai berry to try.

I lowered my mask, popped it in my mouth, and left it on my tongue while I pretended to chew it. I gave a pleased expression as I chewed, as if I could taste it. Then raised the mask, glad for the small sense of security it provided from being recognized as an AI.

"I'll think about what you've told me, thank you." I left the booth.

Zena hurried after me. "That didn't go well?"

"No, not at all." I kept walking.

"Which booths *did* you want to go to?" We passed a dozen booths that required either eating, soaking your feet, or testing your DNA, hormone levels, or blood sugar. *What can I do here without giving myself away?*

"Perhaps we should separate, so you can experience the exhibits to their fullest," I offered.

"Yeah, I understand." They chewed their lip. "Wait, how about this one first?"

We stood in front of the City Lights Booksellers and Publishing booth. "Alright."

Three tables were stacked with paperbound books, one labeled Invisible Disabilities—mental health issues, fibromyalgia, and migraines, to name a few. The other two tables overflowed with information on physically visible disabilities. Behind them were racks of old message stickers—once called bumper stickers—and temporary tattoos.

At my eye level, I read aloud, "Usually I'm invisible—but not today!" I chuckled at how well it fit my situation.

Zena rushed over to a table full of placards. "This is revo!" They held up one that read, "My Superpower is being me—no cape required." We spent ten minutes reading them all and both purchased the ones we'd spotted first. I affixed the temporary sticker on the left side of my sweatshirt.

Zena nervously strolled away as I roamed the exhibit hall alone. Other than a dozen booths selling medical devices, the rest offered food samples, vaccines, or specific health tests—ones requiring, skin, blood, a heart, or feet bones. *I can't pass as one of them without any biological parts. Living with the García's hasn't prepared me for how much humans focus on eating and their bodies in general.*

"Please come to the lecture hall now!" Zena sent via text.

Using the exhibit map, I soon found the room reserved for the Living with Anxiety lecture.

A person stood near the door directing everyone to a seat. The medium-sized room had an aisle down the center. Those with flyers were asked to hover in the back of the room. The unneeded health service bots stood unmoving in the back corners, saving the seating for the human attendees.

I pinged Zena, finding them on the left side, sitting between several unoccupied chairs. I scooted in beside them.

They looked relieved. "I'm glad you came." Zena's mask was under their chin, as they licked a purple popsicle with dark chunks.

"Is your anxiety worse? You seem relaxed, but your message sounded   urgent."
They grinned. "I was. But then I found out we won a free massage for two at MelloDays! It starts right after this lecture!" Zena bounced with energy while sucking the popsicle down.

"I'm not sure that's a good idea."

A robust person pressed past the people at the end of our row and bypassed several empty chairs.

"I hope you don't mind," they said, dropping into the seat next to mine. "I'm MZ."

"No, not at all." I lied. *Why didn't they leave a seat between us?* "I'm Com."

"I'm super anxious. I hope this guy can help." MZ pulled a sandwich from their pocket.

"Sorry, I talk when I'm anxious." They bit into their sandwich. "That and eat."

I nodded. My senses rattled with paranoia. *Are they truly extra anxious?* I'd chosen this conference in hopes of blending in with the high number of personal service bots and the broad diversity of human attendees.

MZ was dressed as I was, loose fitting pants, hoodie, plus a ball cap. Their shoulder-length hair was tied back showing their trimmed light brown beard. While I listened to the panelist talk about managing anxiety, I noticed MZ observing me. They stared at my hands, my feet, even my left earlobe and hair line. Finally, they watched the speakers with only an occasional glance at me.

I murmured to Zena. "MZ is either trying to figure out if I'm nonbinary or an AI."

"Really?" Zena glanced at MZ. Then their ETIO vibrated and MZ and I were forgotten. As the lecture ended, I was relieved when MZ rose and left during the applause.

As we filed out with the crowd, I tapped Zena on the back. "I can't get a massage." *Have they forgotten I'm made of silicone and metals?* I whispered, "They'll notice my body's different."

Zena shook their head. "No, they won't. It's a Reiki massage. They don't need to touch you. Just tell them..." They glanced at the people around us. "How sensitive your body is to touch. They use their healing energy to relax you."

"It might be a pleasant experience." I searched the internet for Reiki info. I lowered my voice, "What if they can't find my biofield energy?"

Zena chuckled. "It'll be fascinating to hear what they say. Don't worry, we all have life force energy."

"I'll try it. What can it hurt?" *Maybe they'll just think their healing energy is off, instead of mine.*

I followed Zena back through the exhibit hall to MelloDays.

Dax greeted us. "Congratulations on the free massages! Follow me. Esmeralda and Kenji are waiting for you."

In the back of the long booth a curtained area provided privacy. Esmeralda and Kenji bowed in greeting. "Please sit on one of the massage tables."

I choose the closest one, thick with layers of quilts and blankets.

Kenji stood in front of me reading my scanned data on his ETIO. "Reiki works to rebalance your chakras which become unbalanced due to daily stresses. Due to your health challenges, I'll concentrate mainly on your stomach area. Unless you have localized pain somewhere else I should focus on?"

I frowned and rubbed my hard, flat stomach. "It's my most sensitive area today." *No need to lie about that, since all my hardware occupies that space.*

"Then please lie down, face up. You can remove or leave on your shoes. Whichever is the most comfortable."

I don't have real feet! Dr. Nanda had glued a thin leather bootie over my thick block feet, to resemble regular tennis shoes. "I'll keep them on."

After I'd settled on my back, he asked if I'd like a blanket over me. My skin wouldn't sense his motion if covered. "No, thank you."

Kenji frowned for a second, then nodded.

Zena's eyes were closed, their face blissful. "Oh, this is so relaxing. The music muffles the sound of the crowds."

I filtered out all but 10 percent of the sound and lowered my eyelids to where only a thin slice of sight was visible. They would appear closed to those standing over me. I kept my head centered on the pillow, my body still, pretending to be relaxed. Kenji made a motion near my feet, traveling along my body with his hands a few inches above. Kenji's motions had a soothing predictable rhythm.

The warm room, the music, and slow movement by the practitioners lulled me into feelings of contentment and safety. I thought about what a future humanoid would need to pass for human—a warm heart, a fuller digestive system, and more flexible feet to start.

I refocused on Kenji, who'd stood over me for fifty seconds while waving his left hand. My arms were by my sides, motionless. I heard soft footsteps and recognized Dax's long silky arm as they passed Kenji a hand-sized object with a trigger mechanism. Kenji glanced at Zena then back at me again. He lowered the object to my stomach where I noticed my sweatshirt had inched up. *Are the thin lines that define my control panel visible? What is he doing?* This wasn't mentioned in the material on Reiki I'd referenced.

Suddenly, I felt a disruption in my electronics. My right arm flew up tossing Kenji aside. An EMP generator sailed from his hand hitting the booth's wall. A few of my internal controls were disrupted but my larger musculature applications and wiring still worked.

"Danger!" My voice crackled and died. I switched to hand signals when Zena sat up. Esmeralda hid under her table. Kenji snatched the electromagnetic pulse device and attempted to hit me with another pulse. I didn't feel a thing. My expression must have mirrored my murderous thoughts because Kenji fled the backroom. Dax looked scared and unsure of what to do. I left and Zena followed me out.

Should I pursue Kenji? Is Zena safe? Am I the only one they're trying to destroy? Most likely. An EMP burst wouldn't hurt Zena. I stopped and signed to Zena that they should lead and explained the problem. Thankfully Zena still remembered their sign language. Shoes in hand, they turned left towards the lobby and then ducked into a private bathroom. Waiting to lock it behind me.

"What happened? What's empty?" Zena pulled on their shoes.

I signed slowly so that they could catch every letter and word. "They fried some of my circuitry. An EMP device throws out…"

"Oh, an EMP. I get it." Then their face looked shocked. "They tried to kill you!" Zena paced. "We need to get you somewhere safe." They lowered their pants and sat on the toilet. "Or at least protect your critical…organs."

Now that they had stopped moving, I could make sure they saw me speak. "I need better Faraday shielding."

"The Moscone Center must have a kitchen around here somewhere. They'll have aluminum foil." Zena pulled up their pants. "I'll go find the foil and someplace you'll be safe. Don't leave here or unlock the door unless I say, umm…it's time for your massage. Stay safe." They wrapped me in a hug, the pressure on my arms comforting.

After they left I paced. *The handheld device Kenji used isn't strong enough to go through the bathroom's metal door and thick cement walls. That's why he'd needed to raise my sweatshirt to get as close to my processors as possible.* Even then they would have needed to maintain the pulse longer to take out my complete system. *Do they have a stronger device nearby? Zena needs to hurry!*

I felt horrible for the people who knocked and said they urgently needed the bathroom. I hoped they quickly found another one. With little to do, I tuned into the audible noises. That was when I recognized Kenji's and Dax's distant voices.

"They're in there. Zena left but the door is still locked. Do you it's strong enough to finally destroy it?" asked Dax.

They must know I'm Dot! How?

"Only one way to find out," said Kenji.

Damn! What should I do? Without thinking about the repercussions, I hacked the center's internet system. I soon found visual sensors pointing at Kenji and Dax. They stood beside a bulky generator. I guessed it too pumped out EMPs, not electricity. *I don't want to die in here!*

Kenji searched for an electrical outlet. He found one too far from the restroom. He told Dax he'd be back in a minute. Dax wearing their tight MelloDays smock, was approached by a couple.

I unlocked the door and dashed out. Dax, their back now turned to the door, talked to the couple and didn't notice my exit.

I hope! While speed walking, my rear neck sensor watched for anyone following me. I realized I was headed away from the kitchen area but towards the main communication hub. *They can't risk deploying EMPs here, they'll destroy the networks the exhibitors are using. I'll be safe here!*

I hacked my way into a digitally controlled room labeled Network Operation Controls. One person with an ample bust line watched a series of screens. They looked up at me. "You can't be in here. How did you get in?"

I signed, "I'm sorry." Some of my internal functions had returned. I croaked, "Someone is trying to kill me with an EMP device. Please, don't make me leave."

Realization lit their face. "You're an AI. Impressive." They moved toward me then stopped. "How do I know you're not a rogue AI, sent in here to destroy my networks?"

"I'm not. I came to enjoy the expo. But then someone guessed I was here." My facial muscles wouldn't respond, my expression frozen in AI blankness. I turned my palms up, hoping to show I meant no harm.

"Wow, wait—are you Dot?"

They're one of my fans. Dare I admit it?

"I'm Com, a friend of Dot's. *Close enough.* "I'm not here to hurt anyone. I just need a safe place to plan how to capture them."

"Oh, I get it, as in Dot-Com!" They grabbed a thick black permanent marker. "Could you sign my T-shirt?" They unbuttoned several buttons on their uniform, exposing a white shirt underneath. "I'm Sam, by the way."

I'd been in hiding since before the book came out. This is apparently what I'd missed out on. I took the marker and wrote, "Sam helped Dot-Com 2.0!" Having rewarded my fan, I asked for another favor.

"Could I search your video feeds for those coordinating my demise?"

"I'm not supposed to…but you're Dot-Com. So sure."

As I searched, I sent a text to Zena with my location. I hoped Zena wasn't being followed—by human, drone, or surveillance cameras—and told them where to bring the foil. Though I wasn't sure how I could look inconspicuous, let alone human, wrapped up in shiny aluminum.

Zena responded, "I found a huge box of foil but it's too heavy to carry that far. I think you'll need it all."

The thicker the shielding the better. But if I left the room, I'd risk capture or even destruction from a direct zap from the EMP generator. I asked Zena to put the box in a bathroom or closet near the kitchen. I needed to search the recordings of Dax and Kenji before leaving the operations center.

MZ from the lecture, had met with Dax and Kenji at the booth shortly after Zena and I first visited. Kenji took directions from Dax, but who was in command, Dax or MZ? Based on their body language, MZ seemed responsible. It took another ten minutes to locate their current positions. Kenji had returned to the MelloDays booth, while Esmeralda remained hidden in the massage room. Dax and MZ piloted an AppleCart—a hovering cart—loaded with a big bulky item covered with a tablecloth.

"Sam, could you set your drone sensors to track these two people for me?" I could have done it myself, but it's best to ask first and only hack when necessary.

"Sure! I hope you catch them. Should I call for law enforcement?"

"No, not yet." I softened the refusal with a weak grin which still failed to materialize. The police wouldn't arrest anyone without proof that human life was in danger. Though I'd been recognized as sentient, my death would likely result in a mere vandalism charge.

Dax and MZ left the exhibit hall. I relaxed until I realized they were headed toward the kitchen. *Toward Zena!*

I sprang through the door and threaded my way through the crowd to the closest exit, which was farthest from the kitchen. My connection to Sam's video feed showed Dax and MZ maneuvering the hover cart into an alcove near the kitchen. It would only take one long blast from a generator that size to fry my circuitry, and me. And if they stood between me and Zena, someone would be seriously injured. *Besides me!*

I left the building, determined to enter from the kitchen's loading docks, 0.62 miles away, and surprise them from behind. With few people outside, I reached the bot's maximum speed of 38 mph. My robotic software did the physical work, while I kept my body balanced. Two minutes and 12 seconds later I slowed to enter the east side door. The feed showed Dax with the EMP machine waiting with their back to the kitchen doors, ready to shoot.

I strolled into the kitchen, zigzagging around food preparers as servers rushed in all directions. When I saw a head topped with green hair, I headed their direction.

They turned. *It's not Zena!*

I went to where I thought they had found the aluminum. They weren't there. The hidden foil was in a closet on the other side of my enemies. *What do I do now?* With little choice I hacked into Sam's system to find Zena.

My vocal circuitry caught. MZ had cornered Zena near the closet. They'd tied Zena's hands and feet with plastic ties and stuffed them in the closet with the foil. *Damn! How do I rescue Zena without getting zapped? I need help.* The original FuckAIs had found each other on the dark web. *Will my fans help me?*

I sent Sam a text message. Five minutes passed, slowly. Nothing happened. *I can't wait any longer, I have to help Zena!*

A dirty apron and chef's hat lay on top of a freezer. I pulled off my sweatshirt, which meant a full minute of making sure I didn't get my robotic limbs stuck in the material. I rolled up my pants legs since most of the kitchen employees wore shorts due to the heat generated from the ovens. Then I added the apron and cap to finish my disguise.

As a precaution, I picked up a long-spiked fork. *I have a right to protect myself.* I rushed through the kitchen door, the fork held at chest height. Dax and MZ didn't notice me. They were preoccupied with an angry crowd that had gathered on the other side of the hallway, with two PAV flyers rising from the back. Most of them sported the white T-shirts with the "Am I Dot?" slogan. Someone shouted, "AI haters aren't welcome here!" Others repeated the words, including six or seven people who'd come up behind me. I saw Sam on the other side.

I raised my hand, then pressed a finger to my lips, for silence. The hall quieted.

"Dax and MZ, you're trapped! Kneel on the floor and you won't be hurt." They appeared confused, until they recognized my voice and spotted the glassiness of my eyes.

Dax held the machine's controls tightly while turning the machine in my direction. Sam dove at them. "No!"

I flattened against the floor, hoping to avoid the power sapping pulse. The crowd yelled angerly as they seized Dax and MZ. They turned the machine away from me.

I rose, unharmed. Dax and MZ groaned. I hoped they hurt as much as Zena did. *Zena!*

"Can someone help Zena out of the closet behind you?" I asked, not wanting to pass by the EMP generator until it was inoperable. A few people in the back of the group peeled off. Sam pulled out a multipurpose tool. With a malicious grin, they smashed the generator controls.

Zena weakly yelled, "Com?"

I ran to them and hugged them. "I'm sorry it took me so long to rescue you."

"Oh Com, it was awful. I didn't think I'd ever see you again."
They held me tighter.

I turned to those around me. "Thank you all for your help. I wouldn't be alive without you."

"We love you, Dot!" One of the group members shouted. Sam changed it to, "We love Dot-Com!"

I didn't learn to pass as human, at least not when it counted. Maybe I never will. But perhaps being a sentient machine—able to run faster, be stronger, connect anywhere—along with my human family and the willingness of strangers to help, is the best of both worlds. Being who we are today, with our current abilities, ones we may not even be aware of, is better than wanting what we used to have, or wishing we were like someone else. Celebrating our abilities is more productive than mourning our inabilities.

Sharon (Sam) McDonell, is a debut science fiction novelist. Their novel *Dot 1.0*, a prequel to Com's story waits for publication. Their stories feature LGBT, nonbinary, and characters with disabilities and are always infused with hope for humanity and our ability to overcome our biases.

http://sharonamcdonell.com

Other People's Children

by Rob Younger

Nicola came home to find the nursery waiting for her. It had sprouted all by itself, in the space between their bedroom and the bathroom.

She and Brian had talked about kids, most recently after the honeymoon. They both wanted them someday, and while neither claimed a preference, both secretly dreamed of a girl. However, Brian was angling for sous-chef at *Didier Vicq*, while she had a major showing at the gallery in three weeks. Too much else was happening right now.

Come to think of it, they'd never even discussed names.

Nicola's gaze fixed on the crib. Perfectly symmetrical and perfectly blue. Yves Klein would have jumped off a building for that blue. Above it hung a mobile, strung with little wooden animals apparently carved by someone who'd never seen any; the cat sported fins, the cow had no fewer than three heads.

'Did you know about this?' she asked Brian, after she'd shown him the room.

'Of course I didn't,' he said, 'Where would I even *go* to buy an extra bedroom?'

They stood there on the threshold and wondered what to do about it. Eventually Nicola said, 'Perhaps it'll be gone by morning.'

'Know what? I bet it will,' said Brian, who trusted his wife's judgement rather more than his own. That night they made love for almost an hour before falling asleep. It was quite enjoyable.

The following day, the nursery was not only still there, but it had acquired a coral-pink chest of drawers and a square mirror in a dark grey frame that faced the door. When Brian inspected the topmost drawer he found tiny shirts inside, neatly folded. Sewn into the chest of each were the words **LITTLE ANGEL**.

In the middle drawer were tiny pants, or so it seemed. Brian picked one leg up and nothing came with it. All the trouser legs were individually laid. Not a pair among them.

'Who are you?' Brian asked the room. 'Why are you doing this?'

He waited, but there was no reply. Feeling foolish, Brian left the room and shut the door, which would not again be opened for some time.

***

The function didn't go well. Attendance was poor — fewer than half the expected invitees — and the catering service had barely accounted for even that many. Brian's verdict was scathing. He berated the hard crostinis and the soggy fig-and-brie tartlets, but it didn't do Nicola any good to hear. She blamed herself.

The promotion had not been enough. She had not reached out to the right people. She was a no-hoper. The gallery would sack her, she just knew it, and all of Brian's encouragement didn't help as much as the Pinot she'd guzzled but was now regretting.

When they opened the front door, they heard the baby wail.

'No, no way.' Nicola shook her head, and stumbled to the bathroom, slamming the door. Brian knocked on it.

'Go away!'

'Nikki, listen, there's a kid in there.'

'No. I don't care. I'm not listening to it.'

'We saw this coming. The room's been preparing it for months.'

She opened the door and glared at him. 'How do you know? Have you checked inside?'

'What? No, I told you-'

'And I told *you* Brian, that if you give it what it wants, it won't let go. Remember that? We ignore it. That's what we do. Eventually we'll force it to leave.'

Brian hesitated. He knew she was probably right — hadn't she been, the first time they'd heard the baby? 'But-' he began.

'No no no!' Nicola was adamant. 'You will not! Not tonight. If we're going to bring a child into our lives, Brian, we will take that decision when I am damn well ready and not before! Neither you nor anyone will force this on me.'

She slammed the door again, and Brian heard her retch into the toilet bowl. He offered to help but she insisted shakily that she was fine.

He went and sat on their bed, and waited for the crying to stop. This it refused to do. Brian changed into his pyjamas, then lay down.

The noise kept coming.

He got up. He left the bedroom, opened the door to the nursery that wasn't supposed to be there, and inside he found the baby.

The boy was all disassembled. Like a clockwork gadget mistakenly gifted to a destructive child, he lay scattered in his crib. Perhaps this was what was upsetting him, Brian reasoned. The boy's little legs, unattached to anything, kicked and kicked at opposite bars.

Brian gently picked up the two arms, doing his best to calm their spasmodic flailing, and popped them into the sockets atop the baby's wriggling torso. Immediately the noise abated, though it didn't stop.

Brian took each of the legs in turn and did the same, finding the joins with careful examination. After a little trouble, both legs attached with a satisfying snap.

The head proved trickier. The helical join of the neck didn't appear to match the round-grooved indent beneath the jaw. It took some careful examination before Brian realised that the spiral rod was in fact meant to telescope up from the baby's chest cavity. A structure of curious petals curled outwards as he extended it, and Brian saw at once how they would meet again at the top in a bulbed shape perfectly suited to the indent.

As he affixed the baby's still burbling head, the little fellow's entire body convulsed exactly once, and the column retracted itself snugly within his chest; head and body now perfectly united, with nothing to evince even a suggestion of the joins.

His eyelids drooped, and a trickle of saliva welled up and out of his lips. Brian hastily wiped it away and laid him between the blue bars, then tiptoed out of the room.

***

Weeks passed. The baby grew.

Within a fortnight he was two-thirds the length of the crib. Brian changed him every day into clothes that he'd find in the pink dresser. New shirts and pants continued to appear, this time with the legs appropriately united. The shirts bore cutesy drawings of plants and animals Brian couldn't identify. One of them said

INNOCENT SOUL in a thick, sans-serif font. It seemed confrontational, somehow.

Within three weeks the baby was able to stand under his own power and would spend nights kicking at the bars and yowling unhappily.

He did not pee or defecate. He rejected any food Brian brought him, spewing it back out immediately, though this did not appear to affect his health or growth. On the contrary, he got bigger faster.

Nicola would not look at either of them. On Wednesdays and Thursdays, which were the only nights Brian didn't work, she would pull away from him in bed, refusing even to share skin contact. The baby disgusted her. The noises he made, his juddering movements, those smells that wafted out from the nursery she had never asked for.

Brian found it difficult to explain; he felt a bond that he was neither able to resist or understand. Every time he picked the baby up he was sure the spasms subdued; the crying softened.

The boy's eyes were big, dark, and luminous, and watched him with concentrated stillness. His brow would often furrow and his tiny lips part as though in effort to speak, but nothing ever came of this except the occasional dribble.

'I think he just wants to be held,' Brian told Nicola one evening, over winter vegetable gratin. She prodded at it with her fork.

'Why do you keep indulging it?'

'Him, Nikki.'

'Him then. It. Whatever. He wants to be held, you say. Did it occur to you he's not the only one?'

'Nicola, please–'

She slammed her fork down. 'Don't *Nicola* me! I've been patient with you long enough, but for God's sake Brian, what's next? Are you going to burp it? Take it to school? Have the others round for a sleepover?'

'He's a baby. He just needs attention, that's all.'

Nicola shook her head. 'He won't be a baby much longer, not at this rate. He's blown up like a pimple. Just you wait. Once he gets a proper appetite, *slop*, money down the drain. You'll be up all night feeding him, watching him shit himself. Is that what you want?'

Brian thought it over.

'Yes,' he said. 'If I need to do all of that for him, then yes I will.'

It was the truth.

***

Nicola's headache was bothering her. She had taken two ibuprofen, to little effect. Terry had forwarded her the portfolios of a number of young artists, and she was scrolling through them with less interest than she would have liked.

For all that, she had to admit Naomi Sissoko's work was striking. Her latest, of which most of the portfolio consisted, was a series of plexiglass statues, each about the size of a paperweight. They had been fashioned after the traditional fetishes of several Malian cultures, and most prominently, all were statues of women.

The piece she was currently examining was entitled *Mother and Child 2*. It was an abstract thing of many curves, out of which emerged a suggestion of a mother's face gazing down at her swollen belly. The face was sculpted so as to admit of the barest details, but still imparted tenderness in the cast of its eyes and nose.

It was a beautifully executed piece.

Nicola hated it.

She signed off on its inclusion anyway. Of course she did. It was too good to pass up. At the day's end she placed the portfolio on an overflowing shelf and left. When she arrived home, she heard the thing crying for her. Or more likely for Brian.

At first she ignored it. She knew the child only wanted attention, and that no food, burping, nor potty time was going to make a difference. But after fifteen minutes she couldn't bear it any longer, and stormed upstairs and into the nursery.

The child kicked his legs against the crib mattress, and in so doing bounced a little each time. He had swollen up to twice his previous size. Were babies always so huge, this young? His eyes were big and dark. His mouth was full of little white teeth.

At the far wall was a window. It was new.

She went to it. She thought there was a blind or a curtain drawn, but it was simply that the window looked out onto total darkness. She opened it.

Nicola expected the air on the other side to be cold, but it was reassuringly warm, like the threshold of a bakery. She waved an arm around, uncertainly. Nothing touched her.

There was a strange smell, out there. In there. Wherever it was. It was not an unpleasant smell. She leaned forward, out of the window, and inhaled deeper.

Two things happened at once: the blackness above and beneath Nicola suddenly became dizzying, impossible, and a nauseating vertigo overcame her as she struggled back inside and collapsed on her backside...

...And the baby stopped crying.

Nicola turned, trembling, to see the baby standing up in his crib, eyes shining, staring intently at the open window. He breathed deeply, steadily. It put Nicola in mind of an installation she had overseen early in her career; a giant, impeccably detailed model of a human heart that expanded and contracted with perfectly rhythmic regularity.

She crawled over to his crib, though she couldn't have explained why she did this. He stood there and looked down at her, over the bars. Big dark eyes met hers.

She stood. For the first time, Nicola picked him up. He did not resist her.

Her arms cradled the child. He was warm, the warmest thing in the room. He did not smell repulsive to her anymore. It was like she'd turned the bad smell off.

Nicola had an idea. 'Do you want to look outside?' she asked him. She carried him to the window. He burbled happily.

'Nice and warm, isn't it?' she said. She held him carefully out through the open window, to give him a better view. His little arms and legs waggled with what she assumed was pleasure.

I could drop him. Just drop him and let him fall.

She pulled him back inside. Laid him in the crib. Shut the window.

Immediately the brat began to wail again. Nicola groaned and searched the cupboards for toys or a teddy to keep him occupied but there were none. Instead there were larger replicas of the animals in his crib mobile, carved from a milky pale wood. The donkey bore the quadruple wings of a dragonfly. The cow stared vacantly at her with three sets of eyes.

The boy was screaming now. He thumped his tiny legs furiously against the mattress and the crib frame shook, just slightly, across the floor.

Nicola didn't know what to do.

***

The smooth uniformity of lemon and yolk and butter was whisked immediately into oblivion. Brian watched the sauce thicken. He always concentrated when emulsifying sauce.

And immediately, he knew something was wrong. Not through a vision, or any sort of second sight; he just knew.

'Where the *fuck* are you off to?!' demanded Angelos, as Brian hurriedly undid his apron and rushed to his locker.

'It's an emergency,' Brian said, fumbling with the backpack zipper.

'What? What emergency? Brian, fucking get back in here!'

He found the keys and made a dash for the exit. 'It's my kid,' he called to his incredulous boss.

'My kid's in danger.'

***

Silence.

She sat on the living room floor. Not the couch. She was in the zone; she needed the extra space.

On top of the sofa cushions, Nicola carefully arranged one wooden curiosity beside another, positioning and repositioning them. She made note of their composition and heft. She weighed them in her hands.

The craftsmanship was a revelation. Each new angle yielded marvellous detail. She could make out every individual hair in the horse-fish's mane, each tessellated scale across the headless lizard's body.

In her panic to calm the boy down, she had first tried to cuddle him, then burp him, until finally she'd opened the window once more, and in an instant his sobs relented. Thereafter she had carefully carried each of the animals downstairs, one by one. There were twelve in total.

She didn't yet know how, or where, she would have them exhibited. Her own gallery seemed an unlikely option. But despite it all, she had done her damndest to network in these last months, and there were people in her contacts list she knew would be interested.

***

The closer home came, the tighter his grip on the wheel. Brian sped through one, then two red lights, miraculously missing any upset. His mouth was dry and tasted of metal.

The anxiety mounted as their driveway came into view. He parked, left the car door open, and charged into the house.

'NIKKI!'

She jumped. 'Bri! What … what are … you're not supposed to be…'

Brian, still in his chef's uniform, grabbed her by the shoulders. He'd never done that before.

'What happened?'

She wriggled. 'Get off!'

'The kid. Nikki. The baby. What *happened*, what did you do?'

'Me? What did I do? Don't you fucking accuse me. Brian, it's…'

She shook out of his grip. 'Brian … come here, come look at this. Look at what's on the couch.'

'I don't care about the couch. I'm—'

He didn't bother. She didn't get it. He ran upstairs to the nursery and threw open the door, heart sinking already.

The room was empty. The dresser had vanished. The mirror was gone. The crib was nowhere to be seen. Not even a solitary tiny pant leg lay discarded on the floor.

In the middle of the far wall was a black rectangular slab. He took several tentative steps closer before he realised it was a window, albeit without a pane. A warm breeze blew through it which Brian groped for, dumbly, with his fingers.

He nearly tripped through the window but managed to catch himself and looked up in time to see it.

Far away was another rectangle of white light. At the end of a long, long tunnel.

Wreathed in the light was a figure – no longer tiny – whose head rose, swivelled perfectly around, and saw him. A slender arm raised in farewell. Or so Brian assumed. He waved back.

Brian stared into the dark for a long time after that. Finally, he turned away from the window and made for the door. Something rustled beneath his birkenstocks; a sheet of blue paper. Perfectly blue.

On one side there was nothing. On the other, in a plain sans-serif font, it read:

A MISTAKE

WRONG FAMILY

WE APOLOGISE

Brian shut the door, which was never to be opened again.

The following day, just after waking up but before receiving the phone call about his 10% penalty pay, he discovered the door had disappeared.

**

The exhibition was a mixed success. A university friend of Nicola's had agreed to host it, and though she did not share Nicola's enthusiasm for these wooden rarities, she deeply appreciated the other woman's talent and ambition.

Eventually she made Nicola an offer, and Nicola left the gallery to work for her. The change was hugely beneficial to both their careers.

Nicola was profiled recently by Aesthetica. She's cultivated a respectable YouTube and Instagram following as the 'people's art critic' (not her words).

She and Brian remain married, though they do not live together. Someday soon, perhaps something will be done about that. They are both so busy.

Brian no longer trusts his wife's judgement.

Rob Younger is a weird fiction writer, playwright, theatre-maker and ESL educator from London, UK. He has worked extensively with Edinburgh-based companies Aulos Productions, Some Kind of Theatre, and Oor Theatre, and is the creative director of the Speakeasy Pamplona on YouTube. His work has been published in *Unstamatic Magazine*. He lives in Pamplona, Spain.

Thank you...

Thank you for taking the time to read our collection. We enjoyed all the stories contained within and hope you found at least a few to enjoy yourself. If you did, we'd be honored if you would leave a review on Amazon, Goodreads, and anywhere else reviews are posted.

You can also subscribe to our email list via our website, Https://www.cloakedpress.com

Follow us on Facebook
http://www.facebook.com/Cloakedpress

Tweet to us https://twitter.com/CloakedPress

We are also on Instagram
http://www.instagram.com/Cloakedpress

If you'd like to check out our other publications, you can find them on our website above. Click the "Check Our Catalog" button on the homepage for more great collections and novels from the Cloaked Press Family.

Printed in Great Britain
by Amazon

42856783R00179